JEAN OF

B

Elinor M. Brent-Dyer

Bettany Press

1996

First published in book form in Great Britain
by Bettany Press 1996
52 Warham Road, London N4 1AT

Originally published in serial form in 1930
by the *Shields Gazette*.

British Library Cataloguing in Publication Data
A catalogue record for this book is available
from the British Library

ISBN 0 9524680 3 4

Designed & DTPed by Green Gosling, London
Printed and bound in Great Britain
by Penshurst Press, London

CONTENTS

ACKNOWLEDGMENTS

The publishers would like to thank the following people, all of whom have contributed in different ways to this volume: Mrs Chloe Rutherford, Elinor M. Brent-Dyer's heir, for permission to publish *Jean of Storms* in book form; Mr Ian Holland, editor of the present-day *Shields Gazette*; and Miss Doris Johnson of the South Shields local history library, who discovered the serialised novel and brought it to the attention of Polly Goerres of the New Chalet Club. For background information we are indebted to Fen Crosbie, Hazel James, Joan-Mary Jones and Helen McClelland. Sally Phillips played a major role in the book's production, sharing the tasks of checking and editing the typescript and helping with the research and liaison. Joy Wotton did her usual professional editorial job on the Introduction and Afterword and advised on the manuscript itself. Elspeth Insch kindly drew the map of South Shields, showing where the story is set, and North Tyneside Libraries, the English Folk Dance and Song Society, Southampton City Heritage Services and Al Blunsdon loaned the photographs which have been used for illustrations. Finally, the book owes its existence primarily to the enthusiasm — and very hard work — of Polly Goerres, who initiated and sustained the project throughout. Her belief in the worth and interest of *Jean of Storms* has added another title to the bibliography of Elinor M. Brent-Dyer. We hope you agree with us that the enterprise was worthwhile.

Rosemary Auchmuty & Juliet Gosling, September 1996

JEAN OF STORMS
IS DEDICATED WITH THANKS
TO THE MEMORY OF ITS AUTHOR,
ELINOR M. BRENT-DYER,
WHOSE WORK CONTINUES
TO BRING SO MUCH PLEASURE
TO SO MANY READERS TODAY

INTRODUCTION

POLLY GOERRES

Jean of Storms first appeared as a serial between 5 April and 31 May 1930 in a provincial local evening newspaper, the six-times-a-week *Shields Daily Gazette*, which served the area now called South Tyneside and always carried one serialisation of a novel. At this time its author, Elinor M. Brent-Dyer, was at the height of her powers as a writer of school stories for girls; this was the year that her eager schoolgirl readers saw the publication of *The School by the River* and *Eustacia goes to the Chalet School*. But *Jean of Storms* is not a story for schoolgirls at all, being a light romance for adult readers.

The heroine, Jean McCleod, is a 23-year-old woman (a lively soul who seems to owe a lot to the then teenage Joey Bettany), who lives a comfortable, middle-class existence with her 35-year-old aunt, Oona McCleod. When Jean's widowed sister-in-law, Doris, dies in India, Doris's two daughters, Jean's niece Allison and her older half-sister Kirsty, are sent to live in England. Jean is to have the care of five-year-old Allison, while Kirsty goes to a paternal aunt on the south coast. During the near-vertical learning curve of child-rearing, Jean is wooed and won, not without some emotional discomfort, by a young doctor, Kenneth Errington. Her best friend, folk-dance teacher Mollie Stewart, is likewise courted by a local curate, Charles Benson. Interwoven into the love story plot are some well-drawn characters such as the fearsome Scottish housekeeper, Morag, Kirsty's irksome Aunt

Gladys, Mollie's troublesome landlady Mrs Taylor, and the serene Moti-ayah from India.

Following its first publication, *Jean of Storms* lay undiscovered for 65 years, bound in copies of the *Shields Daily Gazette* in the local history vaults of South Shields Library. It did not come to light during Helen McClelland's researches for the original edition of her biography *Behind the Chalet School* (New Horizon, 1981, revised edition published by Bettany Press, 1996). Neither did anyone who knew her at the time mention that she wrote for this newspaper, although it is thought now that Brent-Dyer penned a regular women's column.

A column called "Eleanore — Mainly for Women" ran from 1924 to 1931; "Plain Jane" ran from 1931; and "A Shieldswoman's Journal" began in the same year. There were also notes in the *Gazette* on society balls and dinners. On the surface, "Eleanore" could well have been from the pen of Elinor M. Brent-Dyer, since it dealt with subjects as wide ranging and far sighted as "Using your vote wisely" and "Chemistry as a career for girls". However, since Elinor had been living away from South Shields during much of the 1920s, it seems unlikely (although not impossible) that she had penned her copy from the other end of the country and sent it back every week to her home town.

Veronica Cheyne, who left the Misses Stewart's school in 1929, recalls that: "it was assumed by us that the column signed 'Eleanore' was that of Miss Dyer, and 'Plain Jane' by a Patricia Docksey who had also been a pupil at our school, and the social column was written by a man." However, Olga Hargreaves, who as Olga Sutherland had been one of the dedicatees of *Rivals for the Chalet School* (1929), thought that Brent-Dyer could have written either "Plain Jane" or "Mainly for Women", but was certain that she had written the social column, recalling that whenever she and her elder sister went to a society ball, Miss Dyer was always there taking notes, so that they knew they would read reports of what they had worn in the following day's newspapers.

It was only in 1995 that Miss Doris Johnson, who works in the South Shields local history library, was looking up a marriage announcement in the *Shields Daily Gazette* when her eyes fell on *Jean of Storms* — a full length novel serialised in Brent-Dyer's own local newspaper. At about this time, I was passing through South Shields en route home from a visit to Scottish Chalet friends, and decided to call in on some of the people whom I'd met the previous year during the celebrations marking Brent-Dyer's birth centenary (see *The Chalet School Revisited*, Bettany Press, 1994). It was purely on impulse that I did so, and quite by chance that I saw Doris who told me about *Jean of Storms*.

I immediately asked Doris if I might borrow her phone to tell Helen McClelland, Brent-Dyer's biographer, about this amazing find. Helen rang to tell Brent-Dyer's heir, Chloe Rutherford, and that evening I shared the thrilling news with as many of my Chalet friends as possible. As the book was so important to Chalet fans, I felt it was necessary that a copy be taken. This was not as easy as it might sound. For one thing, the photocopied print of the *Shields Daily Gazette* held at South Shields library was very tiny, and every line petered out for the last few words. Sometimes the order of the photocopies did not correspond to the order of the story in the newspaper, and on at least one occasion, paragraphs in the newspapers themselves were actually transposed. On two occasions the newspaper had omitted a chapter heading, so I had fun inventing a couple

(Chapter X: "An Anxious Time" and Chapter XIX: "A Reunion and Two Puzzles").

However, I was determined that other Brent-Dyer fans should be able to read *Jean of Storms*, and brought it to the attention of Rosemary Auchmuty and Juliet Gosling of Bettany Press. They considered that in marking an unusual departure for the author into the field of romance, *Jean of Storms* filled in a piece of the complex jigsaw that is the life and work of Elinor M. Brent-Dyer, a piece that no Brent-Dyer fan had hitherto known was missing.

Once Bettany Press had decided to publish *Jean of Storms* as a companion volume to their three earlier books, *The Chalet School Revisited* (1994), *Visitors for the Chalet School* (1995) and a revised edition of *Behind the Chalet School* (1996), my typescript was checked by Rosemary Auchmuty and another Chalet fan, Sally Phillips, from original copies of the *Shields Daily Gazette* held in the British Museum's Newspaper Library at Colindale. Although some of the episodes in the book, in particular the attitude of Morag to the unfamiliar black face of an ayah, are not politically correct by today's standards, it was agreed that the book would not be edited and updated. Therefore the text is reproduced exactly as it appeared in the serial version, except that obvious typographical errors have been corrected, inconsistent spellings and punctuation made consistent and where sections of the text were misplaced in the newspaper, the correct order has been restored. The book, like all Bettany Press books, is set in the type called New Century Schoolbook, an updated version of the Century Schoolbook type used in the original Chalet School series (published by W. & R. Chambers Ltd).

A little j'ography. I am very grateful to Joan-Mary Jones, whose family is from South Shields, and who grew up in the adjoining street to Brent-Dyer's birthplace, Winchester Street, where her mother's family actually lived, for providing me with a sketch map of the area. She has also researched Brent-Dyer's fictitious place-names and their relationship to real-life place-names as only a local can. She writes:

> To local residents, armed with old maps and reference books of the area, the problem of solving this puzzle becomes quite an easy task and a translation of place-names as follows:
> Aulmbermouth — Tynemouth
> Blyton Sands — Blyth
> Hasnett — Cullercoats
> Noviam — Newcastle upon Tyne
> South Helling — South Shields.

As Joan discovered, Hasnett, like the actual village of Cullercoats, stands on a little circular bay on the north-east coast, and indeed to the south it "straggles and stretches" towards Aulmbermouth (Tynemouth). Hasnett itself, as Cullercoats, is part of the town of Whitley Bay. It has a long stretch of sand and low rocks and a steep bank of grass, the very rocks that Jean could have scrambled over. Until fairly recently the village was very well known for fishing, and a Cullercoats village fishwife, in a traditional costume, was a common sight.

A Quaker family called Dove owned a mill in the area during the sixteenth century, and they were responsible for the subsequent development of the village of Cullercoats. In 1682 (forty years before the date above the door of the fictitious house of Storms), Thomas Dove Junior built a mansion house in Backrow which he called Dove Cottage, but it became known locally as Sparra Hall. It was in continuous occupancy until its demolition in 1979, and there is every chance that Elinor knew this house and intended it for her Storms. Further details about the house are lacking, other than that it stood on the northern peak of a landlocked bay, not quite the north-east coast like Storms.

Around Sparra Hall (a northern corruption of "Sparrow" for "Dove") a number of houses and fishermen's cottages were gradually built, so that the village of Cullercoats developed and thrived with its smugglers, coal trade and finally fishing. By the 1880s, Cullercoats was a very small but distinct community with its own way of life, very much like the Hasnett in which Oona McCleod visits the poor fisherfolk with her bountiful basket. The North-Eastern Railway opened its new coastal line in the wake of the abandonment of the old local Whitley Waggonway route, and Cullercoats station was opened in about 1910. By this time, two tram companies provided a full service on the twelve-mile stretch between Newcastle Central Station and North Shields and on through Tynemouth to Whitley Bay, with an established tramline station at Cullercoats. As we see regularly in *Jean of Storms*, the tram cars are a well-used mode of transport for Jean and Mollie in particular: "Jean McCleod . . . hurried . . . to the car terminus. The run to Aulmbermouth was not a long one — twenty minutes or so — but the cars only ran every quarter of an hour, and she had set off late."

Aulmbermouth, the seaside town, is very likely Tynemouth. It is within walking distance of Cullercoats and has fine old buildings like the Regency ones that Aulmbermouth boasts. It has a promenade and a Northumberland Square, which was the street in the fictitious Aulmbermouth where Dr Errington lived. The large private school, King's

School, at Tynemouth could well have been the school which Jean visited for her dancing classes. The writer Harriet Martineau lived in a fine old Regency house in Tynemouth in the 1840s. Like Aulmbermouth, the town boasted an air of refinement, with a promenade, and a mixture of Regency houses and shops in Front Street.

Joan's research only enabled her to find one smuggler's cave which fitted the location of the final episode, literally a cliff-hanger! This is at Cullercoats itself and she remarks that Elinor described it as the "short bents grass", since the grassy area above the cliffs along the coast at South Shields and Marsden is still known as "the Bents". Another place retaining similarities with the text is Blyth, the real-life Blyton Sands, a small coal port reached from Hasnett by taking the north road past the rabbit-infested fields that Jean mentions. South Shields was depicted, according to Joan, as South Helling; in both cases they were Roman towns famed for their exports. Noviam is of course Newcastle throughout the text, although an actual place called Newcastle is mentioned in Chapter X. Newcastle was the nearest large city to Elinor's birthplace. When writing her not-terribly-revealing potted autobiography, "Something About Me", for the *Chalet Club News Letter*, Elinor admitted to having been born "near Newcastle".

That *Jean of Storms* is set in Elinor's native South Tyneside is fascinating for any Brent-Dyer scholar. Apart from a passing reference to a WAAF from "canny Soo' Shields" in *Gay from China at the Chalet School* (1944), a play, *Polly Danvers — Heiress*, written while living in South Shields, and the possibility that an early school story, *Carnation of the Upper Fourth* (1934), was based around the Tyneside area, Elinor's works are set away from the area in which she grew up. Why, then, did she choose with *Jean of Storms* to write about it? South Shields has its picturesque spots, but even Tom Fennelly, Press and Publicity Officer for South Tyneside Metropolitan Borough Council, would agree that it lacks the appeal of Pertisau-am-Achensee. I would like to think that, being settled back in her home town, she wanted to write about it for a change. Such a setting could hardly have been more appropriate for a serial in her local newspaper.

Brent-Dyer is not on record as ever referring to *Jean of Storms* in later life. She appears to have rejected her past attempt at writing for the adult romance market, just as she rejected her "unfashionable" north- eastern roots. Yet *Jean of Storms* is as clearly her work as any of her school stories, and the same characteristics which have attracted thousands of readers to those books are present in this apparently very different work.

In conclusion, it is marvellous to know that at last *Jean of Storms* is available for present-day fans to read. We must be grateful to Doris Johnson for rediscovering it, and to Bettany Press for making it available to us. View it as you would an old and well-loved friend trying out a new hobby or indulging a new passion. Regard it with the affection that anything by Brent-Dyer rouses in a Chalet fan. There can be no more Chalet titles from Elinor's pen, but here is something new and fresh to us. The plot may be as predictable as that of some of the Chalet books, but *Jean of Storms* is a warm and comforting read with strong characters and a happy ending. I hope you will enjoy it.

A LOCAL SERIAL

by a Local Writer

*****

**The next Serial Story to be Published in
"The Shields Daily Gazette" is entitled**

"JEAN OF STORMS"

*****

**THE AUTHOR IS
Miss Elinor Brent-Dyer**

*a South Shields Lady,
an accomplished writer
who has a number of books to her credit.*

*Her novel, the publication of which will be
COMMENCED ON TUESDAY
has a strong local colouring.
We are confident it will make appeal
to both young and old.
It introduces some interesting young folk,
and has*

AN ABSORBING LOVE INTEREST.

CHAPTER I

NEWS FROM INDIA

Hasnett stands on a little circular bay on the north-east coast. To the south it straggles and stretches towards Aulmbermouth, a pretty little seaside resort of the quieter kind, where dignified old houses, built in the days of the Regency, mingle with shops in the High Street, and others, more modern, rise up along the Promenade. To the north, Hasnett tails off with a few fishermen's cottages, and the big children's Convalescent Home. Then the north road runs on to Blyton Sands, a small coal-port, passing by fields and wild, gorse-covered common, where the rabbits and seagulls hold high revelry. Above the northern peak of the land-locked bay stands Storms by itself. It was built in the year 1722 — the date is above the door — and is set four-square to the winds. Made of the grey north country stone, with thick walls and deep-set windows and doors, it looks sturdily over the North Sea, calmly defying the worst efforts of winds and waters to harm it. A big garden lies all round it, walled in at the back and sides with high stone walls; but in front, they are a bare four feet high, as if the builder had loved the wild sea, and had no wish to shut out its many moods from the main rooms. The land dips here, and, on stormy days, the rose-bushes are washed by the spray of the great waves that foam and churn at the foot of the cliff. The path, which follows the coast-line, is often slippery and wet in the winter and autumn and early spring, and then the dwellers in the old house are fain to use the door cut in the back wall on to the high road.

It was on a certain day in late October that Jean McCleod stood at the dining-room window at Storms, gazing out at the tumbling waste of waters, which tossed fountains of spray up to the summit of the rocks. It was such a day as Jean loved, with a cold gray sky overhead, and a bitter sea beneath. The air was full of the moan of the wind and the roar of the waves, varied occasionally by the shriek of a gull as it winged its way westwards. There was no other sound save the crackling of the driftwood fire that filled the room with a cheery light. The girl had turned her back on the warmth and glow, however, and was standing at one of the deep windows, revelling in the wildness outside. By the fire sat Oona McCleod, her aunt and friend, knitting at a fleecy white shawl intended for the baby of a fisherman who had never come home from his fishing a month before. The widow, a frail girl, had scarcely heart enough to live out the last days before the birth of her baby, and, when he had come, had slipped thankfully out of life. The boy had been taken by a kindly neighbour, who, with five of her own, yet made room for this new mouth. Miss McCleod had been interested in the matter, and had promised some clothes for the poor mite — hence her occupation. As she paused in her work to join in a fresh ball of wool, she looked across at her niece.

"Jean, come away from that window! It's enough to drive one crazy to see you on a wild day like this!"

Jean turned her head with a smile. "Poor Oona! You don't understand, do you?"

"I do not!" retorted Miss McCleod. "But it isn't canny the way you hang over the sea when it's like this! I don't know how you can!"

The tall girl, who was a little more than twelve years her junior, moved away from the window, and came over to the hearth. "I love it when it's in a rage. It seems so mighty I could watch it for hours!"

Miss McCleod looked at her niece. "I hate it when it's like this! I always remember how cruel it is — how relentless. Think of the poor fellows who are out on it now, beating their way to port! It is terrible to me, Jean."

Jean's eyes — splendid eyes of hazel-green — softened as she listened. She knew what was in Oona's mind — the young sailor sweetheart, who had gone down with his vessel in the last year of the war. Oona had only been in the very early twenties then, and now she was nearly thirty-five, but she hated the sea still because of her bitter loss.

"It's some time ago," said the girl, answering that unspoken thought of her aunt's.

"What difference would it make if it were a hundred years?" demanded Miss McCleod. "You are very young, Jean, or you would not talk like that."

Jean opened her lips to refute this, but just then, the kitchen tyrant, Morag McClean, came in with tea and the afternoon letters. The girl sat down instead, and while Oona poured out the fragrant amber fluid from the little melon-shaped teapot, Jean looked at the letters.

"Why — one from India!" she exclaimed.

"From Doris?" questioned her aunt.

Jean shook her head. "It's no writing that I know." She tore it open, skimmed the contents rapidly and uttered a little cry. "Oona! Doris is dead! She died some weeks ago, and they are sending the little girls home to England."

Oona set down the teapot sharply. "Doris dead! Jean!"

"That's what it says," replied Jean. "It's from a Mrs Fortescue. — Here, read it for yourself!"

She handed over the letter, and Oona took it. It

was very brief and to the point. The writer stated
that Mrs McCleod, wife of Jean's only brother, had
died of a sudden heart attack some weeks previously. The two little girls — the elder, a daughter of
her first husband's, the younger Jean's own niece —
were at the time of writing, down with measles, but
as soon as possible they would be sent home. Kirsty,
the elder, was to go to her own father's people, and
the young widow had wished Allison to come to
Storms, to Jean. Word of their departure would be
cabled when it occurred. That was all. The writer,
after a few kindly words of sympathy, signed herself
as "Yours sincerely, Madge Fortescue," and there
ended.

Oona laid down the letter and looked at Jean.

"Poor Doris!" she said quietly. "Well, Jean, we can
scarcely grieve for her, for we never knew her — you
cannot know people through occasional letters —
and she would never come home as we asked after
Alastair died. I am glad, however, that we are to
have the child. I do not know that I should have
cared for the other; but Alastair's little girl should
be with his people. You are her nearest relative, and
it is only right she should come to us."

Jean nodded. Her thoughts were far away to those
days when a letter had come from India where he
was stationed with his regiment, saying that he was
going to marry a young widow with one child. A
year later had arrived the news of the birth of a
little daughter who was to have their mother's
name. Then, a few months later, the unknown Doris
had written to her to say that Alastair was dead —
killed by overwork and cholera, caught while
working among his men in a cholera camp. The
young widow — she was only twenty three, even
now — stayed on in India where she had been born
and had passed most of her life. She wrote occasion-

ally to her young sister-in-law, but there had been little to give them any idea as to what she was like. As Oona had said, they could scarcely grieve for her.

Jean suddenly got up from her seat, and went across the room, and stared out again at the tempestuous sea. The wind was rising with the rising tide, and the water was tossing, fretted and tormented under its pitiless lash.

Suddenly, she turned. "You are right, Oona. I am glad Allison is to come to us."

Miss McCleod, who was full of the clan spirit, agreed. "Allison belongs to the McCleods. She could not go anywhere else. Come and get your tea, Jean, and leave staring at the sea. Draw the curtains, dear, and switch on the light. It will be a wild night." Jean did as she was asked, and came back to the little table by the fire. Outwardly, she was very calm, but inwardly she was seething with excitement. She felt as if everything were to have a fresh beginning. The old, quiet life, of household duties, Guide-work, and folk-dancing, and carefree happiness was over. She stood on the brink of a new existence; new responsibilities would be hers. How would she like them?

"You will not go to dancing to-night?" queried her aunt, as, tea over, and the things carried away, she settled down to knitting once more. "The weather is terribly wild."

Jean laughed. "Oh, yes; I shall go. I feel all churned up inside, and folk-dancing rests me. Besides, you can't think of anything else at the time, and I feel as if I wanted to get away from my thoughts for a while, so that I can get them disentangled and clear. This will make change, you know, Oona."

"Yes. I know," replied her aunt. "Very well, Jean. If you feel like that, it will be better for you to go.

Wrap up warmly and don't attempt the cliff-path, whatever you do. It will be slippery with spray and most dangerous."

"Oh, I'll go the back way," agreed Jean. "I don't want to come to an untimely end on the rocks below."

Miss McCleod shivered. "Don't talk like that, Jean! It's horrible!"

"My dear Oona, this must have upset you a good deal," said Jean. "It's not like you to be nervy and cross. I will take every care. And if you'll take my advice, you'll put that knitting away, and get a jolly book to read while I'm out."

Oona shook her head. "I shall go to Evensong. Don't trouble about me, Jean; I shall be all right."

Jean nodded, and went out of the room to get ready for the Folk dancing she loved so dearly. The class was held in a hall at Aulmbermouth, and she must not be late if she could help it.

Miss McCleod, left alone, quietly put her knitting to one side, and sat gazing into the fire, recalling old times, and wondering about the little great-niece who was to come to them soon.

CHAPTER II

The wind was howling lustily when Jean McCleod slipped out of the door in the big back wall, and hurried along the dark road in the direction of Hasnett village to the car terminus. The run to Aulmbermouth was not a long one — twenty minutes or so — but the cars only ran every quarter of an hour, and she had set off late. When she arrived at the Church High School where the classes were held, most of the people who attended them were there already, and were struggling with the Sleights Sword Dance under the instructions of the teacher, a small, dark girl, with wavy black hair, and twinkling brown eyes. She laughed at the late-comer as she sped past the team who were getting into trouble with the "spin".

"Hullo! Thought you weren't coming to-night — the weather's so bad and you are so late!"

Jean waved her hand, and made for the formroom used as a cloakroom. There, she tore off her outdoor things, changed into dancing-shoes, and was back into the hall with amazing speed. She was pushed into "No Man's Jig" as one of the Toms, and, under stress of keeping her mind on what she was doing, forgot about the amazing letter she had received that afternoon. However, there were only ten minutes left, and then the class, released for a short rest before "Country", thronged round her, demanding to know why she was so late.

"We'd quite made up our minds you'd funked the weather," laughed one girl. "I must say, I was surprised, for it isn't like you! What happened?"

"I forgot the time," explained Jean, "and then I missed a car and had to wait for the next."

"In all that wind? I don't envy you!" put in a small girl, with a halo of fair, bobbed hair.

"Oh, I took refuge in a doorway," laughed Jean. "You surely didn't think I would stand about in the road in this wind."

The first speaker shook her head. "I don't know. You are mad enough for anything!"

"Only when you are anywhere about," retorted Jean.

"What made you so late, Miss McCleod?" asked the instructress, coming up to them.

"Various events," replied Jean. Then, as the others sheered off to talk to someone else, she went on: "Walk with me to the car, Mollie. I have something to tell you."

Her friend glanced at her. "Interesting? Oh, but I can see it is! Your eyes are like the cat's at my rooms. All right; I'll go a little way with you." Then she ran back to the Head Mistress's desk, and called on the class to form sets for "The Health".

The class went laughing to their places and were presently going through the dance with goodwill. One figure went wrong, thanks to Jean's preoccupation, and her set were obliged to walk it carefully, while the others stood or sat on the floor, resting and watching them.

"That's better," said the instructress, when they had finished. "Now, dance it, and see if you can get it right."

The dance went off well this time, and then she turned them on to "Adson's Sarabande." For the rest of the evening the two friends — for they were old and close friends — were too busy to think about what was to come. When the last Morris jig had been danced, Jean went to the formroom to get ready, while one or two of the others clustered round the little teacher, asking questions about steps and movements, and wanting to know whether there would be a party soon. As the younger girl got into her hat and coat, she heard laughter and cries of "Oh, Miss Stewart!" which told her that she would probably have to wait a few minutes for Mollie Stewart. Leaning against one of the desks, she replied to the chaff of Miss Farrar, the girl who had addressed her on her first entry, and presently the others came in, laughing and talking, and there was a wild scramble to get ready.

"Listen to that wind!" remarked the fair girl — a Miss Radley. "I wouldn't be you for something, McCleod, with your walk along the cliffs to-night!"

"Oh, I'm accustomed to it," replied Jean. "Besides, I love it."

"Like to like!" laughed Miss Farrar. "Clouds and wind always go together."

"Rotten pun!" cried Miss Radley. "Well, I must go: I have a pile of history that high to correct before I go to bed to-night. Coming, Farrar?"

Miss Farrar nodded, and they went off together. Then Miss Stewart came up to Jean, and touched her on the arm.

"Come along! I'm ready now and we're late."

"Oh, sorry. Hope I haven't kept you waiting?" laughed Jean, as she picked up her case, and made for the door. "Good-bye till next week, you people."

A gay chorus followed her as she followed Miss Stewart out, and then they ran into a wind that was blowing hard, and obviously meant to blow harder.

"I say, I don't think you'd better come after all," said Jean, as they stopped in a shop doorway to get their breath. "It's getting worse every minute, and you might be blown into the sea."

"What a loss!" mocked her companion. "Of course I'll come! I want to hear your news."

"Well, I'd better tell you here. I can't in all this wind."

"I know something better than that. Come back to my rooms with me, and have cocoa."

"At half-past nine at night? Mrs Taylor won't thank you for bringing a visitor."

"You talk as if it were midnight! Be sensible, Jean, and come."

"Oh, all right! But if she is annoyed, don't blame me!"

The two ventured out of their shelter and were nearly carried off their feet by the mighty gust that swooped down on them at the moment. Half-running, half-blown, they made their way to a cross-street where they found a little shelter, and where Miss Stewart had rooms. It was less of a battle here, and presently they stopped before one of the houses and Mollie Stewart unlocked the door, and they went in. A door at the end of the narrow passage opened as they entered, and a middle-aged woman appeared.

"Oh, Mrs Taylor, I've brought Miss McCleod back for some cocoa," said Miss Stewart. "May we have it now, please?"

Mrs Taylor disappeared with a grunt and the two went upstairs to a small room on the first floor, where the hostess lit a gas-fire before she flung her outer things down on the sofa.

"Take your things off, Jean. The cocoa will be here in a minute. Would you like to wash your hands first? You know where the bathroom is."

Jean nodded and vanished. When she came back, a pile of books had been moved from a small table, which had been brought to the fireside, and supper was ready.

Miss Stewart looked up. "Come along. I washed in my bedroom so as to save time. You oughtened to stay very long, for the wind is rising still. You don't want to spend the night on that couch, do you?"

"I should simply hate it!" said Jean cordially. "Oh, the wind will rise all right. It's coming up on the tide and it isn't flood till midnight. Steady with the sugar. I don't like things as sweet as you do!"

She took her cocoa and when they were settled, Mollie Stewart turned to her friend, exclaiming, "Now!"

Jean ate a sandwich meditatively before she answered "Mollie, do you remember my brother, Alastair?"

"Only vaguely. He came to school once, and took you out. I was to have gone too, but had had an unfortunate difference with Mademoiselle, so it didn't happen. But why?"

"Alastair went to India, you remember," said Jean slowly. "That was a final treat before he went off."

"He married out there, didn't he?" asked her friend, racking her memory for details of the big, faintly-remembered officer who had been Jean McCleod's brother.

"Yes; the next year. She was a widow with one little girl."

"I remember. You told me the day before we broke up. It was my last term."

"Yes; I was only fifth form, and feeling miserable because you were going and we'd always been such chums. Do you remember I wrote to you a year later and told you I had a niece?"

Mollie nodded. "Of course. And I got another letter later saying that your brother had died in cholera camp."

Jean nodded in her turn. "Yes. Well, this afternoon, I got a letter from a Mrs Fortescue in

India, saying that Doris — my sister-in-law — was dead, and they are sending both children home to England as soon as possible."

"What — both to you?"

"Oh, no! Kirsty, the elder, is to go to her father's people. But little Allison is coming to us."

Mollie Stewart was silent. She was not very sure what to say. Jean, watching her with smiling eyes, waited. Presently, she spoke.

"When will Allison arrive?"

"I don't know. But Mollie, it's going to make a difference to me. You see she is a delicate kiddy from all accounts, and I can't very well go off and leave her to Oona for any length of time. I'm afraid this is going to spoil our summer holiday."

"How old is she?" demanded Mollie. She was upset, but Jean was not to know it yet. She hoped the arrival of this small child was not going to upset things altogether. She and Jean had been friends ever since the day when Jean, a very shy new girl, had been found in the Middle School cloakroom, weeping desolately, by Mollie Stewart, who had taken her to her heart with characteristic impetuosity, and had comforted her with the assurance that school really wasn't bad.

When Miss Stewart had come to Aulmbermouth to teach Folk Dancing in the district, they had both rejoiced. In class, they were careful not to obtrude their friendship; but out of it they were still on the same terms.

Jean guessed what was going on in her friend's mind. "It shan't make all that difference, Mollie," she promised. "Only I shall be more tied, now."

A dash of rain and wind against the windows turned the current of their thoughts at that moment. Jean hastily gulped down the last of her cocoa, and stood up to put on her hat and coat.

"Yes; you'd better go before it gets worse," agreed Mollie. "It's going to be a wild night and Miss McCleod may worry if you turn up late."

No more was said about the afternoon's news but both thought the more, and when she had closed the door on Jean racing to catch her tram, and was back in her little sitting room, Mollie Stewart sighed.

"It's going to make changes," she said aloud, "and I hate changes!"

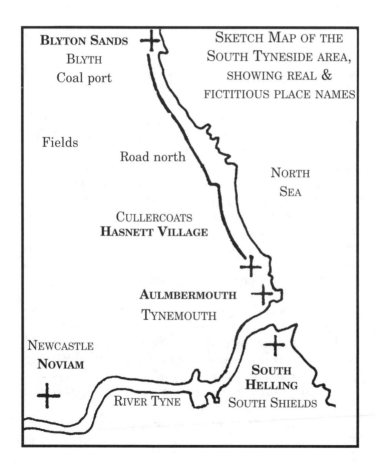

CHAPTER III

"Given two bachelor women and one small child, the question arises, where is the said small child to sleep? Oona, wake up and give me some advice."

Miss McCleod looked up from her book and smiled. "My dear Jean, it wouldn't be much use if I did. You'll get your own way, whatever I may say, and well you know it. What are you thinking of doing?"

Jean collapsed on the floor against her aunt's knee, and leaned her black head back. "I haven't an idea. Don't be so squashing, Oona. I've had a row with Morag about ushering in people on me unannounced, and I did think I could come to you for a little sympathy! If you fail me, I shall go down to the rocks and howl like a dog. Put your book down — it can't be half so interesting as my problems — and lend me your ears for a few minutes!"

Oona closed her book resignedly, and laid it down. "Well, what do you want?"

"Where shall I put Allie to sleep when she comes?"

"In the little dressing room over the door, I should think. She'll be near us both then, and can have some place to call her own, too."

"But she's only five. Do you need that when you're just five?"

"I should think it might be useful. Besides, every girl should, if possible, have her own private room.

It is so here, and I certainly think it would be the
wisest plan. You are accustomed to reading till all
hours of the night, and you couldn't do that if you
had a small child in with you. I am a bad sleeper
and too restless to be a good room-mate. Give her
the little room and let her have the door between it
and yours open during the night. Then she can call
if she wants you, and you can continue your evil
courses."

Jean heaved a sigh of relief. "Do you really think
so? I was afraid I ought to have her with me. I never
even dreamed of her sharing with you."

Miss McCleod nodded. "I never supposed you did.
There's only one thing, Jean. I won't have you
making a slave of yourself to her. As for having her
in your room, I won't hear of it, so please don't
discuss it again."

"But supposing she's afraid — such a wee thing!"

"She won't be. She will go to bed early, and most
likely be asleep when you go upstairs. If the door is
open, she will feel you near and, in any case,
children of that age usually sleep the clock round."

"I hope she'll be happy with us," said Jean
anxiously. "It must be rather dreadful for her,
coming to entire strangers by herself."

"Most likely she won't think about it. Besides, she
ought to be at home with you pretty soon —
especially if you continue to sit on the floor as you
are doing at present! Well, if that is all you want to
say about Allison, I think I will get on with my
book!"

"Oh, but it isn't," Jean hastened to reassure her.
"I've got heaps to say. So don't go and bury yourself
again till I've finished!"

Oona looked resigned, but she left the book where
it was, and turned her gaze on the serious face lifted
to her. "Go on, then, I'm listening."

"I want to know if you think I ought to send her to school," said Jean. "She is only five, I know, but Alma Radley says they have tinies at the High School in the K.G. there. You see, Oona," she went on, "there are no other children here for her to play with, and if she has been with Kirsty all the time, she may feel lonely with only grown-ups. What do you think?"

"I certainly should not dream of sending her anywhere before the summer term," said Oona, decidedly. "Five is much too young for school."

"But it isn't really like school," urged Jean. "They play most of the time."

Miss McCleod shook her head. "It doesn't matter. If the child had had the life of the average Anglo-Indian child, she would hate it. And you've got to remember that she must be acclimatised first. A delicate baby of five won't take kindly to our nipping winds and heavy sea frets all at once. If you did send her to school, I don't suppose she would be there for half the term. Let her wait till May when the weather will be better and you can send her then if you think fit."

"Well, what am I to do with her all day?" demanded Jean. "I don't know the first thing about children, and I don't believe I could teach them, either. She ought to be starting to learn to read, oughtn't she?"

"Jean, you are making mountains out of molehills! Wait till the child comes, and see what she is like. Is that the bell? Who on earth can be coming to see us on such an afternoon as this?" And Oona glanced at the streaming window-panes against which the rain was beating a brisk tattoo.

Jean, with a belated remembrance of her position, got up from the floor, when Morag opened the door, a dour expression on her face. "It's Miss Mollie, Miss

Jean. Will I let her in on ye?"

"Mollie? You silly old woman! Of course!"

Jean dashed hastily past her, and ran to the door which Morag had carefully closed behind her before coming into the dining-room, and disclosed Mollie Stewart in its deep embrasure, her pretty face pinched with the cold.

"Mollie! Come in at once!" Jean caught her by the arm, and dragged her in. "Morag is an idiot! I never included you in my remarks, but she is annoyed with me, so I suppose she's trying to get back at me this way."

"I don't know what you are talking about," shivered Mollie, as she slipped out of her Burberry. "That had better go to the kitchen — thank you, Morag — I've got an unexpected holiday, so I thought I'd come round and see you. Can you put me up for the night? I've bought my pyjamas with me."

"Rather! Can you stay? Oh, good! Oona and I are on the verge of scrapping, we are so bored with ourselves and each other, and I've put Morag's back up with a few words on the inadvisability of showing visitors straight in on us, and she is furious."

"Oh, is that why I was left to cool my heels on the doorstep in all this torrent of rain? I wondered what had happened!"

"Morag was doing it to pay me out for the aforesaid remarks. She knew I should be mad about it. Come along in! Oona, here's Mollie come to spend the night with us. She's got a holiday."

"The school where my Frampton classes are held was burned down over-night," explained Mollie as she sank into an easy chair. "They couldn't get anywhere else in such a hurry, so they wired me not to come till next week. I got the wire at midday, so I thought I'd come out and see you people. What happened last week, Jean? We missed you."

"Toothache," said Jean, with a reminiscent grimace. "I went to see Mr Tomlinson the next day and he stopped the brute — when I hoped he'd take it out and have done with it!"

"Poor Jean! You have my deepest sympathy. Was it very bad?"

"Rotten! It's all right now, thank goodness. Did I miss much?"

" 'Chelsea Reach' and the beginnings of 'Running Set'."

"Oh, Mollie!" Jean sat up with a wail. "I do think you might have waited till I came! You know I was dying to begin 'Running Set'!"

Mollie laughed unfeelingly. "Oh, you'll soon pick it up! We didn't go very far, I can assure you. A good many people were absent, though one or two absentees were present, notably, your pet aversion."

"Was that awful woman there again? When she hadn't turned up for three weeks, I'd hoped she wasn't coming again."

"Who is this?" asked Oona.

"Oh, didn't I tell you?" Jean turned her bright face to her aunt. "She's an awful creature named Clapham. I don't know much about her, but I can't endure her."

"Why not?" asked her aunt.

"Oh — I just can't! She's so dull — and so podgy and sloppy. She talks with her teeth shut and she has a ghastly voice at any time! And she talks nothing but council school shop. I can stand it when that pretty red-haired kid, Miss Bannister, tells us about her tinies. But I get sick of all the rot Clapham tells us. I never go near her if I can help it, but you can't always avoid it! She arms so fiercely. I loathe it! Besides, she tries to teach me and I know as much as she does and if I don't, Mollie is the one to do the teaching. I choke her off when I can, of course — ”

"Notably in 'Picking Up Sticks'," put in Mollie. "Oh, I saw you, Jean! You were downright rude to her."

"Well, I do know a sheepskin hey when I do it, and I don't need anyone to pull me right."

"Still you needn't have snapped at her as you did. However, there's no sense in talking to you about her — it only upsets you. I've got some news that ought to cheer you up."

"What is it?"

"We've got three men, now. They've all done some dancing and I'm in hopes they may get others to join. Then we can have a men's class. At present, they have to be with you folk."

"I wish we could have a men's class! Who are they, Moll?"

"One of them is the new doctor from Northumberland Square. I've met him at Vacation schools and he's very jolly. The others are the new curate at St. Simon's, and one of the men from the boys' school. They've both done a good deal of morris, and some sword. The curate wants to introduce dancing at the boys' club. I advised him to begin with sword, which they will all love, for short-sword — Rapper dances, you know — ought to be in their blood. We are near to Newbiggin and Walbottle, and all those other places where they do the Rapper dances still; and I've no doubt the forefathers of these lads had their own dance, too, only it's been discontinued and forgotten."

"More than likely," agreed Jean. "Hullo, here's Morag with tea." Morag entered the room, still looking dour. Jean had offended her mightily by her plain speaking, and she was not prepared to forgive her young mistress yet. She laid the little table in a chilly silence, and then departed to her own quarters, still gloomy and standoffish.

"Morag is wild with me!" chuckled Jean, as she held out the muffins to her friend. "Mollie, after tea, I want you and Oona to help me to decide about further arrangements for Allie's room."

Mollie took her muffin, and during tea, she discussed the room and its future occupant with great animation. When the meal was over, they went up to the little dressing-room over the door, and Jean and Mollie proceeded to go into detail.

"This will be charming for her," declared the latter, as she gazed round the dainty room, with its rose-spattered paper, white paint, and wicker chair with pink cushions. "I should put a pink shade over the light, I think, Jean, and you could move in that little white bookcase you used to have in your own bedroom. Where will you put your own frocks, though?"

"Oh, somewhere," said Jean easily. "Was that the bell? Heavens! What a peal! I wonder it isn't broken!" Steps were heard ascending the stairs and then Morag put in an appearance bearing a cablegram which she handed to Jean, still in offended silence. Jean tore it open.

"From India!" she said.

"What does it say?" asked Miss McCleod, eagerly.

"Children sailed October the twenty-fifth. Arrive early December," read Jean. "Well, I must say I think they might have let us know sooner!"

"So do I," said Mollie. "What a queer idea to pack them off like that without letting you know sooner!"

"Will there be an answer, Miss Jean?" said Morag stiffly. "If there isna, I'll be sending the bit laddie aboot his business."

"No, Morag. No answer," said Jean, absently. She turned to her aunt. "Oona, one of us must go to Southampton to meet the boat, and I suppose it had better be me."

Miss McCleod agreed with her. Various committee meetings were due from which she ought not to absent herself. Jean could be more easily spared.

"I wonder when they will arrive," said Jean. "They may be delayed, of course. The papers say they've been catching it in the Mediterranean."

"Isn't there a shipping gazette downstairs?" asked Mollie. "It will give you the Indian boats, won't it?"

"Good idea," said Jean. "Come along, Oona. We'll go and see what we can gather in the way of information from it."

They went off downstairs to the dining-room where they found the gazette under a pile of magazines, and the two girls bent over it eagerly. Suddenly, Jean uttered a cry, and put her finger on a column. "Here we are! 'S. S. Indian Queen. Left Bombay October 25th. Port Said' — oh, that doesn't matter! — 'Valetta on the third'. That's all. How long does it take from Valetta to Southampton, anyway?"

Oona shook her head. "I'm afraid I can't help you. Doesn't it say when she's due? Let me see, Jean."

Jean handed her the paper, and she looked at the place. "Yes; here you are. 'Due December the sixth'."

Jean looked at the place. "Good heavens! And this is the fifth! I must wire them at Southampton, and set off at once. What time is it now?"

"Ten to six," said Mollie, with a glance at her watch. "You should catch the nine-fifty from Aulmbermouth, Jean. Then you'll be in plenty of time for the midnight train to Southampton. Tell me what you want to take, and I'll go and begin packing at once."

"Will you? Mollie, you're a real friend! My McCleod frock for travelling — see if it wants fresh collar and cuffs — and my big brown coat and beret. One change of everything and my green dinner dress."

Mollie left the room, and Jean turned to her aunt again. "Oona, how much money have you? I have enough for my fare, I think, and a pound or two over, but I don't want to run short."

"I can let you have fifteen pounds," said Oona quietly. "Luckily, I cashed a cheque this morning, and I only used a pound of it. You ought to be able to manage on fifteen and what you have yourself. You will be coming straight back, won't you?"

"Oh, I think so. Southampton in this weather won't be very inviting, and the sooner the child is here, the better, I think."

"If the boat is delayed, you can wire me and I will send you a money order at once. If she arrives all right, you must put up at Southampton overnight and come on in the morning. You will have to break the journey at York, I think, so I will not expect you till Saturday."

"Yes, I think I'll stop at York," said Jean, thought-fully. "It would make too long a day from the kiddy otherwise. She's only five, after all, and not strong at that."

"I think it would be wiser," said Oona. "I shall be glad of the time, too, for there is the room to get ready. If you stop at York, Jean, you can catch a train at about ten the next morning, I think. That will mean you will be here in the afternoon."

"Then if Allison is tired, she can go straight to bed," observed Jean. "Thank you, Oona. Now I must go and interview Morag about sandwiches for to-night."

"I will do that," said Oona, getting up. "You had better go and see what Mollie is doing."

"Very well. She'll stay, of course, just the same, and she had better have my room."

"I will tell Morag to change the bed linen, then,"

said Oona, and she went off to the kitchen, while Jean ran upstairs to see what Mollie was after.

She found her friend sitting beside the glowing fire, putting fresh collar and cuffs on her tartan frock. On the bed lay her dinner dress, with a little pile of under-things. Her beret and coat were hung over the back of a chair, and her strong, brown shoes were warming at the hearth."

"It does need clean ones, then?" said Jean, indicating the frock with a wave of her hand. "Have you put out any pyjamas? And what about hankies?"

"Your blue 'jamas are on the bed, but I forgot the hanks," admitted Mollie. "I say, Jean, what about money? I can let you have a pound or two if you are short. It's a heavy train fare, and you ought to have plenty with you, for you don't know how long you may be away."

"I'll have plenty, I think," replied her friend from under the bed where she was burrowing in search of her suitcase. "— Come out! Oona can give me enough to go on with, and I have some of my own, for a wonder. Thanks all the same. If I needed it, I'd take it and be glad." She began to pack with a swift deftness that told of long custom. "Heigh-ho! I never thought when I left my comfy bed this morning that I should be spending to-night in the train! By the way, you'll stay, won't you, Moll? Oona wants you, and I'd be relieved to know you were with her. I loathe leaving her. This is a bad time for her. — She remembers — well — what happened during the war about this time."

Mollie nodded her head comprehendingly.

"I know. All right, Jean, I'll stay. I can get the rest of my things to-morrow, and bring them out here after the class. To tell the truth, I shan't be sorry to get away from my landlady for a while. I'm convinced she's going mad! What do you think? Last night she landed into my room at one o'clock in the morning to ask me to admire her beautiful curly hair! I was simply wild!"

"I should think so!" returned Jean drily. "Mollie, did she really?"

"Honour bright, she did! I locked my door when she had gone, and I shall keep it locked at night for the future."

"I should think so! I don't see why you should stay on with her. You hate her, and she's a most unpleasant person. The very sight of her makes me feel queer. If she had lived a hundred years ago, she'd have been ducked for having the evil eye."

"Yes; I feel like that sometimes," said Mollie thoughtfully. "I know the poor thing can't help her face, but that awful, dropping eyelid of hers, and her ugly smile make me feel creepy at times."

"I think you ought to change your rooms," said Jean with decision.

"I know I ought, but I've tried to do it twice, and each time she's wept to me, and offered me all sorts of benefits if I'll only stay. I can put up with her as a rule, so long as she doesn't come and talk to me. I feel ill then. Jean, that woman has the most ghastly mind! She can talk about nothing but diseases and things of that kind!"

"The sooner you leave her, the better for you," said Jean firmly. "Is that finished, Moll? Thanks very much. I'll change now, and then I'm ready."

"All right. I'm coming downstairs to tell Oona I'm staying while you are gone. The trams run till eleven-thirty and the only day in the week I'll have to walk out will be on my Frampton day. I don't get into Aulmbermouth till nearly twelve then."

"Indeed, you'll take a taxi!" protested Jean. "Walk along the road at twelve o'clock at night! I can see Oona letting you — even if Morag agreed, which she never would."

Mollie laughed. "Morag is not my slave-driver, thank you. However, we'll see. It's not for another week, and you may be back before then. Buck up and change, and come down. There must be heaps to see to yet."

Mollie left the room with her swinging, graceful walk, and Jean changed rapidly for her unexpected journey. When she went downstairs, she found the other two busy with all sorts of details, and joined them in their work. Morag brought an ample supper at eight o'clock, and at ten, Jean and Mollie set off for the station, where Mollie was to see the traveller safely off. The rain had ceased but the wind was blowing great guns, and the sound of the waves as they thundered on the rocks below the cliffs filled the air with a continuous booming.

"It's going to be a wild night," said Mollie with a shiver as she pulled her coat collar closer round her throat. "Just listen to that sea!"

Jean laughed. "I love it when it's like that."

"Stormy petrel," mocked her friend.

There was no breath for more, and when they had turned the corner, and the wild north-east wind came rushing to meet them, so that it was a struggle to reach the tram terminus. They got to the station just in time for the train to Noviam, where Jean would change for the Southampton express, and there was time for no more than a hasty goodbye, as the porter bundled Jean and her belongings into the nearest compartment. Mollie waved to her and then, as the train moved out of the station, she turned away, to make her way back to Storms. Jean gave a little sigh as she settled down with a book till Noviam was reached. Arrived there, she quickly found the Southampton train, and finally settled down for her long, night journey.

CHAPTER IV

ALLISON

The great ship, storm tossed and weather beaten, had at last reached port in safety, and passengers were all greeting friends and relatives who had had a long and weary wait, for it was nearly a week since she was due. She had been driven out of her course by a gale which had arisen shortly after trouble with one of her screws. The wireless had broken down, and, for thirty hours or more, she had drifted at the mercy of the elements before temporary repairs had been effected. At length, she had entered the long stretch of Southampton water, and was moored safely and at rest for the time being. On board, Jean McCleod was looking anxiously round for her little niece. She saw several children, but all seemed to be with relatives already. Presently her gaze lighted on a little girl, dressed in deep mourning, and she wondered if this could be Allison. The child was pretty with the rounded prettiness of childhood. Long brown ringlets hung over her shoulders, and she was rosy and dimpled. Jean crossed the deck to her, and the child, hearing the step, turned at once, and looked up, displaying a pair of big, red- brown eyes.

"Are you Auntie Jean?" she asked in quick, clipping accents.

"Yes; if you are Allison McCleod, I am your aunt," said Jean.

The child's brows were contracted in a quick frown. "I'm Kirsty," she said. "Allison is over there with Ayah. But you're my aunt, too, if you're

Allie's."

"Not quite," said the girl. "If you want to call me 'Auntie', you may, of course, but I am no relation of you, really."

Kirsty shrugged her shoulders and pouted. "You are very stiff! Mamma always said you were my auntie, too. Auntie Jean, I'm not going to live with you, I know, but I want to come and stay with you in the big house in the funny little village by the sea that Papa told me about. When can I come?"

Jean had a horror of spoilt children, and it was quite evident that Miss Kirsty was a remarkably spoilt child. Still, she had no wish to snub the child, so she said, "You must wait and see what your aunt says. If she agrees, we shall like to have you in the summer. Now will you take me to Allison?"

"She's over there," said Kirsty ungraciously, pointing in the direction of a handsome Madrassi ayah and a little girl also in black. "I'm going to wait here for Aunt Gladys. You can go, if you like."

Jean raised her eyebrows at this rudeness, but she said nothing as she turned away and went across to the other two. She thought the more, however.

"I hope to goodness Allison isn't like that," she thought to herself as she skirted an excited family party. "Oona will be horrified if she is!"

By this time she had reached her objective and was holding her arms out to the little figure which had buried its head against the Indian woman on her approach.

"You are Allison, aren't you?" she said gently. "I am your Auntie Jean, your daddy's sister. Won't you kiss me?"

The ayah stooped over her little charge, trying to unclench the desperately clinging hands. "Missy-baba speak to the Mem sahib," she said gently.

"No — no!" wailed a frightened little voice.

"But Missy-baba must do as she is told," said the low, murmorous tones that were bringing back a flood of memories to Jean. "Come, my little princess!"

The baby hands were freed, and the woman turned the child round to face her aunt. She lifted sad dark eyes to the girl's face as she did so. "My Missy-baba not naughty. Only being frightened — and shy."

Jean dropped on to her knees and took one of the small hands in hers.

"Allie," she said, pleadingly. "Won't you look up? Won't you kiss me, dearie? I have so longed to see you — Alastair's little girl."

The little face, shadowed by the deep black hat, was kept obstinately downbent. The child had made up her mind to have nothing to do with this aunt who was taking her away from Moti and Kirsty, all that remained of her small world. Moti was obviously distressed at her charge's behaviour. She tried to put the child a little from her. But, at the first movement, Allison had twisted round again, and was clinging to her, sobbing, "No-no! No-no, Moti!"

Things were at a deadlock, when there was the sound of steps, and Kirsty, accompanied by a small, bird-like lady, came over to them.

"And so this is Allison?" said the newcomer with a marked Hampshire accent that grated on Jean. "Look up, child, and let me see if you are like your mother. What? You won't?" as Allison made no attempt to leave her shelter. "But that's not a good little girl! Let go of her, my good woman!"

Jean thought well to interfere at this moment, since it was evident that Kirsty's relative was fully prepared to prise the child away from her refuge, and she rather dreaded the scene that might follow.

"Excuse me," she said, in her soft, Highland voice, "but I am Miss McCleod, Allison's aunt."

"I am Mrs Page," replied that lady briskly. "Chrissie's aunt, you know. So you are the one to have charge of poor Doris' youngest? You look very young."

"I expect Allison will find me all the better playfellow for that," said Jean, quietly, though inwardly she was highly annoyed at the remark and the impertinent scrutiny that had accompanied it. "She is tired, of course, and very shy. I won't bother her just now, Moti," she went on. "Can you bring her to the hotel? You need not leave us yet."

"I staying two — three days," said the soft, plaintive voice. "Perhaps, even more."

"I will come with you and show you our taxi," said Jean. "Excuse me, Mrs Page. I will see them established, and then I should like to ask you something, if you don't mind waiting a moment."

"Oh, I'm in no hurry," said Mrs Page. "Come along, Chrissie, and show me your hand- luggage."

"Come, then, Moti," said Jean.

Back on the ship she saw to the final arrangements, and then turned to Mrs Page.

"It is all so hurried," she said, apologetically. "Are you spending the night here?"

The elder lady shook her head. "Oh, no. I live in Fareham, near Portsmouth. We shall get the six train back, and get home as soon as possible."

"Then you haven't much time," said Jean, feeling thankful that this was the case. "Will you come back to the hotel with me and have tea? Then Kirsty can say 'good-bye' to Allie and Moti. You will have time if we go now."

"Well, I don't mind if I do," agreed the lady. "I came in early this morning, so I have finished all my

shopping, and there is nothing to do but wait for the
luggage. My husband is coming to see it through the
Customs for me. What are you doing about
Allison's?"

"I have arranged for it, thank you," said Jean. "I
want to get Allie out of this cold wind. And Kirsty
looks as if she would be the better for getting to a
good fire," she added, with a smile at the child.

"Oh, Chrissie is going to be a healthy, open-air
girl," said her new guardian, airily. "But what did
you call her, Miss McCleod?"

"Kirsty!" said Jean. "That is what I have always
heard her called."

"Papa called me that," put in the lady herself.

"I see. A Scotchman, I suppose," said Mrs Page.
"But she's going to live in England, so we'll make it
'Chrissie'. She was named 'Christian' for her poor
father," she went on.

"I will try to remember," said Jean, gravely. "You
must forgive me if I make slips, but I have known
her for six years as 'Kirsty', so I may find it difficult
at first. Here is our taxi. I see Allison means to sit
on Ayah's knee, so there will be plenty of room for us
all. Will you get in?"

They got in, and were driven rapidly from the
docks to the quiet, residential hotel where Jean had
been staying. Arrived there, she took them all up to
the big bedroom where Allison was to sleep with
her, and, after seeing that they had all they needed,
slipped away to arrange for a room for Moti. When
she came back, Kirsty and her aunt were ready, and
Moti had succeeded in persuading Allison to have
her hat and coat removed. The two children were
dressed alike in white serge frocks, with narrow
black belts. Kirsty's brown curls were tied back with
black ribbons, and Allison's linty-white locks needed
nothing.

Jean looked at her with a feeling of dismay. Her brother had been a handsome man, and her sister-in-law a pretty woman, but their child was as plain as she could well be. Her hair was lank and stringy; her skin, pasty; her mouth had a decided droop; and she was very thin. So far as could be seen, her best feature was her nose, which was delicately modelled, with sensitive nostrils. Her eyes she kept obstinately on the ground, so, beyond the fact that her black lashes were long and curling, nothing could be learnt about them. Kirsty, on the other hand, had her mother's pretty if indeterminate features. Her colouring obviously came from her father, since Jean remembered that Mrs McCleod had been very fair.

The elder child was very different from the younger, being a merry, healthy child, though it struck Jean that she was accustomed to having a good deal of her own way. Secretly, the girl wondered what would happen if she and Mrs Page ever came to loggerheads. It was plain that the lady would stand no nonsense, and Jean rather wished she had been able to take both little girls to Hasnett for the first few weeks, in order to give Kirsty a partial breaking-in. That, however, was impossible. Oona would not have liked it, and Mrs Page would certainly have resented the suggestion. Jean said nothing as yet, but decided that Kirsty's visit to Storms would come as soon as possible. She knew very little about children, but she had an idea that it was wisest to draw in the reins gradually. Mrs Page looked as if she would not understand this, Kirsty would be curbed from the beginning.

All the time they were at tea, the elder lady rattled on about things in general, while the children took what was given them, and Jean thought this over. When they had finished, she sent

the little girls with Moti for Kirsty to put on her hat
and coat, and detained the lady to ask if Allison's
step-sister might come north for March and April.

"I'll see," said Mrs Page. "It would be a pity, don't
you think, to upset them by letting them be together
so soon, though. And then, Chrissie is a big girl —
eight years old — and she will be going to school
after the holidays, and I don't want to break in on
the term so soon."

"I know there is much to be said for all that," said
Jean pleadingly, "but don't you think they may
settle down better if they know they are not going to
be apart too long? I feel sure they will miss each
other dreadfully at first."

"I'll see," said her guest again. "If Chrissie is good,
and gets on well at school, I may let her come to you;
but it must lie with herself."

And with this, Jean had to be contented, though it
seemed to hold a very shadowy hope for the future.
She could not see Kirsty as good as all that.

When the visitors had gone, to the accompani-
ment of tears from Moti, who seemed devoted to the
two children, and a small kiss from Allison to her
step-sister, Jean returned upstairs to the bedroom
to try and make friends with her small niece.

She found that Moti had undressed the child, and
was sitting by the fire with her, crooning an old song
which Jean remembered hearing her ayah sing in
those far back days in India. The sound brought
back to the girl the vision of her own little cot in the
centre of the room, the mosquito-nets drawn back
for her, while ayah's charpoy in the corner awaited
her faithful attendant. She could hear the rustle of
her mother's silken skirts as she came to hear her
little daughter's prayers, and kiss her good-night.
She savoured again the faint aromatic perfume of
the nicotina flowers that grew outside the window.

"Moti!" she said. "Oh, Moti! It is so long since I heard that song!"

Moti stopped her crooning, and looked at her, the child in her arms. "Memsahib been in Hind?" she asked wistfully.

"For seven years," said Jean.

With a sudden inspiration, she dropped down on a low stool, and, with hands clasped loosely round her knees, dreamy eyes fixed on the fire, she began to tell her memories. They were not many for the deaths of her parents, following so soon on her coming to England, had obliterated many of them. Jean could recall sunny mornings, when she had ridden out on her waler pony before chota hazri with a sais in attendance, and her mother's tender kiss to welcome her back home again. She remembered the merry romps on the verandah with Meeta Ayah, and the bearer and the funny little kids that frisked about the compound, while their mothers bleated after them. There were stories told her by the adoring servants who thought missy-baba a little queen, and petted her and would have spoiled her, had it not been for her mother who never permitted a command to be disobeyed or disregarded.

Sitting there, Moti opposite her, cradling the child in her arms, Jean poured it all out, gradually forgetting where she was until a little movement brought her back to the present. Allison had slipped out of Ayah's arms, and was standing beside her. The long lashes were lifted, and for the first time, her aunt saw her eyes, and caught her breath at the loveliness. Real McCleod eyes they were, deeply green, and beautifully set with their heavy fringes of lashes.

Allison put a scrawny little hand on her knee. "Auntie Jean," she said shyly.

Jean caught her in her arms. "Allison! Alastair's little girl! You will try to be happy with Auntie Jean, won't you, dawtie?"

Allison nodded her head. "Yes; 'cause you love India, too," she said.

Jean bent and kissed the sallow little face. She had to put Allie to bed after that, and when the child was sleeping peacefully, she had to draw her slender fingers from the clinging grasp of the child's. She stood looking down at her with a smile. Allison's heart had been won that night. A big step had been already taken.

CHAPTER V

"Mollie, for pity's sake come and sit down! You make me feel ill the way you are wandering about! You remind me of Satan going up and down, seeking what he may devour!"

Mollie Stewart strolled back from the window, and took up her stand on the hearthrug, with a smile for Miss McCleod who lifted a protesting face to hers.

"I'm sorry, Oona, but I'm rather excited, you know. Ten years have I known Jean, and never did I think to see the day that she should bring home a child to bring up! Her own — yes! I can see Jean with three or four babies of her own being perfectly sweet with them. But a niece is different. There's poor Doris to take into account, you know."

"I've brought up Jean, and was far younger than she is when I began," said Oona.

"Was Jean's mother like Doris?" asked Mollie quietly.

Oona shook her head. "Jean's mother was — wonderful. Jean has her features and her sweet gaiety — though she has the McCleod colouring and feyness, too. But my sister-in-law was a beautiful woman both in face and character. Hasn't Jean ever told you about her?"

"Very little. She says she was so young when she left India that she only remembers a few details here and there. And then, Mrs McCleod died so soon after! I always get the impression that Jean regards her mother as a cross between an angel and a fairy

47

princess. It's difficult to tell, from that sort of thing, what anyone is like."

"Yes; I suppose so," replied Oona thoughtfully. "Allison was a very lovely person. I adored her from first seeing her — when I was a small child. When my own mother died, she wrote to me so lovingly. I was only seventeen, you know, and very lonely. She wanted me to go out to them when my schooldays were ended. She died three weeks after the end of my last term — when I was eighteen, and my brother couldn't live without her. He followed a year later. Alastair was nineteen, then, and Jean only eight. It may have seemed rather an undertaking for a girl still in her teens to take a child of that age to bring up, but I knew what Jean was, and I have never regretted it. She has been a great comfort and consolation to me, and what I should do without her, I could not say."

"You'll be keeping her a while yet," replied Mollie. "After all, she is only twenty-three."

"Oh, I will not be selfish about her," said Miss McCleod drily. "If the right man comes along, I will not allow Jean to sacrifice herself for me. So far, he hasn't appeared, but I expect he will, any day. Jean was made for marriage."

"You'll have a business, persuading her of that," said Mollie.

"I know. I shall expect your help there, Mollie."

"You'll get it. I should hate you to be left, but you are right about Jean. She ought to marry, and I hope she does."

"Well, we needn't trouble about it just yet." Miss McCleod got up, and went to the window where she stood looking out at the sullen sea which washed heavily up against the rocks. There was no wind, but it was a dull day, with evidence of a coming storm. It was bitterly cold, and the sky was overcast.

"It'll snow if this goes on," said Mollie, joining her.

"Yes; I wish Jean would come. From this morning's letter it sounds as though Allison were very delicate."

"Anglo-Indian, and never been out of the country before — what else could you expect?" asked Mollie. "What I should like to know is, why on earth Jean wants another room prepared. It can't be for the other child, for Jean said she and the aunt went off at once."

"Jean may have arranged to bring her north with Allison for a while," said Oona. "It might be rather a good thing at first. I wish we had thought of it sooner."

"Can't say I like the sound of the aunt, either," said Mollie. "If Kirsty's spoilt, as she is almost certain to be, there'll be a few tussles before she settles down. I know what a little brute I was when I first came home. The servants there had treated me like a little princess, and it was a shock to meet Grannie's prim parlour-maid who refused to be called 'pig' and shook me when I kicked her!"

Oona laughed. "I remember your grandmother telling me all about it at one Speech Day when we foregathered. She said you were decidedly of the opinion that you belonged to the Heaven-born. Smithson, I gathered, did not see it in the same light."

"That she did not!" said Mollie with a chuckle at the recollection. "She was most shocked at my behaviour. So was Grannie, though she forgave me, for she said I didn't understand."

"And did you learn soon?" asked Oona with a twinkle.

"In about six months. Oh, how I hated England those first few weeks! I used to howl for Ayah who had let me treat her as I liked, and only called me her little princess. I can hear her now." Mollie's dark eyes grew very soft. "That gentle voice so murmorous that many of them have, and her pet-names. It never mattered to Ayah how naughty or unkind I was; I was her Missy-baba through it all."

At this moment, the door opened, and Morag appeared, with a plate of cakes which she placed on the table. Then, with a sidelong glance at her mistress, she coughed.

"Mphm! Will they be coming soon, Miss Oona?"

"Any minute now, Morag," replied Oona. "Have you put the ham on the table?"

"Aye, hev I. An' the eggs is ready for boiling. Will Miss Mollie be having her tea if the train's late?"

"Yes; but I hope it won't be," said Mollie. "I'm dying to see Allison and Kirsty, if it's she Jean is bringing."

"Ye're no sae ill for a dying body," was all Morag vouchsafed ere she left the room.

"Good old Morag!" laughed Mollie. "I love her for all her snippy ways!"

"Oh, I daresay it's very good for you," said Oona drily. "If they don't come soon, you must start your tea, Mollie."

"I knew it. And I shall be cross if that happens. I think I'll just run upstairs to the staircase window and see if I can see the taxi coming, Oona. Will you come, too?"

"Looking for them won't bring them any sooner. No thank you, Mollie. I'll stay in the warm room, I think. Don't wait up there too long or you'll catch a cold, and that won't be a comfort, my dear."

"I won't stay long," Mollie promised as she ran out of the room, leaving Oona alone with her thoughts.

It had been just such a day as this on which Jean had come to her. She remembered waiting at the staircase window, looking down the white road to Aulmbermouth to see if she could see the cab coming. She had caught the cold she had just prophesied for Mollie, and Alastair had been so angry. He had always treated the aunt who was a year younger than himself as if she were a sister, and he had scolded roundly.

"You never can show sense," he said. "Where's the use of catching cold for nothing? You are an ass, Oona!"

She had sneezed violently, lending gratuitous point to his remarks. Jean had stared at them both — such a lovely child, with her streaming black hair and green eyes, and delicate face.

"Poor Auntie Oona!" she had said. "I think you are very unkind to her, Lal." It had been "Auntie Oona" till the death of the young lieutenant who had taken the best of Oona McCleod's life with him when he sank beneath the grey waves of the North Sea. Then, the pretty schoolgirl had tacitly understood that she might drop the appellation, and it had never been resumed. After all, there were barely twelve years between them. Well, Alastair was dead, and Jean was bringing his little girl home to them. The entrance of Morag at this point cut short her reflections, and she turned round to behold the faithful handmaid bringing the teapot and two eggs on a tray. "You and Miss Mollie had best tak' your tea," said Morag. "Sit you down, Miss Oona, and I will give her a cry."

Oona meekly obeyed, and Morag stalked from the room and called Mollie, who was flattening her pretty nose against the window panes. The next moment the sound of flying footsteps was heard and Mollie made her appearance, blue with cold.

"My dear girl, how silly of you to stay there so long!" Miss McCleod exclaimed in dismay. "Come to the fire and warm yourself. What a good thing we decided to have a high tea for Jean and the children! You will catch cold, Mollie, if you do such mad things. Now drink this tea at once."

Mollie gulped down the tea and sat down by the fire, looking much better.

"I'm warmer now," she said as she chipped at her egg. "I wish they'd come, Oona. I shall have to be off very soon. I told the beginners to be there promptly to-night, and I simply must be there myself. I've been furious with them lately because they've been coming in at all times. After all, they asked me to have the class at six, and I arranged it to suit them, so I think the least they can do is to be there and not keep me waiting."

"You'll see them when you get back," said Oona, referring to Jean and her party.

"After ten? The children will be in bed by then, I hope."

"Well, there's always to-morrow."

"To-morrow I go back to my dear landlady. I should think she's about given me up by this time. It has been nice here, Oona. I don't enjoy the prospect of returning to her after Storms."

"Well, it's your own fault. Jean and I both want you to come here, but you've refused every time. Come, Mollie, change your mind, and come to me for the rest of the year at least."

Mollie shook her head. "It's dear of you, Oona, and I know you mean it when you say you want me. But it's better for me to be at Aulmbermouth — I'm more get-at-able there. Besides — " she hesitated, and then came to a full-stop.

"Oh, I know your Scots pride won't let you accept any favours," returned Oona. "But you can pay something into the house-keeping every month if you feel like that."

"It isn't only that. I ought to have a place of my own where people can come who want to discuss business with me. Don't make it too hard for me, Oona. You don't know how I long to come."

"Very well. But one thing I insist on, Mollie. You must change your rooms as quickly as possible. You have no close relations in England to look after you, and I've always looked on you as another niece, ever since you were so good to Jean at school. I don't feel happy about you in that place, and you must flit as soon as possible. Promise me to see about fresh rooms on Saturday."

"I'll do my best, but it's no easy matter to get permanent rooms in Aulmbermouth. Still I am really getting frightened of Mrs Taylor, and should be glad to leave her if — what's that?"

"That" was the sound of a taxi, and the next moment, the pair were on their feet and racing to the door. Morag was before them. She got it open as the taxi drew up, and saw what it contained before they did. With a face full of horror, she turned to her mistress, "Maircy me! Miss Jean's brocht yin o' they blackies!" she ejaculated, aghast.

CHAPTER VI

Morag's words meant little to Mollie and Oona at the moment. They ran down the narrow path which led from the front-door to the wider one that ran round the house, and, in a moment, Jean was in her aunt's arms. Mollie followed, but the delay was brief. Moti had time to get out of the taxi, and lift Allison out, and then the three turned to the child.

Jean stooped, and lifted her up. "This is Allison," she said.

Oona took the little girl from her, Allison acquiescing silently.

"Little Allison! So you have come to us at last! We have wanted you, dearie."

Allison kept her black lashes against her cheeks. She made no effort, however, to turn away from her young great-aunt, which was something gained. Mollie drew nearer.

"Won't you speak to me, Allison?" she said coaxingly.

Allison submitted to being kissed, but she made no attempt to look up, and Jean turned to Moti who stood near, looking miserably cold in spite of her many wraps.

"This is Moti, Allison's ayah," she said. "She was to have returned to India by the next boat, but she loves Allison, and has agreed to stay with us for a time at least."

Mollie held out her hand. "It is good of you, Moti," she said. "Allison will be happier if she has you, I know. I remember how I missed my ayah when I first came to England."

A gleam of white teeth showed in the dark face as Moti replied, "The Memsahib has lived in Hind?"

"I was born there," explained Mollie.

"It is well. My Missy-baba will be with those who understand."

"Come," said Oona, who was still holding Allison. "Let us go in."

They all entered the old square hall, where Moti gazed appreciatively at a big log fire, leaving Morag to settle with the chauffeur to her own satisfaction. The chiming of a clock recalled Mollie to her class, and she gave an exclamation.

"Half past five? I must go! The class will be waiting for me, and after all I've said, it won't look well. Will you kiss me good-night, Allison? I expect you will be in bed when I get back."

Allison smiled a tiny smile, and gave the kiss, lifting her eyes to the speaker's face as she did so. Mollie, like Jean, was taken aback at their loveliness. So was Oona.

So was Morag, who came in at that moment in excellent good humour, having come off victorious in her encounter with the man.

"Eh! It's the McCleod eyes she has!" exclaimed the good woman. "Come to old Morag, my dearie. I nursed your feyther when he was as auld as ye!"

Allison glanced at Jean who seemed her sheet anchor just now, and, obeying the look she received, went over to Morag, holding out a little scrawny hand with the air of a princess.

Morag took it, and shook it heartily. "Eh, but ye're a bit lammie," she said warmly. "Ye look fair starved. Come ben ma doo, and warm yersel'! Morag'll gang to the kitchen to bile an egg laid fer yer ain sel' this verra morn."

She held open the dining-room door, and Oona

took the child's hand in hers, and led her in.

"Welcome home!" she said. "Welcome home, little Allison."

Jean followed them after she had put Moti into Morag's charge — not without some inward qualms as to how that person might treat the Madrassi — and turned to Mollie regretfully.

"I forgot all about that early class, Mollie. What hard luck! There's such lots to talk about!"

"Can't be helped," said Mollie philosophically. "You won't be in bed when I get back, will you?"

"At ten o'clock? Talk sense, Mollie! If it's fine, I'll come along the road and meet you from the car."

"Decent of you, but it's beginning to snow already. I thought it would. No; you get your talk with Oona over first, and I'll have my innings after supper. Now I must fly! Good-bye for the present."

She went off, and Jean returned to the dining-room, where Oona had taken off Allison's coat and cap, and was removing her shoes.

"Get her slippers, Jean," said Miss McCleod. "Poor bairnie! She's starved with cold and hunger! And change your own things. Morag will be here in a minute or two. She has the eggs to boil, for we thought you'd rather have a good tea now, and wait for supper with Mollie."

"True for you! Allie, here are your slippers, honey. Put them on, and then come with me, and I'll show you where to put your things."

Oona looked mildly surprised at the last sentence, but she had made up her mind not to interfere with Jean's training unless she thought it absolutely necessary, so she said nothing. Allison did as she was bidden and then Jean took her upstairs to wash her face and hands, and brush her lank, thin hair before she allowed her to sit down to tea. She had made up her mind that Allison must learn to wait on herself as soon as possible. Knowing from experience how children are treated in India, it seemed best to her to break in the child as soon as possible. Moti was not to be with them always, and Morag and her satellite had no time to run after a small child.

When they were seated at the table, and Allison was making short work of the egg with the pinky-brown shell that had been placed in front of her, they left her to herself, only seeing that she had plenty of everything. Her appetite was small, however, and she soon leaned back in her chair, watching them as they made a leisurely meal. It was not possible to talk much before the child, but Jean described the journey, and Oona gave her some of the local news, Allison listening to them in silence.

Oona glanced at her once or twice. The child's lack of beauty was puzzling her. She was not a McCleod, except for her eyes, and she did not appear to resemble her mother, either. Jean and Alastair had both been lovely children, but there was little sign of even future prettiness in Allison.

When tea was over, it was after six, and Jean decreed that the child must go to bed at once. They took her upstairs to the rose and white room with its glowing fire in the little grate, and Moti waiting for her charge. Allison was tired, and made no demur as Jean undressed her, the ayah moving quietly about, putting things away as she unpacked the big trunks. Then Oona got her first shock. When Allison was in her nightgown, she was tucked into bed straight away, with no question of saying her prayers. Miss McCleod opened her eyes, but said nothing till they were well out of the room, and on the way downstairs, Moti having been left to watch over her Missie-baba's slumbers.

"Jean, I am not going to interfere," she began, "but don't you think it rather a mistake to let that child get to bed without saying her prayers? If children do not form the habit young, they are apt never to form it."

Jean glanced at her aunt, but said nothing until she had closed behind them the door of the little study they generally used in the evenings.

"I agree with you," she said very seriously. "The trouble is that Allison has learnt none."

"My dear Jean!"

"Yes; I was rather shocked, too. One assumes naturally that a child of that age has learnt something. Allison knows nothing. Apparently Doris didn't bother herself, and, of course, Alastair died when Allie was a baby. I haven't troubled her with anything yet, she seems so tired, poor little soul, and all these new experiences must be so bewildering to such a baby. So I left it till we got home."

"Well, the sooner you begin, the better, I consider," said Oona, who had the true Scots feeling for religion. "It seems awful to me that that child should go off to bed like that. You could say 'Our Father' when you were only five."

"But I was a well-brought up child," laughed Jean, "and I gather that Allison is not. So far as I can find out, she knows nothing about God or Christ, and angels are not in her scheme of things at all. She was nervous about being left while Ayah had her evening meal in the London hotel, and I told her that her guardian angel would watch over her. She said, 'What is a guardian angel, Auntie Jean? Is it a new ayah?' I wasn't very sure what to say."

"Jean!"

"Well, how does one explain such a thing to a child that doesn't know the first thing about Heaven?"

Oona was floored for a minute. Then she said, "I

think you will have to begin at the very beginning, and begin at once. And, for pity's sake, don't let Morag hear you. She would be — "

"Horrified to the depths of her gude Scots soul!" finished Jean for her. "You may be very sure I shan't let her. She would be sure that poor little Allie was foreordained to Hell! Morag is a dear, but her Calvinism gets on my nerves at times. She is so hatefully gloomy about it all. Religion is not a subject I discuss much, I can't. But I'm perfectly sure that God doesn't predestinate some people to Heaven and others to Hell in the ghoulish way she makes out. It wouldn't be fair, and whatever else God is, He's fair, I know!"

"Jean, I don't like to hear you talk in that way. It doesn't seem reverent," complained her aunt.

"Oh, I'm reverent enough; only I think my God and Morag's haven't much in common. Mine likes people to be happy, and Morag's prefers to have them calling themselves miserable sinners and worms of the dust and so on."

"Jean, my dear!"

Jean laughed. "Don't be so shocked, Oona. Anyone would think I was talking rank blasphemy to see your face! As for Allie, she shall learn about 'Gentle Jesus' and God our Father but I won't have her scared by talk about hell-fire, and the devil, and 'the worm that dieth nor', so please warn Morag."

"My dear girl, if Morag sees fit to tell Allison what her future destination may be, no, not the whole Royal family, nor the entire body of presbyters will stop her, so how do you imagine that I can?"

"Well, luckily, Allison will spend most of her time with me, and Moti is staying with us till the summer, so we ought to be able to manage for the present."

"I'm sure I hope you will," said Oona with a

backward glance for the little girl who had been herself, and who had lain awake night after night, quaking with dread of the devil who might be lying in wait for her.

"Of course we shall. And now, tell me what you have been doing while I've been away. Letters aren't much use, really. One is so apt to skim over the interesting details. How is the Burn baby getting on? And has Mrs Vicar been behaving herself, or has she been setting everyone by the ears as usual?"

They lapsed into what Jean called "Parish gossip" after that, and went on until the sound of hurrying footsteps outside the window told them that Mollie was coming, when Oona vanished kitchenwards to make the coffee, and Jean ran to open the door.

"Well, what sort of a class?" she began. "I say! What a night!"

"I feel like a snowman," returned her friend. "I'd better go straight through to the kitchen to peel. Don't come too near me, Jean, or you'll get wet."

"You must be soaked," said Jean, as she followed her down the long passage into the bright kitchen, where Morag promptly hustled Mollie into the scullery, and took off her coat, hat, and gloves, with a brief "Get yer boots off this minute, Miss Mollie! Maircy on us; but yer fair drookit!"

Mollie obeyed meekly, and then put on the dry shoes and stockings Jean had run to fetch her. Her short blue frock was dry, but her pretty hair was wet, and the maid produced a towel, and proceeded to give her head a good rubbing, ejaculating all the time. When at length the kitchen tyrant had pronounced her to be dry enough, they had supper over the study fire, and Mollie listened to all Jean could tell her about the children.

"Poor kiddy!" she commented, after her friend had described Mrs Page. "I'm sorry for Kirsty, Jean. Do you think that woman will let her come here as you suggested?"

"I hope so," said Jean. "All the same, 'ah ha'e ma doots'. If it has to depend on Kirsty being good, I'm afraid we shan't see her for some time."

"We must hope for the best," said Oona. "All the same, Jean, I wish you could have brought her straight here."

"I rather wish it myself," admitted Jean. "Only I'm afraid it wouldn't have done to suggest it."

"I suppose not. Well, if you two have finished, Morag had better clear away. Are you going to bed soon, Jean? You have had a long journey, and must be tired."

"Not very. Moti was a great help, though. She attracted rather more attention than I quite liked. I'll just run up and see if she is all right, Mollie, and then I'll come back. I want to know what I've missed while I've been away."

"Lots," called Mollie after her.

Five minutes later, having seen that Moti was comfortable, she was downstairs again, and they settled round the study fire for a cosy talk. Oona in her low chair; the two girls on the hearth rug. At eleven, Miss McCleod went off to bed, reminding them that it was getting late, and that they ought to be going upstairs before long.

"All right," said Jean. "We'll come presently."

"Presently" was half-past twelve, for there was a good deal for Jean to hear, and she had much to tell. Also, she spent some time in trying to persuade her friend to leave her present landlady and come to Storms. Mollie refused to do the latter, but she agreed that she would be glad to leave Mrs Taylor.

They stole in to peep at Allison before they parted for the night, and found her sleeping sweetly snuggled up into a ball.

"Poor baby!" said Mollie. "Well, your hands will be full enough now, Jean."

"Oh, I don't mind," said Jean, serenely. "So long as Morag doesn't get wind of the fact that she's never been taught to say her prayers, I don't mind."

"Better start teaching her to-morrow," advised Mollie. "Well, I'm tired. Goodnight, Jean."

"Goodnight, Moll. Pleasant dreams," replied Jean, as she softly closed the door of the little room, and bent to kiss her friend.

Then they parted and an hour later the lights were all turned out, and Storms lay sunk in sleep.

CHAPTER VII

THE FIRST TUSSLE

The next day, they woke to find that the ground was covered in a thick coverlet of snow, a whistling wind from the north tossed the waves to yeasty foam: the heavy sky gave promise of more snow to follow; and bitter winter had descended on them. Moti could scarcely get Allison dressed for her excitement. She had never seen snow before, and she would break away from the patient ayah to run to the window and gaze out with all her eyes. Jean, hearing the gentle remonstrances which were all Moti administered, came to the rescue at last. She hurried through the last of her own dressing and went into the gay room. Allison, half-clad, stood by the window, looking out, while Moti was standing by, a little white woollen frock in her hand, waiting till it should please her Missie-baba to come and let herself be finished.

"Good morning, Allison," said the young aunt.

The child turned round, showing a beaming face. "Good-morning, Auntie Jean. Oh, Auntie! Just see! How beautiful, isn't it? Who did it, Auntie? Tell me!"

"God did it," said Jean, with a feeling that so she might approach the child's ignorance. "He sent it through the night to cover up the plants, and keep them warm and safe till Spring comes. Allie, let Moti finish dressing you, and then you can come downstairs and see it from the morning-room window."

Allison turned from the window with a sigh, and Moti slipped the frock deftly over her head, and then gave her hair some finishing pats with a brush. Jean stood looking on till the child was ready. Then she held out her hand.

"Got a clean hanky? Come along, then, and we'll go and see if Auntie Mollie is ready." Allison took the hand, and they went along the passage to the door of Mollie's room.

"Mollie! Are you up yet?" called Jean. For answer the door was flung open, and Mollie, gay and fresh in a gown of her favourite dark crimson, faced them.

"Up!" she repeated indignantly. "Of course I'm up! Considering it's half-past eight, I should have said there was nothing extraordinary in that, for all your eyes, Jean McCleod! Good-morning, Allison. Sleep well?"

"Yes, thank you, Auntie Mollie," said Allison shyly.

"Do you mind?" asked Jean, answering Mollie's questioning eyebrows. "You are with us so much, and I don't want her to use your given name just as we do. I thought it the best way out of the difficulty."

"Oh, I don't mind. I hadn't thought about it — that's all, and it was rather startling at first. Are you two ready? Then let's get down to the fire."

They ran downstairs, Allison between the two girls, to the morning room, where Morag was putting the finishing touches to the breakfast table. She returned their greeting dourly, for she considered that she had a grievance against Jean for bringing Moti to Storms. Morag was properly sorry for all Indians, and gave all she could spare to foreign missions; but she thought that they ought to stay in their own country, and not come fashing a decent Scotswoman.

"Sic' blethers!" she thought, as she moved briskly about. "I'm no sae auld that I couldna hae done for Miss Allison. It wad be better gin she was wi' an honest Chreestian that wad teach her the Holy Scriptures, and no fill her heid wi' whigamleeries, as I dinna doot yon puir heathen will."

She meant to have it out with Jean later on, but would wait till Allison was out of the way. Morag's ideas of the respect owed by the young to their elders — and, therefore, betters — were immense. Jean, partly guessing at what was in her mind, inwardly shook in her shoes, and resolved to avoid the handmaiden as long as possible.

"I shall catch it about Moti," she said to Mollie Stewart later on. "I can see it in Morag's eyes. As you love me, Mollie, stick to me like seccotine."

"I don't mind as long as I'm here," replied Mollie, "but what will you do when I've gone?"

"Glue myself to Allison. Morag won't find fault with me before her. She'd think it wrong!"

"That's a blessing," said Mollie.

"It is! Oh Mollie, I foresee all sorts of difficulties in bringing up Allie as I want. Oona won't interfere — she never does. But Morag will make up for it! She helped to bring me up — or thinks she did, which comes to the same thing — and she'll be convinced I'll make a hash of things if I'm left to myself. What she'll say when she learns that I don't let her have a finger in the pie I shudder to think!"

"I think you and Oona give in far too easily to Morag," replied Mollie. "She simply rides rough-shod over you as she thinks fit."

"Not always!" Jean's mouth took a peculiarly obstinate curve. "I'm not going to give her any chance to scare Allie as she scared me when I was small. Her awful predestination or whatever it is used to make me terrified to go to bed. And as for not giving in to her, what about yourself?"

Mollie laughed ashamedly; but her only answer was, "Well, you'll have your work cut out!" This,

however, came later in the day. At the moment,
Morag finished her work, and then rang a bell
which brought "the lass" from the kitchen and Oona
from the dining-room where she had been attending
to one or two details. Morag set "the Books" before
her mistress, and the others sat down, Jean
drawing Allison on to her knee, while Oona read a
small portion of St. Luke's Gospel. A few prayers
followed, when Jean set her small niece on her
knees beside her, whispering to her to close her
eyes, and fold her hands. Allison did as she was told,
with a silent wonder as to what it all meant. Then
Prayers over, the two domestics retired to their own
meal in the kitchen, and the ladies sat down to
theirs. Allison was nearly as silent as she had been
the night before, but her big eyes were taking everything in. Mollie and Jean discussed folk-dancing
with vigour most of the time, and Oona sat listening
to them, and attending to everyone's wants. When
they had all finished, Jean took her small niece
upstairs, and gave her various odd jobs to do.
Allison was to learn to make herself useful, for the
girl had a vague idea that if you keep a child
occupied, it is usually happy and, therefore, good.
When everything was finished, she took the little
girl down to where Mollie was sitting darning
stockings, and Oona going over accounts in the Den.
She brought with her a certain box which the child
eyed with interest. When the door had been shut, a
tray and needles and cotton were produced, and the
box was opened, and quantities of brightly-hued
beads were emptied on the tray. It was the work of a
few minutes to show Allison how to thread them for
rings and bracelets, and when she was happily
employed with them Jean reached for her own work,
and the conversation went on.

"What about rooms, Mollie?" she said as she

stitched at some delicate embroidery. "Do you want to go and look for them this afternoon?"

"I suppose I'd better," replied Mollie, surveying a neat darn with complacency. "I don't want to, but I simply can't endure that woman any longer! She gets on my nerves!"

"Do you think she might harm you?" asked Jean curiously.

"I — don't — know," replied Mollie slowly. "I have a funny feeling that she might go right off at any moment, and it isn't pleasant."

"I shouldn't think it was," said Jean. "You'll be an ass if you stay there."

Mollie nodded. She really was beginning to feel frightened of her eccentric landlady, but she hated a fuss. She knew she ought to have moved long since, but Mrs Taylor's lamentations when she had suggested it upset her, and she had yielded — weakly, as she knew.

"If only she wouldn't be pathetic," she said now. "I do so hate rows! I believe you rather like them, Jean; but I'd do almost anything to keep out of them."

"That's weak of you, Mollie. You are feeble at times, you know."

Mollie laughed, but her face was still troubled as she said, "Well, she cries, and does all she knows to make me comfortable for the time. Last time, she stood by my table, offering me all sorts of privileges, and saying, 'So you will stay, won't you?' till I felt quite daft!"

"It doesn't matter what she says, Mollie," came Oona's quiet tones from the corner. "You have your work to do, and if you are perpetually worried by scenes at home you cannot give your best to it. That is not fair either to your pupils or yourself. You owe them a duty and you must think of it. I don't think

Mrs Taylor is at all the sort of woman with whom you ought to be, and I wish you'd change as soon as possible."

"Mrs Taylor ought to have some good, husky young man in her rooms," said Jean. "I don't think she's straight, either. I'm convinced she reads your letters! I caught her with one one day when I called to leave your shoes. It was raining, you remember, and suddenly it got worse, and she asked me in to wait till it was over. There was one of your letters from Burmah on the table, and it was open. She made some silly excuse of having carried it down with her dusters, but I didn't believe her — and neither did you."

"As that letter had been in one of my drawers when I went out, I did not," said Mollie with vigour. "Also I know she lies in wait for me when I come home late. What she imagines, I can't think; but more than once I've seen her dash into the house in a hurry as I turned the corner, and more than once I've seen the curtains move when I've come in."

"She's a thoroughly nasty-minded woman," declared her friend. "You and I will go and see what we can get this afternoon, and then, when you are settled up, Oona shall come with you, and break it to her."

"All right, Jean. This afternoon we'll go and see if I can get anything."

"And if you can't," added Oona, "you'll just come back here like a good lassie. Yes, Mollie," as Mollie tried to negative the proposal, "I mean it. I had no idea she spied on you like that. She is obviously a most dangerous woman, and I will not hear of you staying there any longer."

Mollie gave in. She said no more on the subject, but rolled up the last of her stocking and proposed that they should play with Allison.

"Let's teach her some of the singing games," she said. "Come on, Jean. Push the table back; and Oona, put your old bills away. Pack up the beads, Allie, and we'll have a romp."

"Morag will think we've all gone mad," laughed Jean as she helped to clear the room.

"Oh, bother Morag! Come on, Oona, we'll play 'Wallflowers' first."

So when Morag entered the room twenty minutes later she found them in the middle of the floor, solemnly dancing round and singing.

"Juist like bairns!" said Morag to herself with a contemptuous sniff.

The mad skipping came to an abrupt end on her entrance, and the dancers broke up in confusion. Mollie might say what she liked, but she was as scared of the old woman as any of them.

"There's a wee laddie at the back door, Miss Oona," said Morag with another indescribable sniff for "sic whigmaleeries". "He says he's fra Mistress Burden at the Cottages. Yin o' her bairns is gey sick and she'd be gled if ye wad gang doon."

"Of course," said Oona. "Who is it, Morag?"

"Wee Jock Stoddart. Whit he's daein' oot o' schule this hoor o' the mornin' I'm no sayin'. I brocht him ben an gied him a feely-piece. Wull I tell him ye'll gang the noo, Miss Oona?"

"Yes. And Morag, give him that can of broth in the larder to take home. I'm afraid they get little enough to eat, poor bairns, and it's bitter weather."

"Gin Geordie Stoddart wad leave the beer an' gang tae wark like ither decent bodies, his bairns wad no be dependin' on ither folk for their meat," said Morag, leaving the room, still with that disapproving air.

Oona shook her head. "Morag blames poor George Stoddart for his poverty; but if that shiftless, silly little wife of his could give her mind to keeping her home neat and clean and cheerful, she would find he would probably leave the Hare and Hounds to look after itself. What else can be expected of a man who comes in tired after a day's work, only to find the children screaming about the house, the hearth piled up with yesterday's ashes, dirty china on the table, and only a 'tin o' sumthing' for comfort? I don't blame the men half as much as I blame the women."

She left the room to get ready for her tramp, and the two girls sat down by the fire again, Allison having betaken herself to the window to watch the falling snow as the conversation bored her.

It was after one when Oona returned, tired out with helping a distracted mother with a very sick small boy, whose breathing told a sorrowful tale of bronchitis.

"Lunch will be ready in a minute," said Jean, as she helped her aunt to shed her wraps. "Oh, you poor Oona! You look done!"

"What was wrong?" enquired Mollie, returning from the kitchen whither she had carried Miss McCleod's snow-clogged boots.

"Little Tom Burden is down with bronchitis," said Oona, sinking into her chair with a sign of relief. "I'm afraid it's going to be a bad case. By the way, Mollie, your new doctor was there — at least, I suppose it's the new one."

"Dr. Errington?" said Mollie with interest. "Oh, I'm so glad. What did you think of him, Oona?"

"Very clever, I thought. And very gentle and good. Tom seemed to take to him at once. He seems attentive, too. He promised to call again in the evening. I am afraid he thinks there is some danger of pneumonia from the way he spoke. I could see he didn't like the child's condition. Luckily, Mrs Burden is a good housewife and Tom will be carefully nursed. But it's a heavy burden for the poor soul, with five other little children and a husband to see after as well."

"The parish nurse will go in and help with the night-nursing," said Jean. "She really is a boon at times like this. I'm thankful we've got her, or you would be insisting on trotting off there every night, and I won't have it."

"Oh, yes; Nurse Cayley will be in and out, and the neighbours are sure to lend a hand. It's amazing how good the poor are to each other."

Allison came up, and laid a tiny hand on her great aunt's knee.

"Is it a little boy who is sick?" she asked curiously.

"Yes, dear. A little boy just as old as you are. And there are some little girls, too, who have very few toys to play with, and must be kept quiet because their brother is so ill. Wouldn't you like to send them some of your beads to play with? You have so many, and a lot of other toys as well."

Allison shook her head. "I want my beads myself," she said.

"But you have so many," pleaded Oona, who was the soul of generosity herself, and wanted the child to know the joy of giving.

"No!" said Allison. "You can buy them some in the bazaar — you, and Auntie Jean and Auntie Mollie."

"But we are not going to do so," put in Jean, "because you are going to send them some of yours, Allie."

Allison's mouth set in a hard, unlovely line. "No!" she said.

Oona looked grieved; Jean raised her eyebrows; Mollie shook her head but said nothing. She felt that Jean had made a mistake in speaking so arbitrarily, but she had no idea of interfering.

"You must never speak to me like that, Allison,"
said Jean, quietly. "If you are told to do anything,
you must do it. You have plenty of beads for yourself
and the little girls at Burdens, and you must give
them some."

Up to this time, Allison's feeling of novelty had
kept her from rebelling at anything, but that was
wearing off, and she had been badly spoilt in India.
There had never been any question of sharing for
either her or Kirsty, and unselfishness was a quality
in which she was lacking. The bright beads had
captured her childish fancy, and she had no
intention of giving them up. She promptly followed
a plan which, so far, had always brought her her
own way. She flung herself on the floor, screaming
and kicking with rage. Her mother had always
given in to this at once. It was to be expected that
Auntie Jean would do the same. To her great
amazement she found herself picked up, and carried
upstairs, shrieking like a small demon all the time.
She was borne to her own room, where Moti, who
had been sitting by the fire, sewing, rose in alarm,
and was deposited on the bed.

"Moti, please undress Miss Allison, and put her to
bed," said Jean rather breathlessly, for the child had
struggled vigorously, and it had been all that she
could do to carry her. "You may go and sit in my
room when you have done, and please shut the door.
You are not to speak one word to her — you understand."

"Yes, Memsahib," said Moti meekly. She understood very well, and dared not disobey, such was the
awe Jean's manner roused in her.

Jean turned and left them, and, in ten minutes,
Allison found herself alone, and in bed, and almost
too startled to cry. She had never been treated like
this before, and presently, she sobbed piteously. The

delicious smells from Morag's cooking reminded her of the fact that she was hungry. Were they going to starve her, and give her no dinner? That question was answered a little later, when Jean appeared with a bowl of bread and milk for her.

"Sit up and eat your dinner, Allison," she said briskly. Allison sat up. The entire lack of anger rather overawed her, and she ate the bread and milk without a murmur. When she had finished, her aunt set the bowl on one side and then sat down on the edge of the bed. "Allie, haven't you a lot of things you like?" she said gently.

"Yes," said Allison.

"Do you know that those little children of whom we were speaking have not two toys each while you have more than twenty-two? See here!" She went to a cupboard and opened the doors, showing three shelves laden with the child's playthings. "You have all these and yet you won't give a few of your beads to those other children."

"You can buy them some," came the quick answer. "Send Ayah to the bazaar with a rupee, and you can buy many — many."

"No; I'm not going to do that," said Jean, still gravely. "I want you to spare them some of yours. Haven't you ever shared with Kirsty?"

"No."

"But when you had something and Kirsty wanted to share it, didn't you?"

"No; Mama bought her the same."

Jean was at her wits' end to know what to do. She had made up her mind that the child should send some of the beads, but it would be better if she sent them of her own accord. Just where to begin with the kind of teaching most children get in babyhood, she did not know.

"I am sorry for you, Allison," she said finally.

"Why?" Allison was interested.

"Because you don't know what fun it is to share."

Allison turned this over in her mind. "You don't share, Auntie?"

"Oh, indeed, I do! Auntie Oona and Auntie Mollie and I always share. And now you have come, you shall, too."

Another silence. This was something quite fresh to Allison. Jean watched the little face anxiously. Would her argument succeed?

It did. The child held out her hand. "Give me my beads, please, Auntie Jean."

Jean went off to fetch them, and presently returned. Allison took the box and opened it.

"May I have another box?" she asked. Her aunt got one, and the little girl carefully poured half the treasured beads into it.

Then she put the lid on and held it out. "You may take these," she said with difficulty.

"Thank you, Allie." Jean took it, and bent and kissed the child.

"You may say I sent it," said Allison. "And — and I'm sorry I was a little budmash."

"Never mind now, darling," replied her aunt, gently. "Lie down and get a nap. When you wake up, Ayah may dress you, and you can take your toys to the Den and play with her there till tea-time."

She saw the child tucked in, and then went downstairs with the box in her hand.

"Well?" queried Mollie, as she entered the room.

"She's given in. But oh! What a time we're going to have of it! She's the veriest little heathen!"

"Poor baby," said Oona. "You pudding is in the fender, Jean."

Jean rescued it and sat down. "Bringing up children isn't all jam!" she said. "I foresee lively times before us!"

CHAPTER VIII

At half-past two, Jean and Mollie sallied forth to seek rooms, and if there was time, to beard Mrs Taylor in her lair. The snow had ceased to fall for the present, and though the sullen sky gave promise of more to come, they were well-wrapped up with strong boots and furry gloves. A bitter wind blew from the north, and the sea was breaking on the rocks with a heavy sound, betokening a storm. Mollie shivered as she looked at it, but Jean stood, drinking it in with deeply gleaming eyes.

"Jean! Come away at once!" cried Miss Stewart when she could endure it no longer. "It's freezing cold, and I'm in a blue funk already. Don't stand there, seeing visions. For pity's sake, let's go and get it over!"

"Sorry," laughed Jean. "I forgot you had to face the Gorgon."

"That just describes her," declared Mollie, as they left the cliffs, and struck inland. "She has a Medusa-like appearance, and I'm scared of what she may say or do when we break the news to her."

"She can't do anything very bad!" retorted Jean. "I'll see you through it — whatever it is!"

"Better be prepared to help me pack on the spot," said Mollie ruefully. "Oh, we're in for a sweet time, I can assure you. I expect we shall have all her defunct relatives dragged out and spread before us at the very least. Also, I'm sure you'll get some extraordinary information about my character. I only hope she doesn't try to weep on my shoulder."

"Oh! she'll never do that!"

"Heaven knows! I wish this were well over — that's all!"

They walked briskly along, the half-frozen snow already beginning to crunch under their feet. Down the village street they went, where the glow of firelight through the windows of the fishermen's cottages gave a cheery aspect to the day, and where the little post office was already lit up. The old Norman church, with its steeple-crowned tower, which a pious and inartistic generation had so adorned — Jean could never make up her mind whether it was intended for a signpost to Heaven or not — and its graveyard, where the long, low mounds lay quieter than ever under their mantle of driven white, and the black yews and sycamores made Mollie shiver, though Jean glanced at it with a smile, and a tender thought for the sleepers who rested so quietly there 'after Life's fitful fever'.

"I should like to lie there when I die," she said as they passed the vicarage. "It is so near the life of the place! The children play round the graves in summer and the sea croons its lullaby to them all the year round, and in winter it is so still."

"Jean! Don't be so gruesome!" protested Mollie. "It won't matter where your body lies. You will be There!"

"I know that. But I like this old churchyard where men and women have mingled with the dust for so many centuries. Just think, Mollie. The fishermen of Beauclerc's reign were laid here with their nets just as old Simeon Burn was last week. What a wonderful company to have found rest here."

"There will be a far more wonderful company Beyond," said Mollie, softly, gravity touching her pretty face to beauty. "I don't worry where the dust of me lies, Jean. I'm so sure of meeting mother there."

"And all the others," added Jean. "All the dear people we have loved, and all those we have read about and heard of. I don't know about you, Mollie, but as soon as I've had a few centuries of Father and Mother, I am going to seek out Joan of Arc, and Drake and Raleigh, and poor, ill-fated Mary of Scotland, and gallant Flora Macdonald, and her yellow-haired Laddie, and countless others."

"Morag would be shocked if she could hear us, wouldn't she?"

"I know. Morag expects to wear a crown of gold and a white robe, and to play on a harp when she has finished with the earth. As for lovely Mary and Prince Charlie, she is certain they are anywhere but in Heaven! Did I ever tell you about the row I had with her when I first came to Oona?"

"You've told me about a good many rows, but nothing on this subject so far as I can remember."

Jean began to laugh. "It was rather funny. I had been doing something wrong, and she threatened me with the devil and hell-fire if I continued in my evil courses. I said, 'I don't care! I wouldn't want to go to Heaven! It sounds awfully dull, I think! Hell seems to me as if it will be heaps more fun!' She nearly had a fit."

"I wonder she didn't expire of horror! I'm sure she thought you terribly blasphemous!"

"Of course she did. What did you expect? From that day to this, she has always had her doubts about my sanity."

"She will certainly have her doubts about poor Doris if she ever gets to know how very little that child has been taught! How did you manage her in the end, Jean?"

"Oh, just said that we all shared, and should share with her. She gave in then. But, honour bright, Mollie, I was beginning to wonder how I was going to work it if she still stood out."

"She's a weird kiddie," said Mollie, thoughtfully. "You have to treat her like a tiny baby, and begin at the very beginning."

"All very well if she were a tiny baby!" said Jean ruefully. "Unfortunately, she's old enough for some reasoning, and I can't blame her if she wants to stick to her possessions if she's never been taught anything else. I suppose Doris was too frail to bother much with her, and gave in for the sake of peace. Luckily for the young lady, I don't mind any number of fusses, and she'll have to learn to do a little giving in herself, now."

"I should hope so!" Mollie spoke with decision. "She'll have an awful time of it otherwise when she goes to school!"

"Oh, well. She's not going till after Easter at soonest. I may not send her then, even. It won't hurt her to play for a while, and she's not a slow child, so she will soon pick up her lessons."

"Radley says the babes have a very good time of it at the High," said Mollie.

"Glad to hear it. I want her to go, for there are so few children round our way. The only one near enough is Rosie Winter, and as Oona and Mrs Winter are on terms of the iciest politeness, I doubt if Rosie would be allowed to play with Allie."

"She'll do very well as she is for the present," said Mollie consolingly. "In any case, the weather is much too severe for her to go out much, and she'll probably be quite happy with you two and Moti. By the way, how long is Moti staying?"

"Till the summer, at any rate."

"And how is Morag taking to her?"

"She isn't," Jean laughed. "She calls her 'yon puir heathen body,' and treats her with a pitying scorn."

"How does Moti stand that?" asked Mollie, curiously.

"Don't think she notices," returned her friend. "She is to have one of the dressing-rooms fitted up as a sitting-room for her till I can get the big attic turned into a nursery. She won't have much to do with Morag — which is as well."

"I think it is," agreed Mollie. "There's Aulmbermouth looming up! Oh, Jean! I wish it were well over! I'm sacred stiff of it all!"

"You needn't be," returned Jean. "After all, she can't bite you, and she won't try to keep your things. Perhaps she'll be out when we get there, and we can get your trunk packed before she returns."

"Let's hope so anyways! It would save a lot of trouble. I know you think me a terrible coward, but you don't know her, and I do!"

They hurried on, and had reached the town just as the first white flakes of snow began slowly drifting down again. The shop-windows were all lighted by this time, and the streets were full of children hurrying home from school. At the gates of the High School, they met Miss Radley, and two other mistresses who belonged to the folk-dance class.

"Hullo, McCleod," said one of them. "So you've got back? Have a good time?"

"Not bad," returned Jean.

"Have you heard the news about the class? Oh, but Miss Stewart would tell you!"

"Do you mean about the three men? Yes, isn't it good? Now, perhaps, we shall get a men's class, and then we can send in mixed teams for the Tournament classes, as well as men's morris teams."

"What are you going to do in town at this time of day, Miss Stewart?" asked Miss Radley in friendly tones. "I thought you were going to stay at Hasnett for the rest of the winter."

Mollie shook her head. "Oh no! I was only there till Miss McCleod came back. I'm now going to inform my present landlady that I'm not returning to her after all. I can't stand her any longer, and want to find fresh rooms as soon as possible."

"I'm not surprised," said the girl who had not yet spoken, a tall graceful person, Miss Black by name. "I know someone who was with her for a term, and she cleared out at the end of it — said she couldn't endure it any longer."

"Wasn't that Dorothy Weston?" said Miss Radley. "Didn't she have to go before the governors because of the awful things that woman said about her?"

"So she did! I'd forgotten that. Yes; I remember it now. Poor Dorothy had a fearful time clearing herself. That horrid Mrs Taylor went to the head and told her Dorothy used the most awful language and smoked in front of the girls, and came home late with young men, and all sorts of rubbish."

"How much foundation was there?" asked Jean.

"Oh, her brother came over and took her to the theatre at Noviam once or twice, I believe, and she said 'damn' when she picked up a hot poker by the wrong end. She did smoke in her rooms, but that was no more than all of us do; and we could all vouch for it that she never let the girls see her. Still, it wasn't pleasant for her, though they accepted her explanations, and even sent Mrs Taylor a letter advising her to be careful how she talked about people or she would find herself landed with an action for libel some day."

Mollie looked worried. "Heaven knows what she may cook up about me!"

"Oh, but you don't teach children. It would have been bad if Dorothy had let them see her smoke or hear her swear. But you only do what we all do, and never before us even. I don't see that it can matter much what she says about you in that line."

"It doesn't do anyone any good to be talked about," said Jean.

"And if people hear me talked about in that way, they will reflect it back on the Society," added Mollie.

"Let's hope she got such a fright last time that she manages to hold her tongue about you and your doings," said Miss Black, laughing. "I know the Head warned her that she must not expect to be recommended to any of our staff again."

"I should think not!" said Jean indignantly. "It was a wicked thing to do, and might have cost Miss Watson her post. People like that should be shut up as lunatics. I'm sure they do far more mischief than they ever realise!"

"Oh, she meant to do harm," said Miss Radley with conviction. "It wasn't her fault she didn't. And though the governors' letter shut her up to a certain extent she went about hinting things to outsiders for ages. I believe she stopped when Dorothy left us to get married, but not till then. She's a spiteful, malicious woman, and thoroughly dangerous."

"That sounds a cheery outlook for me," said Mollie ruefully.

"More likely for me!" laughed Jean. "She'll be sure to blame us for taking you away. Luckily, I don't care what she says about me. Don't worry, my dear. She'll hold her tongue if she has any sense at all."

"Where are you going, Miss Stewart?" asked Miss Derwent, the other girl. "If you haven't decided, I believe my landlady's sister wants someone, and I can recommend her. She is very nice, and a good cook. Our art mistress used to dig with her, but her people have come to live at Noviam, so she's at home now. Would you like to try Mrs Woodhouse?"

"It sounds promising," said Mollie. "Thanks, I will try her, I think, and see if she can take me."

"If you like to go now, I'll come round with you," offered Miss Derwent.

"Will you? That would be jolly of you. But what about your tea? You must be dying for it after teaching all the afternoon."

"Oh, it's my prep. day on Wednesdays, so I'm in no very evil case," returned Miss Derwent. "Come along, it's only down this next street."

"Well, I must go back. I've heaps to do, and no time to do it in," laughed Miss Radley. "Goodbye, everybody! Coming, Eva?"

Miss Black nodded, and went off with her to the rooms they shared. Miss Derwent led Jean and Mollie down a quiet little street, facing the High School playing-fields, with small houses all bright and cheery-looking. Before the gate of one she stopped, and presently they were admitted by a tiny woman with snow-white hair framing a strangely youthful face. She wore widow's collar and cuffs on her black dress, and was daintily fresh to look at.

On hearing their errand, she welcomed them in, and led them into a little sitting-room which, she said, was vacant.

"There is not much furniture," she said, "but you can bring anything of your own that you want. This fireplace is an open one, and there is a gas fire in the bedroom, worked by a slot-meter. Would you like to see it?"

"Yes, please," said Mollie; and they were led upstairs to a little bedroom where everything showed the same dainty freshness. There was a good cupboard in one corner, and the house was lighted by electric light. The bathroom would be at Mollie's service every morning, and most nights.

"And what are your terms?" asked Jean, in

obedience to a poke from Mollie.

"Well, ma'am, I charge thirty shillings a week for the two rooms. Light is half-a-crown extra and so are fires. As for food, I suppose the lady will board herself, but I shall be pleased to do any cooking at any time."

Then, with a murmur about "bread in the oven", she left them and the three girls drew closer together to discuss it.

"It's dearer than Mrs Taylor," said Mollie, "but I can afford it all right. She seems a decent sort, too, and that's something."

"I should think you might try it," said Jean. "If you don't like it, you can always leave." "You will, though," said Miss Derwent confidently. "When my landlady was in the infirmary last term for six weeks, I came here, and if I hadn't been so well satisfied with where I am, I'd have stayed on. The Vicar of St. Simon's will speak for her personal character — she's a great church worker; and I think you'll like her."

"Well, I'll try it," decided Miss Stewart. "At any rate, it's yards better than Mrs Taylor, and I can't face going back there."

Mrs Woodhouse returning at that moment they came to terms, and Mollie arranged to move in the following week. Her things would go to Storms from Mrs Taylor's, and then from there to Mrs Woodhouse's. When all this had been settled, she paid a week's rent, and was given a latch-key, after which they took their leave, and said "good-bye" to Miss Derwent, whose rooms were in the other direction.

"And now for Mrs Taylor!" said Jean. "I wonder what she will say?"

"As long as she doesn't weep over me, I can put up with it," said Mollie.

"What shall you do if she is out?"

"Come again to-morrow, I suppose — Look out, Jean!"

Her warning came too late, however, for heedless Jean, in crossing the road, had not troubled to look, and she was so nearly under the motor car which shot round the corner at this moment, that even Mollie's clutch on her arm would have been of no avail to save her had not the driver, swinging forward, swept her aside with his arm, catching her across the chest, and flinging her away. Mollie caught at her as she went down, and helped to break her fall. Even so, she fell against the kerb, and when the driver, after performing some remarkable convolutions with his car, stopped it, and came tearing back to them, she was struggling to her feet with a half-stunned look on her face. He slipped an arm around her shoulders, and helped her to her feet.

"I'm sorry I had to be so rough," he said, in pleasant, well-bred tones. "It was that or a nasty accident."

"Dr. Errington!" cried Mollie.

He turned to her with a look of surprise. "Why, Miss Stewart! I didn't recognise you!"

"I saw you didn't," returned Mollie. "Jean, are you all right? This is Dr. Errington. Doctor, this is Miss McCleod."

"I have heard of you, Miss McCleod," said Dr. Errington genially. "I know your aunt, I think. And now, will you come to my surgery, which is only round the corner in Northumberland Square, and let me see that your head is not damaged? My housekeeper can give us tea, I expect."

With an effort, Jean pulled herself together. "It is very kind of you, Dr. Errington. I struck my head as I fell and I think I was a little stunned, I felt so stupid for a moment."

"Then come and let me see it," he said, in gravely professional tones. He beckoned to a small boy who had been watching the scene, heedless of the falling snow. "Keep an eye on this car, till I come back, will you, sonny?"

"You bet," replied the youth, removing his fascinated gaze from Jean's face to the car. Having relieved his mind about the machine, the doctor took them to a pretty, old-fashioned house, with a red lamp over the door, and ushered them into a large room, obviously a man's room for there were none of the prettinesses that show the presence of a woman. A huge fire of logs burned on the hearth and a bowl stuffed full of chrysanthemums on the big solid table was the only attempt at beautifying it.

He made Jean remove her hat and let him examine her head. Luckily, the thick hat had prevented more than a nasty knock and he soon satisfied himself that there was nothing badly wrong.

"You will feel shaky for a day or two, I'm afraid," he said. "You will certainly have a bad headache. But that is all."

"It serves me right," said Jean, as she sat down. "I simply didn't look to see if the road was clear. I'm always doing it. Miss Stewart vows I shall end up under a 'bus or a lorry."

"Oh, I hope not," he said. "And now, I will ask Miss Grant to bring us some tea and then, I hope, you will allow me to run you over to Hasnett."

"Oh, I can get a tram, thanks," began Jean.

"Don't be silly," broke in Mollie. "You'll have a raging headache before long, banging your head like that. You won't be fit to go anywhere. No; you must accept Dr. Errington's offer, and I must catch my

train to Murrow or I shall be late for my classes
there."

"Have you to go to Murrow to-night?" asked the
doctor as he rang the bell for his housekeeper.

"Yes," said Mollie. "This is my Murrow night.
Tomorrow I have Frampton, and on Friday, Blyton
Sands. Saturday morning the junior classes are held
here. It's a busy life!"

He laughed, but Miss Grant came into the room
just then, so he asked her for tea, and left Mollie's
remark unanswered.

It was a simple meal, for Miss Grant had no
cakes. The bread and butter were cut thin, however,
and there were girdle cakes. Mollie enjoyed a hearty
meal, though Jean, with the threatened headache
already beginning, could only drink some tea.

She was silent for the most part, and the other
two left her to herself, and discussed folk- dancing
till Mollie found she must run to catch her train.
Then the doctor went to see about his car which he
had brought round while tea was preparing, and
packed Jean into it.

The snow was falling dizzily, so he was obliged to
drive carefully and slowly, and it took up most of his
attention, but, subconsciously, he felt the presence
of the slender girl at his side at every moment, and,
when he dared, he stole glances at her delicate face
with its Greek purity of contour, so unlike what he
would have expected from a Scotswoman.

As they reached Storms, Jean aroused herself to
thank him, and to beg him to let her get out and go
in the back way. She had no wish to alarm Oona.

"You have been so kind," she said, forcing a weary
smile. "I am grateful to you, but please don't come
any further, or my aunt may be frightened."

He looked sharply at her, and stopped the car.
Then he helped her out, and across the road to the

door in the wall.

"Can you get to the house all right?" he asked.

"Yes, thank you," she said. "It's only across the drive."

He let her go at that, and, with a farewell wave, he vanished. He heaved a sigh as he went back to the car, and got into it to drive back to his lonely house. Somehow, he felt, as he had never felt before, the want of a woman to sit facing him as he read a new book on pulmonary complaints.

"A man needs a wife," he thought, as he laid it aside at one o'clock, with three pages only read, and went off to bed.

CHAPTER IX

MRS TAYLOR

When Mollie returned from Murrow, it was to find Jean in bed and sleeping quietly while Oona was sitting by the fire in the Den, reading. She looked up as the girl entered, and greeted her with a smile.

"Come away and get warm, Mollie. Has it stopped snowing?"

"Yes — thank goodness," replied Mollie, sitting down by the fire, and taking off her shoes. "But it's freezing hard, Oona. The wind is rising, and I think we're in for a windy night."

"More snow later, I expect," said Oona. "Did you have good classes?"

"Oh, fair to middling. There are some idiots in this world."

"What's gone wrong?"

"Oh, just I tried to teach the Advanced class 'Whirligig', and they made a mess of it."

"Is it a very difficult dance?"

"Not ad — not if people will use their brains. Oh, thank you, Morag!" as Morag entered the room with her supper-tray.

Oona said no more till Mollie had begun on her scrambled eggs. Then she asked "What happened to you and Jean this afternoon?"

"Oh, we nearly had a nasty accident. Jean's in bed, I suppose?"

"Yes. She went straight there, and her head seemed so bad, I didn't like to bother her with questions. Tell me about it, please."

Between mouthfuls of egg, Mollie told the story, and then went on to describe her new rooms.

"I'm thankful you've finished with that woman," commented Oona, when she ended.

Miss Stewart made a face. "That's just what I haven't done. By the time I had fixed up with Mrs Woodhouse and had tea, I had to run to catch my train, so I have to see Mrs Taylor to-morrow."

Oona looked troubled. "I think I had better come with you myself. Jean will not be fit for anything. That was a nasty bump she got — there is a big lump on her head, and she looked very poorly when I was last in. I don't think you ought to go alone, I had best come. I don't like what you tell me of what those girls said. I wish you had left her before, Mollie."

"Not half so much as I do," returned Mollie ruefully. "All right, Oona. If you really will, I shall be thankful. I don't believe I could face her by myself. If once she started to weep on me, I should be done."

Oona smiled. "Oh, no, you wouldn't. You have more backbone than that. But she may try to make it unpleasant for you, and I may act as a slight deterrent on her. Can you get up early for once?"

Mollie laughed ashamedly. "Yes, of course. It's only because I have no real reason for rising that I lie in bed so late. What time do you want to go?"

"Well, I think we ought to get there about eleven. Breakfast at nine, say, and we can catch the ten car. That will mean we shall be in Aulmbermouth by ten-twenty. We will tell her you are leaving, pack your things, and bring them here in a taxi. You haven't much, have you?"

"No. Only one trunk and one suitcase. A good many things are here already."

"So much the better. Very well, then, Jean shall

sleep as long as she can, and Moti can take charge of Allison. You and I will get that very unpleasant piece of business done before lunch, and we can arrange later about your going to this new place."

"All right," said Mollie, submissively.

"For the future, Mollie, you will spend your week-ends here. I blame myself very much that I did not insist on it sooner. I should have seen then that something was wrong, and you would have left Mrs Taylor some months ago."

Mollie nodded. Then she stood up and stretched herself. "Thanks, Oona. Well, I'll take my tray to the kitchen and get to bed. I'm dead tired."

"Don't go into Jean," said Miss McCleod, rising, and beginning to tidy up. "She was asleep when I looked in last, and that's the best thing for her."

Mollie nodded, and vanished kitchenward with her tray. Morag was sitting knitting and looked up grimly when the girl entered.

"Whit ha'e you and Miss Jean been daein', Miss Mollie?"

"Having adventures," replied Mollie.

"Ay, ye wad! At your age, ye ought tae hev mair sense! Gin ye canna luke tae sae whit's comin' doon the rod, ye needna expect bairns tae dae it! It's yer deid bodies that wull be broght home next! Ye thochtless lassies!"

Morag had known Mollie for nine years and considered her as one of the family. In her eyes, both she and Jean were mere children to be scolded for the good of their souls, and she was not in the habit of sparing them.

Had she dared, Miss Stewart would have fled before the storm but she knew that Morag would merely bide her time, and the lecture would be worse than ever. She had ruled too long at Storms for them to refuse to be schooled by her if she decided that they needed it. Even the dignified Miss McCleod could only listen when Morag spoke her mind. She had been a faithful servant and had stood by them and theirs for more than fifty years now, so that they almost felt it their due to listen to her. To-night, Mollie had a lengthy lecture on the wickedness of being foolhardy, and was only thankful when, at the end of fifteen minutes, Morag waved her away with a "Awa' tae yer bed and be thankful ye hevna tae lie thinkin' o' the sorrow ye've brocht tae Storms! Whit time did ye say ye wantit tae be ca'ed? Half past eight? Ye must be ill! Aweel. I'll ca' ye — and see and get up when yer ca'ed!"

Mollie said "good-night" meekly, and then fled upstairs, and locked herself in in case Morag should think of something else to say and follow her to say it. Later she went to see that Allie was all right, and after tucking the blankets more closely round the child ran back to her own room, where her pyjamas spread before the blaze, and a hot bottle in her bed, all told of Morag's care.

With a little chuckle, she undressed, and tumbled into bed, where she speedily fell asleep, and slept till a heavy knock on the door, and the adjuration, "Miss Mollie! Get ye oot o' yer bed, else yer water wull be cauld!" brought her on the floor. Twenty minutes later, she was downstairs, whereat Morag gave a grim chuckle. Allie, attended to by Moti, was there before her, and then Oona came in, and after breakfast and prayers, the elderly lady went to see to household matters, while the younger kept the child amused till it was time to set off. They went over the hard, crunching snow, waving as they passed the window, to Allison, who stood there to watch them off. "Much too cold for Allison, poor bairnie," said Oona, as they crossed the road to the tram terminus. "Mollie, you look blue! You aren't a true Scotswoman if a little cold upsets you like this."

"I hate it!" said Mollie rebelliously. "Give me the tropics and plenty of warmth!" Luckily, a tram came along almost at that moment, and they were soon speeding along Aulmbermouth, where the treacherous pavements sent people slipping and sliding, and even Mollie and Oona, in rubber boots, found it none too easy to get along.

"Mercifully," said Mollie as they turned into the street where Mrs Taylor lived, "it isn't far."

They had nearly reached the house, when she grasped Oona's arm. "Oh, Oona! I wish it were over. I feel like the dentist's!"

"English as she is spoke!" said Oona. "Mollie, you goose! It will soon be over, and then think how glad you will be!"

Mollie stopped dead in the street, and burst into a peal of laughter, "Oona, that's just what I've heard you say to us both many a time when we were going to the dentist's!" Oona joined in the laugh, and it did them both good. When they were serious once more, they went on, and presently Miss Stewart was using her latch-key for the last time, and had ushered Oona into the passage. A door at the end of it opened, and a head was poked out.

"Is that you, Miss Stewart?"

"Yes," said Mollie. "May I speak to you upstairs, Mrs Taylor?"

"In a moment. I'm just putting a pie into the oven."

The head vanished, and Mollie led the way upstairs and lit the gasfire. Almost immediately, steps were heard ascending the stairs, and then Mrs Taylor entered the room. Oona looked at her with interest, and a sense of repulsion. She was a tall, gawky woman with a long horse-like face, of sallow complexion. Her eyes were brown, and the lid of the left one drooped conspicuously, giving her a sly appearance. She had a wide, ugly mouth with yellow teeth, and a one-sided smile; her hair, which was her sole beauty, was white and wavy and arranged on the top of her head in curls. Her dress was brownish-yellow — obviously a one-time "best" dress — elaborately trimmed with scrolls of black braiding and it fitted tightly over a badly-corsetted figure. Altogether, Oona thought she had never met a more repulsive woman in her life.

She advanced smiling her one sided smile. "Well, Miss Stewart, I thought you were never coming back to me again."

"That is partly a mistake," said Mollie, her nervousness making her voice very clear and icy. "I have come to get my things. I am leaving you today."

"Leaving me, Miss Stewart? You can't mean it! After all I've done for you! Aren't you comfortable?"

"No," said Mollie quietly. "I am not."

"But why? What can I do for you that I haven't done? A fire in your bedroom while this cold weather lasts? I'm sure I should be pleased — and no extra charge."

"It isn't that," said Mollie. "I object to being spied on — that is all."

"Oh, bravo, Mollie!" thought Oona. Aloud, she said nothing, but she watched the two closely.

Mrs Taylor's cheeks flushed at the words. "Well — I'm sure!" she exclaimed in a high key.

Mollie held up her hand. "Wait! I want to finish what I am saying. I will pack my things now — Miss McCleod will help me — and, as I am leaving you at a moment's notice like this, I will, of course, pay you a fortnight's rent. My things will go to Hasnett, where I am staying for the present, and I will send my address to my correspondents, so that you need not be troubled with forwarding my letters."

Mrs Taylor looked at her. Then she sat down, and burst into tears. "Oh, Miss Stewart! I did think you were kinder than this! What have I done that you should leave me like this? I'm sure I did my best to make you happy! I'd willingly have made a friend of you, and taken you about with me — "

Oona rose. She felt that there had been enough of this, and Mollie did not seem very sure how to deal with it. "Will you go and pack, Mollie," she said.

Her voice brought Mrs Taylor to her feet in sudden fury. "Yes! Go and pack!" she cried. "It's you and that stuck up bit o' goods she's forever bringing here that's made her do this! Taking the bread out of an honest woman's mouth! But she's no better than she ought to be — a brazen little hussy — "

Across the frothing torrent of the woman's words, Oona's voice struck calm and cold.

"Mollie, will you please do as I tell you at once!"

Mollie fled. What happened, she never knew, but when she came back, Mrs Taylor was helping Oona to tie up her books and pictures, and there was a cowed look in her eyes. She took very little notice of the girl, and when Mollie laid the money on the table, she barely said "Thank you."

"Have you everything?" asked Oona.

"I think so," said Mollie.

"Ah! Then Mrs Taylor, if you would be so good as to call a taxi, we will trouble you no longer."

Mrs Taylor vanished, and presently the taxi-horn sounded outside the house. The man came up, and carried down Mollie's possessions, and when the last was on the taxi, and the girl herself inside it, Oona turned to the landlady.

"If ever I hear of your slandering or attempting to spread gossip about Miss Stewart," she said, "I will communicate with my lawyers. Please remember that."

Then she got into the taxi, and directed the man to go to the post office.

"Why that?" demanded Mollie.

"To give them Storms as your address. I don't trust that woman one inch, and there is no reason why she should be given the chance of tampering with your letters. Storms will do until you can tell your correspondents your new home, and if any letters come after you leave us for Field Terrace, one of us can always send them on to you."

Mollie slipped her hand into Oona's and squeezed it. "Oona, you are a dear! I could never have gone through that to-day by myself — anyway, I know she would have been fifty times worse than she was, even! What we got was enough for me!"

"More than enough, I think," said Oona. "Well, you are finished with her now, at any rate. Don't bother about her again."

But that was where Oona was mistaken. They had by no means finished with Mrs Taylor, nor she with them.

CHAPTER X

AN ANXIOUS TIME

"I'm going to walk into Aulmbermouth to-night," said Jean, six days after her accident. "It's a gorgeous night, and I'm quite fit again, so I'll get ready as soon as tea is over."

Miss McCleod looked dismayed. "Walk in, Jean? Do you think it wise?"

"Yes," said Jean. "I haven't been out all day, and I'm longing to stretch my legs."

Oona said no more. In the main, she could control her niece, but there were times when she knew it best to let the girl go her own way. Besides, Allison was there, watching them with great eyes that took in everything. She had not been very well all day, and she was fractious. With Jean in her present restless mood, Oona had felt rather driven between the pair of them. Tea went on in silence, and when it was over, Jean rose, and went to the window, and stood looking out at the moonlit sea with a restless expression that made her aunt quake inwardly. She sent Allie off to find Moti, and rang the bell for Morag to clear. Then she went to the girl.

"Come along to the Den, Jean. Moti will look after Allison till I go to put her to bed."

Jean followed her aunt to the Den, and wandered about, while Oona sat down with her knitting.

"I'm bored, Oona," said the younger girl, suddenly.

"So I see," said Oona quietly. "I understand, Jean. You are not accustomed to having a child perpetually with you, and Allison has been very trying today. I don't think she is well."

"Oh — cold or tummy!" said Jean. "Better give her something to-night. She'll be all right. She is dreadfully spoilt, Oona, and I won't give in to her."

Oona raised her brows but said nothing more on the subject. Instead, she asked if Jean really meant to walk to Aulmbermouth, for, if so, it was time she was getting ready. Jean nodded curtly, and went out, to return presently, ready for her walk.

"Bye-bye," she said, casually. "I'll be back about ten."

"Very well," said Oona. "Don't walk back, Jean."

"Oh, I'll see!"

Jean went out, and Oona heard the crunching of the snow under her feet as she passed the window. Miss McCleod sat back, wondering what had gone wrong. It was not like Jean to be so captious.

Meanwhile, Jean herself went on briskly. It was a glorious night, with bright moonlight and no wind. She met no one on the road, for the cold held no attractions for the stolid matter-of-fact fisher-folk, and they mostly kept to their own cosy homes, or else went off to the nearest public-house. Just outside of Aulmbermouth she heard the steady "purr-purr" of a car, and, turning, saw the doctor. He had obviously seen her, and he slowed up as he neared her.

"Good evening!" he called. "Can I give you a lift?"

"No, thanks," replied Jean. "I'm only going to classes, and it's just ten minutes' walk to the school now."

"Have you walked all the way?" he asked, thinking how lovely she looked in the moonlight.

Jean nodded. "Yes; I felt restless, and thought I'd walk it off. Are you going to class now?"

"Got one call to make first," he said. "It's a Mrs Taylor. She fell down and sprained her ankle, and I

haven't seen her so far. I was called out suddenly at
two before I got off on my afternoon round, so I've
had to make a late one."

"Mrs Taylor!" said Jean, a sudden black depression creeping over her.

"Yes; she lives in Front Street. Do you know her?"

"Miss Stewart used to room there," said the girl.
"Well, I mustn't be late." She moved away a little,
her mouth drooping, her whole aspect one of
weariness. He looked at her in dismay.

"Miss Jean, are you quite fit to dance, do you
think? That was a nasty knock you had last week."

"I'm all right," said Jean, sharply. "You'd better go
on, or you'll miss everything."

He looked at her; then he started up his car again,
and with a valedictory wave of his hand, called, "See
you later!" He drove away, and she went on to the
school, trying vainly to throw off the heavy cloud
that had settled over her. At the gates of the High
School, she met one or two of the others, who
welcomed her gaily. "Last lesson of this term," said
Miss Farrar as they went in.

"Party on Saturday," said Miss Derwent, cheerfully. "That's something to look forward to."

"Anyway, don't borrow trouble," added a third.
"Come along and get ready, or we shall be late."

Laughing and chattering they swept into the
school, where Mollie and her two hostesses of the
afternoon were waiting for them. At sight of Jean's
face, she left them, and came running to her friend.

"There you are at last! Did you bring my shoes? I
forgot them." Then, as Jean moved to get the shoes
from her case, she added in lower tones, "What's up,
Jean?"

"Idiocy!" replied Jean. "Just that and nothing
else!"

Mollie, engaged in changing her shoes, looked up

enquiringly. "Don't understand. Can't you explain better than that?"

"No," said Jean curtly. "Let me alone, Mollie."

Miss Stewart stood up, gave her friend a curious glance, and then left the room. Jean having changed, followed in silence, and was thankful when they were called to take their places for the sword dance. Her mind was too overburdened for her to give proper attention to what she was doing, and, before long, her set was tangled badly. Mollie, coming up to set them right, was troubled. Jean was totally unlike herself, and she could not imagine what was wrong. Allie had been poorly, but if she had grown worse, Jean would have stayed with her, so it could not be that. She could think of nothing which could account for this, and finally, seeing that Jean would do no good, requested her to sit out, since she was spoiling the set. Jean went off to sit down and watch the dancers with absent eyes, and to try to pull herself together.

With a mighty effort, she did it, and when country dancing began, she was able to take her part without upsetting the others. They, having heard of Allison's indisposition, put her manner down to worry over the child, and left her to herself, thinking it kinder. The doctor came in in time for this, and one glance at his face as they met in the side and honour of "Newcastle" set Jean's mind at rest for the time being. Why she should be so anxious for his respect and friendship, she had no idea. For her years, Jean was curiously young in mind. Her training, both at home and at school, largely accounted for it. Oona had never allowed her niece to hear silly talk, and the school had been at one in condemning any "soppy" talk. In consequence, Jean, and also Mollie, were as fresh-minded on such subjects as they had been as schoolgirls of fourteen.

The dance ended, and Miss Stewart bade them take partners to learn "Step and Fetch Her." The doctor came for his partner, and led her off in quiet triumph. Jean might not know what was her real feeling for him, but he knew that, from the first moment, he had fallen in love with this slim, green-eyed girl with her moon-light beauty and her slender grace.

He meant to go slowly, for some occult sense warned him that Jean would not be easily won, and he meant his wooing to be a happy one. But he intended to make her his wife sooner or later. So he made the most that he dared of his opportunities, and prayed for others. Had anyone told him that night that those were soon to come, he would have gone down on his knees in thankfulness. Had anyone told him that estrangement was to make those very opportunities a sheer agony to him, he would have dashed his fist in the face of the informer. The dance continued, and both had forgotten themselves in sheer enjoyment of it, when the swingdoors at the end of the hall were suddenly flung back. Jean looked up in surprise to break away next moment, and go racing towards them. Standing there, her face white and her eyes frightened, was Oona.

Allison? Jean caught her aunt by the arm, and shook her slightly. "Oona! What is wrong with Allie?" The doctor had followed her. He knew that he was wanted, and, knowing also of Allison's extreme delicacy, he guessed that it was something serious.

"Dr Errington, will you come at once?" said Oona, paying no heed to Jean. "Allison has croup — diptheretic croup, I am afraid. She is very ill already. I rang up your house, but they told me you were out. Then, I remembered you were here, so I came to bring you. Mollie told me that the telephone here had gone wrong."

He left her without a word, and Jean fled to the formroom to get into her hat and coat. They were both on the doorstep at the same moment, and into the taxi which had brought Oona.

"Round to my house first," said the doctor. "I want one or two things."

The driver, knowing what was wrong, put on his best speed, and when they reached the house the doctor barely gave him time to slow up before he was out of the cab, and into the surgery, where he selected what he needed with a steady haste. Then, back into the taxi once more, and away down the moon-litten road to Storms, where a little child fought with the deadly membrane that was closing up the air-passages.

When they reached the house, the doctor sprang out, and went off upstairs. His one remark in the cab had been to ask which was Allison's room, and he knew where to go. Jean and Oona followed him, and the driver, knowing them, removed himself and his taxi without comment.

In the little bedroom they found Allison in bed, held up in Morag's arms, fighting and struggling for breath. Moti, with the ipecachuana bottle, stood close at hand, tears in her dark eyes. Bessie, "the lass", was putting more coal on the fire, and a huge bath of water nearby showed what remedies they had tried. One glance at the child's face warned the doctor. It was touch and go already. Allison had very little reserve strength, and she was dangerously ill. There had been no time to get another doctor, and tracheotomy must be performed without delay. That meant that someone must hold the child's head since the doctor could not administer chloroform and perform the operation at the same moment. He turned to Jean. She was white, but there was a steadiness in her face that told him she could do what he wanted.

Swiftly, he gave his commands. A table was carried into Jean's bedroom, as there was more room, and the light was better there. Certain instruments were dropped into a pan of boiling water and boracic powder; the doctor was washing his hands in more hot water and disinfectant, and Morag was tying a spotlessly clean apron round his waist. His coat was off, and his shirt sleeves turned well back.

Moti was holding Allison, who was only half-conscious, and Bessie was keeping the fire going, and weeping at the same time.

"Bring her along," said the doctor. "Miss Jean, you must hold her head."

Jean took up her stand at the head of the table. She was white to the lips, but she was curiously composed. He showed her what to do, and she took Allie's head between her palms with a quietness that showed plenty of self-control.

The operation was a short one, mercifully, and quickly over. From the time the doctor made the quick, clean cut into the larynx to the time when, the little tube in place, and that awful grey look dying out of Allie's face, he stood back to watch the result, was only a few minutes in reality. To Jean it seemed an eternity.

At length, from a long distance as it seemed, she heard his voice. "That will do, Miss Jean."

Her hands fell to her sides, and she looked at him with a mute question in her eyes.

He nodded. "Safe, I think. She ought to do now."

Oona, overwrought and tired, burst into tears, but Jean gave him a smile he never forgot.

"Thank God — oh, thank God!" she said, her voice thrilling deeply in the words.

CHAPTER XI

A llison remained poorly for the next few days, and the doctor felt justified in calling in every day. He had spent the whole night at Storms, being anxious to see to those first hours himself, though he felt fairly sure that the child would be all right now. He had rung up his housekeeper, to tell her to send on any messages that came for him, and then had turned his attention to arrangements for the night. Oona decided that Jean had better share Mollie's room, and then hers would be made ready for the doctor. She herself would sit up with the little patient for the first few hours then Moti would take charge. Morag was willing, but was too old a woman to be allowed to lose her night's sleep unless it was absolutely necessary. Mollie and Jean were already tired out, and Jean at any rate had already had as much as she could stand. Oona knew that the girl would have undertaken the night-nursing completely if she were allowed, but, in the circumstances, it was not needful, therefore the elder woman quietly decided she should spend her night in bed. As for Mollie, she was wearied out with teaching, and was not strong for all her spirit. She had spent most of the morning in getting her new rooms put into order, for she was to move in the next day, so she, too, needed the night's sleep. To say that the two Oona had thought for so carefully were grateful would be utterly untrue. Jean at first refused to go to bed. She protested that, as Allison's aunt, she had the best right to sit up with her, and,

whatever Oona and Moti chose to do, she meant to
be beside her.

"You have done your share," said Oona. "You will
have to be responsible for a good deal of the day
nursing — for to-morrow, at any rate. I have that
meeting of the Women's Unionists and, as I am
secretary, I must go if it is at all possible. Mollie has
to settle in at Field Terrace, so she won't be with
you. Morag and Moti will fight if they're left alone —
you know what Morag's opinion of Moti is, even
though there are no grounds for it. She will be
convinced that 'a puir blackie' could never do all
Allison wants. You must be able to take charge, and
you must have a good night's rest, or you won't be fit
for it. Please say no more, Jean, but go and get what
you are likely to need, and be quick about it."

When Oona spoke like that Jean knew there was
nothing for it but obedience, so she meekly went to
find her pyjamas and washing paraphernalia, as
well as a morning frock from the bedroom where
Morag was busily re-making the bed so that the
doctor might lie down if he felt able to do so.

By ten o'clock Mollie came in, tired and anxious,
and, therefore, cross. Everything was ready for
them, and Allison was sleeping quietly, though her
temperature was still rather too high to please the
doctor. Moti sat beside her while the gentleman
discussed a good supper in the dining room, before
going up to take over his duties. Jean sat opposite
him, her face mutinous. She still considered that
she had a grievance, for Allie was her niece and
ward. Apart from that, it was not until she had
known the child's danger that she had realised how
dear she was to her. When her friend appeared,
eager questions on her lips, she scowled slightly at
her aunt, who answered Mollie's queries quietly.

"Better now. The doctor performed a tracheotomy

and she is sleeping. He will stay the night in case of need, so you and Jean must sleep together."

"Was it as bad as that?" asked Mollie in awed tones. She had the usual layman's ignorance of operations, and "tracheotomy" had a fearsome sound.

"It was touch and go at the moment," said the doctor. "I saw that at once, so I wasted no time, though it was awkward having no anaesthetic. Miss Jean proved herself a heroine, though, and I think all will go well now."

Jean's brows slightly relaxed under his praise, but she was not her usual sweet-tempered self yet, as the other two knew.

"Did Benson come in for the morris?" asked the doctor, presently, as he passed his cup to Oona for more coffee.

Mollie shook her head. "No; he must have been sent for somewhere."

"More than likely. The clergy seem to get as little sleep in their beds as we medicos. At least, the St. Simon's clergy do. If I am ever called to an urgent case in the night, I am always sure of finding either the Vicar or one of his curates on hand, ready to do anything they can, from making a poultice to fulfilling their own office."

"That's more than you can say for our Vicar," said Jean, coming out of her sulks with an unexpected-ness that made Mollie jump. "He sleeps sound enough o'nights!"

"Jean! That's neither fair nor kind," said Oona reproachfully. "Mr Semple is an earnest hard-working man, and if he doesn't visit the sick in the night, you may be sure it is because he is not called. He would go if he were wanted."

Jean was in argumentative mood. "He might! I suppose he would think it his duty. But doesn't it just show what sort of a man he is when he isn't called?"

Oona was silent. She knew her Jean, and it was little use contradicting her when she was like this. She was perfectly capable of twisting arguments round till she gave strangers a most exaggerated idea of the shortcomings of the poor Vicar who was a well-meaning man, if he had only been left to himself. The fact that he never was so left, meant trouble at the parish. His wife was at the bottom of most of the disputes that were perpetually arising, and she was always urging him to courses that made trouble for the congregation. Mr Semple was badly handicapped; of that there could be no doubt. In her better moments, Jean was one of the first to admit this. At present she was more likely to blame him entirely for anything that went wrong.

The doctor, not understanding these wheels within wheels, looked puzzled. Jean was showing herself all prickled to-night. His "ladye fayre" would not be easy. He realised that. At the same time, he was more than ever in love with her. With Meredith, he might have said "Hard, but O, the glory of the winning were she won!"

Mollie calmly turned the conversation. Not that she had much sympathy for Mr Semple whom she cordially disliked, but she felt that Jean was all on edge, and, to her loyalty, it was a pity for her friend to show herself in such an unlikeable character.

"Mr Benson has taught his boys three dances," she said. "As far as I can make out, they rather scoffed at them for 'girls' nonsense!' But they worship him, so they agreed to try them. Now, he says, they are crazy to learn as much as he can teach them. At my suggestion, he taught them 'Rigs' and 'Bean Setting', and they took to them like ducks to water."

"How on earth do you know that?" asked Jean suspiciously. "You say he didn't come to class at all."

To her surprise, Mollie changed colour. "I sometimes meet him in town," she said. "He always tells me how they are getting on — of course, he knows I'm interested in anything connected with dancing. He's so keen to give them something to keep them off the street. Even in a sleepy little place like Aulmbermouth, there's plenty to set the boys wrong. Pitch and toss on the rocks in summer, and billiards at the billiard saloons in the winter, for instance."

"Pitch and toss on the rocks!" exclaimed the doctor.

"They go there because then the town police can't interfere with them," explained Jean. "It's out of the borough, you see, and means the county police. Of course, they are always having raids and so on, but the lads are very cute, and they keep sentinels posted about, and are very wary of strangers."

The doctor nodded. "I see. Well, it's better than that abominable rabbit-coursing so many of the miners round here seem to indulge in. I like sport as well as any man, but wherein lies the sport of setting racing dogs after a terrified little animal that does not know its ground, and is certain of death, is more than I can say."

"Or anybody else with a sense of decency," cried Jean hotly, her colour rising as she spoke. "It's a cowardly, damnable thing, and I only wish the men could be in the rabbit's place occasionally, and know what it's like! That might check them!"

"Hear-hear!" said the doctor as he rose from his seat. "I fully agree."

Then he turned to Oona, and asked her to excuse him, as he wished to go back to his little patient, and see how she was getting on. When he had gone,

Oona went off to the kitchen, and the two girls were left alone.

"I got such a fright when she came in like that!" said Mollie, pouring out more coffee for herself. "I was afraid it was something really bad."

"It was quite bad enough," retorted Jean, sharply. "The kid was nearly choking to death when we got here! I had to hold her head while he performed the operation, and she looked ghastly! I don't know how much worse you would like it to be, of course!"

Mollie opened her lips to reply, but she caught sight of Jean's white face, and realised that the girl was on the verge of a breakdown. Her mouth was quivering like a baby's, and her eyes were dark with unshed tears. Jean would have hated nothing so much as the falling of those tears, so Mollie shut her own lips again. She drained her coffee, badly scorching her mouth in the process, and then offered her cigarette case.

"Smoke?"

Jean nodded and took one. She was by no means such an habitual smoker as her friend, but she felt the need of something to steady her nerves just now. They lit up, and smoked in silence for a few moments. Then Jean turned to Mollie with some casual question about the classes and managed to get rid of the lump in her throat and those inconvenient tears. The conversation became desultory, and at length Mollie suggested that bed would not be a bad plan. Jean agreed, as they gathered up their possessions, and went upstairs.

"I'm going in to see Allie," said the young aunt as she tossed her book down on the bed. "Coming with me?"

"Rather!" Mollie slipped her arm through the other girl's, and they went quietly along the passage to the little rosy room, where Allie lay sleeping sweetly, drawing in fresh life with every breath. Moti sat by the fireplace, and the doctor was by the little bed. He looked up with a smile as the girls entered, and moved away, so that Jean slipped into his place. Lovingly, she hung over the little white face on the pillow, marking how much better it looked already.

Mollie, after a murmured, "Poor little dear! But she really does look quite like herself now, Jean!" slipped out, and left the two together. Jean raised to the doctor's face eyes green as beryls. "She is much better, isn't she?" she asked imploringly.

He nodded. "Very much better, Miss Jean. It will be a few days before she is quite right again, of course; but, in the long run she ought to be her usual self by the end of a week or so. You really have no need to worry. I am only staying so as to be on the spot in case the membrane should grow again, though I am not anticipating it in the least."

Jean drew the bedclothes closer round the child's shoulders. Then she stood up.

"You are very good, doctor. I am more grateful to you than I can say. If you had not been so quick, Allie might have — might have — " She paused, unable to finish her sentence.

"Nothing would have happened to her," said the doctor gravely. "You would have found some way out, I am sure. That ancient domestic of yours — what do you call her? Morag — would have evolved some marvellous old wives' cure. Mind, I am not in favour of that sort of thing; but I should be a fool if I did not acknowledge that such things have worked wonders in the past. However, the worst is over now, and there is no necessity to talk about it. Any other doctor would have done what I did. As a matter-of-fact, it was partly your own steadiness that helped to save the child."

Jean gave him a wonderful smile. "I shall always feel that I owe her life to you," she said. "Oh, you may put it off as you like, but I know that, under God, you saved Allie for me. I shall never forget that!"

Then she smiled at him, and left the room quietly, leaving him thrilling with hopes and dreams.

CHAPTER XII

The days that followed were rather anxious ones, for Allison did not recover as quickly as the doctor had hoped, and she was very fretful and irritable. The heaviest part of the work fell on Jean, who spent most of the day in her room. At night, Moti took charge with instructions to call Oona if anything were needed. When Saturday came, Jean was worn out, and looked it. She had never had much colour, but what she had had vanished, and her eyes were heavy. Oona noticed it with dismay, and sent for Mollie post haste. Mollie arrived looking worried, for Bessie, "the lass", had said that the mistress wanted to see her about Miss Jean, and, on being pressed for further information, had replied that Miss Jean was looking ill. "What's wrong?" asked the girl as she ran into the Den.

"Jean is poorly for lack of fresh air," replied Oona, coming straight to the point. "Is not your party to-night? I want you to go and get her case which I have packed, and take her off to your rooms, and keep her there for the rest of the day — or, rather, to take her out this afternoon. She's scarcely left Allison all this week, and she's not accustomed to confinement. She'll be ill if this goes on."

"All right," said Mollie. "We can walk over to Blyton Sands this afternoon; and this evening, she'll be fully engaged. But who'll look after Allison?"

"I shall. I have had such a plethora of meetings lately, that I have had no time to help with the nursing, and that is why Jean has had so much to do. Morag would have helped, but I think Jean is afraid of what she might say to the child. Allie is much better to-day, and the doctor said that he wasn't coming till to-morrow, so Jean can leave her easily. It will do her good to get right away from it all for a while. Allie is not the best of patients, and Jean has never been too patient. No; I'm not trying to be funny, so don't look at me like that!"

"Well, I thought it didn't sound like you," said Mollie demurely. "I'm glad the kiddy is going on well at last. You've had a benefit of it since she came!"

"Never mind. It's over now," said Oona, placidly. "The doctor thinks she ought to be all right after this. Of course, she will need great care as long as the cold weather lasts, but once she is acclimatised, he thinks she will be all right. You can look in on her as you go up. She may have visitors, now, and she seems to have taken a fancy to you."

"Weird taste!" commented Mollie lightly. "Very well, I'll pop in, and collect Jean. Then we'll go off for the day. I'm coming here on Tuesday, you know, so I shall see you then. I've got to go over to South Helling on Monday — they want to start a class there, and the girl who is going to act as secretary wants to see me. I had a letter this morning, and she's asked me to go over about three and have tea with her. I would have come on Monday if it hadn't been for that."

"So they are going to have a class there?" said Oona. "Won't it take some of your people from Aulmbermouth?"

"I shan't mind that," returned Mollie. "The classes are getting on the large side, and it's difficult to give everyone the proper amount of attention."

"When can you fit in your class over there?" asked Oona.

"On Mondays. I can move that advanced morris

class at Aulmbermouth to Tuesday night, after the others, and that is all I have on Mondays at present."

"It will mean that Tuesday is a very heavy day for you," said Oona, frowning. "If you begin at six, and go on till ten, you will be very tired."

Mollie laughed. "Oh, nonsense!" she retorted. She went out of the room laughing, and ran upstairs leaving her friend to shake her head over this new venture. Mollie was full of spirit, but she was given to thinking herself much stronger than she really was, and Oona sometimes worried over her.

Her mother had died when she was a baby, and her father was in the Indian Civil Service. Her only relative in England was an old cousin who lived in London, and whom she and Jean had dubbed "the Gorgon". This was an elderly maiden lady of all too certain age, who disapproved thoroughly of her young cousin, and spent most of Mollie's periodical visits in fault-finding. To the McCleods the girl was like one of themselves, and Oona, at any rate, troubled about her at times.

"I wish Mollie would marry," she thought.

Her own tragedy had made the elder Miss McCleod realise that marriage for a girl of Miss Stewart's temperament was the ideal life. She hoped that both girls would marry some day; and though she was no match-maker, Oona wondered about the young curate at St. Simon's. She had met and liked him, and he certainly seemed very interested in pretty Mollie. As for Mollie herself, Oona was fairly sure that she was by no means indifferent to the tall young man who walked through the streets as if he were striding across his native veldt — he was a Rhodes scholar from South Africa — and who was so enthusiastic about his work.

The sound of the girls coming downstairs roused

her from the reverie into which she had fallen, and she went to see them off.

"Allie is asleep, Oona," said Jean. "Thanks awfully for packing my things, and for offering to sit with her. You are a sport!"

"I shall expect you when I see you to-night," said Oona. "If it's very late, take a taxi. Have you any money?"

"About ten shillings," replied Jean. "All right. Farewell until we meet again. Oh! Don't let Morag be alone with the kiddy. She may mean well, but I don't like all her acts!"

"Oh, nonsense! You needn't worry. I'll look after Allison quite safely. After all, I've had several years of experience."

"I dare say! But I won't have Allie frightened."

Oona laughed and waved them away. "Go along and get your walk! Have a good time to-night."

"Always do at parties! Come along, Mollie. She doesn't want us!" They set off, laughing and talking, and Oona mounted the stairs to Allison's room, and settled herself by the fire with her book.

What Jean and Mollie talked about at first has little to do with this story. It was desultory conversation mainly; but presently they drifted off to the question of the classes at South Helling. Jean was wildly interested. South Helling, an important coal port at the mouth of the Aulmber, and just opposite to Aulmbermouth, has a large population, and does a great deal of export business. It is very old, part of it dating back to the time of the Romans — notably the Roman Remains at the site of the Church of St. Hilda, which is said to be the same as that on which Hild, a daughter of the royal house of Northumbria, established her church when she came to this place — then a river island — to found a convent later left in charge of St. Verca, one of her nuns. There had

been no folk-dance classes there before, and the fact
that they were keen to begin, now meant something
to all who were interested. One of the leading vicars
in the town had offered them — with the full
concurrence of the parish council — his church hall
at a nominal sum, and a girl who was very musical
had been found who would play accompaniments.

From South Helling, they drifted to
Aulmbermouth, and from there, to various people in
the classes. Finally, they came to the Reverend
Charles Benson, who was doing splendid work
among the lads and young men of the parish, and
was already talking hopefully of being able to send
a morris team to compete in the Musical
Tournament held each year at Noviam.

"I like Mr Benson," said Jean thoughtfully. "He is
such a boy!"

"He's no such thing!" retorted Mollie sharply.
"He's a man, and he's doing a man's work among
those lads. If all clergy were like him, we'd hear less
about empty churches than we do."

Jean raised her eyebrows, but something in
Mollie's aspect kept her tongue quiet. She changed
the subject, and made complaints about Morag's
latest whim. "She says I'm telling Allie lies when I
tell her about Father Christmas!" she complained.
"She actually told me the other day that I ought to
be ashamed of myself for letting her think such
things! I've forbidden her to say anything to the kid
about it."

"And much good that will do!" struck in Mollie. "If
Morag thinks it her duty to enlighten Allison, she'll
do it, whether you like it or not. You ought to know
that by this time. She fears no man — nor woman,
either. You've probably just set her back up for no
purpose."

"Morag will do as I say this time!" said Jean with

a tilt of her pretty chin. "There'll be such a fuss if she doesn't!"

"There'll be a fuss all right. But how you propose to bridle her tongue unless she chooses, passes my comprehension!"

"Oh, I'll do it," said Jean. "For one thing, Allison will never be left alone, and she isn't likely to start anything before Oona or me."

"Think not?"

"She'll be choked off pretty quickly if she does!"

"Then may I be there to see it! It'll be well worth seeing! — I say, Jean, you look tired. Hadn't we better get the bus? No sense in wearing yourself out before to-night?"

"Very well. Here is a bus coming, so we shan't have to wait, thank goodness!"

They clambered into the bus, and were presently bowling away to Aulmbermouth, where they were set down at the end of Field Terrace. Mrs Woodhouse had tea ready, and they sat over it, chatting gaily while they sampled her excellent scones and cakes, and drained the teapot dry.

"Rather different from Mrs Taylor's wash," observed Mollie. "That woman never made tea worth drinking."

"Rather different from Mrs Taylor's altogether," said Jean, as she looked round the room with its dainty curtains, and glowing fire, and soft lamplight that touched Mollie's charming face to fresh beauty.

"Yes; I feel at home here," agreed the mistress of the little domain. "More tea? I can water the leaves again."

"I think not, thank you," decided Jean. "That would be wash! I say, Mollie, I've news for you — very nearly forgot it. Mrs Taylor has a new boarder, and who do you think it is?"

Mollie shook her head. "No idea. Tell me, and

hurry up. We ought to be changing for the party now. I want to be early so as to see that everything is all right."

"It's Mr Benson," said Jean.

Mollie went silent while she digested this unwelcome piece of news. "What a — weird thing," she said at length.

"Just what I thought. I hope she makes him more comfortable than she made you. There's one thing," added Jean with a chuckle, "She's not likely to disturb his slumbers by asking him to admire her hair at one o'clock in the morning."

"But why isn't he staying on at the Clergy House?" asked Mollie.

"Some idea of the Vicar's that one of them ought to be in a less rarefied atmosphere, I gather," said Jean. "I got it from Mrs Semple, and that's what she says."

"Oh?" said Mollie.

She was silent for a minute or two, and when she spoke again, it was to suggest that they ought to change. They went upstairs to the pretty bedroom and changed into their evening frocks — Mollie's of rose-pink georgette, Jean's jade-green of the same material. When they were sure that all was right, they slipped on their coats and caps and set off for the High School, where some of the members of the branch were already. Mollie slipped off her coat and hat and then went down to see that everything was ready. Jean followed a moment later, with Miss Farrar and Miss Derwent, and the buzz of their chatter rose as more and more people came in. At length, Mollie mounted a chair, and announced that they were about to begin. The pianist played "Mary and Dorothy" once through, and then they ran to make up sets.

Mollie was busy seeing that they had enough

room, and that some sets were not too big while others were too small. She stood out for the first time, for she had promised the dance to the doctor who had not yet come, and was on the little platform, watching it and enjoying the prettiness of it when a tall figure stopped before her, and she looked down and saw Mr Benson.

"Good evening, Miss Stewart. Aren't you dancing this?"

"Good evening," replied Mollie. "I was — Dr Errington asked me for it; but he hasn't come."

"Then may I have it? We can join on at the end of that set, I think."

Mollie hesitated, but he gently escorted her to the place, and she was dancing with him almost before she realised that she was there.

Three dances later the doctor turned up, full of apologies for his lateness, and she was dancing with the curate again, and he was unable to speak to her. He turned to Jean, next to whom he was standing.

"I'm sorry I'm late, Miss Jean. I hope I haven't missed much!"

"Just the first three," said Jean, cheerfully. "This is just ending. The next is 'Newcastle', and I have that with Miss Stewart. Excuse me, please."

She slipped off, and joined Mollie on the platform, where that busy person was giving some directions to the accompanist.

"Do we dance first or second time?"

"Oh, second, I think."

"All right!" She glanced at her friend with a mischievous twinkle in her eyes. "You're 'in face' to-night, as they used to say! That frock suits you, Mollie, my child."

Mollie opened wide eyes at her, but someone took her attention at the moment, and Jean went to sit down till the first time "Newcastle" was over.

The party went with a swing, and by the time they reached supper, the last restraint had gone from it and the air thrummed with the merry "Folk" atmosphere. Even strangers who had come as guests were chattering away with people as if they had known them for years instead of a short two hours. Mollie, looking round at the laughing faces, felt that this was the biggest success of the branch, and glowed with pleasure. Jean, waited on by the doctor, was her happiest self, and filled him with ecstasy by her friendliness. There is no disguising the fact that she was wont to show him more of her prickly side than the other, and it was a revelation to him, now, when he got it in full force. As for Mr Benson, the only wonder was that he didn't capture his lady and make her promise to marry him as soon as possible when she danced "Haste to the Wedding" with him. A small modicum of sense remaining to him, however, he refrained, and the evening passed off without any contretemps.

It ended with "Sellenger's Round" when they formed big circles, one inside the other, and danced as if they had just begun. Then the pianist played "God Save the King", and the term was ended. There was a scurry for wraps, and they went home. Jean, looking for a taxi, was met by the doctor with an offer to motor her back to Storms. She agreed after some demur, and Mollie and Mr Benson walked with them to the doctor's house in the quaint old Northumberland Square, where the latter two said "good-night", and went on their way, since Mr Benson had announced his intention of escorting Miss Stewart to her rooms.

As they separated, a woman passed them well-wrapped up, and with a big scarf round the lower part of her face. As she saw them, her eyes grew very evil, and she glared at them with a hatred which Mollie felt. The girl turned round, but all she saw was a muffled figure, walking with a limp, and she had no idea that the casual passer-by was Mrs Taylor, who had vowed to make them smart for treating her as they had done. Mollie had made a bad enemy when she told the woman her mind so plainly. The warped brain — Mrs Taylor decidedly had a kink in her brain — laid a good deal of the blame at the doors of the McCleods, and it would be strange if she did not manage to do them harm in some way or other. Meanwhile, Jean, seated at the doctor's side in the little car, was being carried swiftly along the road to Hasnett and Storms. It was an ideal night for motoring. The crisp air brought a glow to Jean's cheeks, and her eyes glowed as she sat, humming scraps of the country-dance tunes.

"You like dancing?" queried the doctor as they turned into the straggling street with its fishermen's cottages on one side of the road, and the big public house on the other.

"Oh, like!" said Jean. "That doesn't begin to describe it!"

"I am glad," he said, quietly.

Something in his tone struck Jean, and she turned, and glanced sharply at him. What she read in his face, deepened the colour in her face, and she hurriedly changed the subject to Allison's illness, and kept him to it till they reached Storms. But when she was saying "good-night" to him, he leaned out of the car and took her hand.

"I wish we might always love the same things, Miss Jean," he said, softly.

It is true Jean snatched away her hand and bade him "good-night", with some incoherence, but he drove away with a satisfied smile, and as for her, she lay awake till the small hours of the morning, smiling absurdly to herself in the dark.

CHAPTER XIII

WHAT SUNDAY BROUGHT

The next day, Jean walked into Aulmbermouth to go to church with Mollie. Allison was getting on splendidly, and she was able to get up next day for a while. They hoped to have her downstairs on Christmas Day if she went on well. The frost had continued, much to the surprise of everyone, and daring people were prophesying a white Christmas. The sun was shining out of a pale blue sky and a fresh breeze was ruffling the surface of the water to little, white capped waves. Jean strode buoyantly along, revelling in the beauty of it all.

"It's almost too fine to go to church," she thought. "I'd rather have a walk along the cliffs."

However, she knew her friend was expecting her, so she made the most of her walk, and arrived at Field Terrace, glowing and fresh. Jean found Mollie ready and waiting and the two set off for St. Simon's. At the door, they were encountered by Mrs Taylor, who promptly turned her back on them. Jean grimaced to herself as she turned into the seat, a proceeding which greatly interested some small children who had turned round at the moment, and got the full benefit of it. They were so enthralled by the face she made that they kept turning round to stare at her, much to the discomfiture of their mother, who could not imagine what had happened to her usually well-behaved trio. Jean herself was rather startled, for she had acted unconsciously, and had no idea why they were so interested in her.

During the singing of the first hymn, she leaned

towards Mollie, and whispered, "I say, is there anything wrong with me? Is my hat on back to front, or anything?"

Mollie opened her eyes, glanced over her friend, and shook her head.

When the sermon came, and Mr Benson was in the pulpit, Jean settled herself to her own thoughts, while Mollie listened with deep interest to what he had to say. That it was very ordinary meant nothing to her. At least the preacher had a breezy manner of his own, and he made use of some picturesque illustrations which attracted even the restless children in front.

Jean sat very still, pondering many things. Her thoughts were mainly on the doctor, rather to her disgust. She had no idea why he was always coming into her head, and she resented it strongly. She glanced at Mollie, who was sitting with her eyes fixed on Mr Benson, her whole attitude one of attention.

"I wonder?" thought Jean to herself. "It would be rather decent if it happened. I can say nothing to Mollie yet, of course; but I might be able to help them somehow. What fun if it really came off! The wedding would have to be from Storms. I should like it so much. He is very nice — nearly good enough for her, and she would make a topping little wife."

The end of the sermon brought her back to the service once more; but when it was over, and she and Mollie were walking briskly in the direction of Storms, she recurred to her idea. Not that she could say anything to her friend. Oona's training told, together with Jean's own temperament, and it would have been very difficult for her to say anything. At this moment, Mollie turned to her friend, "You're very quiet, Jean! What's wrong? And what on earth did you mean by your question in church?"

"It was the kiddies in front," explained Jean. "They stared at me as though I were a circus freak!"

"I noticed nothing," said Mollie. "You look all right, now, anyway. It must have been your imagination!"

"It was no such thing!" protested Jean indignantly.

"Then you must have been making faces at them," returned Mollie, with no idea how near the truth she was.

"As though I should in church! You forget I've been brought up by good Scots folk! I'd as soon dream of walking up the aisle on my head as of making faces in church! — I say, Mollie, must you go to Farrar's to tea this afternoon?"

"Yes. She asked me ages ago, but I've always put her off, and I can't go on doing it."

"Well, I wish you wouldn't," grumbled Jean. "I thought we might have had a walk this afternoon. It's a lovely day!"

"Walk with me as far as Aulmbermouth," suggested Mollie. "You walked in this morning, and we are walking back. If you do it again this afternoon, I should think you'll have had enough, even for you."

Jean shook her head. "No; I want to go over the rocks. I feel like climbing."

"Then I'm afraid you will have to go by yourself — unless Oona will come with you."

"Oona won't come. She said this morning that she felt tired, and should lie down this afternoon. All right; I'll go by myself."

"We'll be able to have a walk on Tuesday," said Mollie. "On Wednesday, I want to go into Noviam, to finish my Christmas shopping."

"So do I. It's fun having a child in the house for

Christmas. Won't Allie stare when she sees the tree?"

"Hasn't she seen one before?"

Jean shook her head, "Never. I asked her, and she didn't know what it was, so I got Hans Anderson, and read her 'The Little Matchgirl' and 'The Christmas Tree'. She loved them."

"Sensible child. I love fairy tales yet!"

"I should hope you did! I shouldn't have you for a friend if you didn't."

Mollie laughed. "It's not likely to happen, so you needn't be afraid."

They reached Storms at this point, so no more was said on the subject. After the midday dinner, they ran upstairs to see Allison, who was sitting up, looking better than they had yet seen her. The sallow tinge had left her face, and her eyes were bright. She at once demanded "more stories from the green book — please".

It had taken Jean and Oona all this time to teach her to say "please" when she wanted anything. As her aunt said, she was the veriest little heathen in all her ways when she first came, and had considered it sufficient for her to demand anything for it to be forthcoming at once. What sort of a time Kirsty was having if her behaviour was on a par with her little sister's, Jean shuddered to think. She guessed that Mrs Page would not be a patient or gentle teacher.

"Poor kid!" thought the girl, as she got Hans Anderson from her own room. "What a time she must be having of it!"

Then she dismissed Kirsty from her mind and read the story of "The Constant Tin Soldier" to Allison, who listened with absorbed attention. When the tale was at an end, Jean closed the book, and told her small niece that she was going out for a while, but that she would not be long, and then she would come and read again.

"I wish you would stay with me, Auntie Jean," said Allison, wistfully.

"So I will when I come back," promised Jean, with a kiss. "Don't fret, Allie. I'll stay with you till bedtime when I come, and Auntie Mollie is coming here on Tuesday for Christmas, so we shall have a lovely time together. Shall I tuck you up for a nap?"

Allison agreed, and when they had seen her lying down well on the way to dreamland, the two friends went off to get ready. It was nearly three o'clock when Mollie finally caught the bus to Aulmbermouth, and Jean set off in the opposite direction for her scramble over the rocks — a project she was careful to keep secret from Morag when she ran into the kitchen to inform the good woman that she was going out, but that Allison was all right, and Moti would be with her till her aunt returned.

"Ou ay," said Morag non-committally. "An' wull ye be in tae yer tea, Miss Jean?"

"Yes," said Jean, "but Miss Mollie won't. We'll have it with Allie."

"Aye? Well I suppose ye'll be in aboot four," said Morag, and ruffled the leaves of her Bible as a hint that she wanted to go on with her reading.

Jean took it, and vanished circumspectly from the house till a bend in the road hid her from sight. Then she made for the cliffs, and climbed down them to the sands which had been left hard and firm by the receding tide. Once there, and assured that there was none to see her, she gave rein to the restlessness that had been oppressing her for the last few days, and raced and danced madly along till she reached the rocks. There, she had to be more careful, for she had no wish to slip and hurt herself or mark her clothes. That would have meant

Morag's knowing all about it!

She scrambled about, enjoying herself to her heart's content, till the sinking of the light warned her that dusk was drawing near and she had promised Allison not to be long. With a sigh she took off her hat, ran a pocket comb through her hair, and then, after deciding that she would pass muster, set out up a narrow path which led to the top of the cliff. It was an easy scramble and she soon reached the end. Then she stopped short in dismay. Standing not ten paces away was the Rev. Charles Benson, his face to the sea, his hat in his hand, evidently enjoying the loveliness of the scene. With a guilty feeling Jean went forward with a brave smile.

"Good afternoon," she said. "Isn't this a lovely day?"

He turned to her with a grin which lit up the wholesome ugliness of his nice face. "Miss McCleod! I didn't know you were anywhere near!"

"I've just come up the cliff," explained Jean. "I expect that boulder hid me from sight."

"Is Miss Stewart not with you?" he asked.

"No; she has gone in to Aulmbermouth. She is coming out on Tuesday till the day after Boxing Day, though."

Jean salved her conscience for this gratuitous information by reminding herself that he would be sure to learn it somewhere, so he might as well know at once.

"Are you going home?" he asked as he fell in beside her, and they walked on.

"Yes, I've been a long time away from Allison, poor baby."

"Oh yes; your little niece. How is she now? You must have had a nasty fright about her!"

"Much better thanks," said Jean. "Won't you come in to tea, and meet the lady?"

"No thank you," he said. "I have to get back, and then go off to St. Andrew's Mission. Something has gone wrong, and I want to see the caretaker before the service."

They walked along in silence for a minute or two. Then the curate said, "How long did you say Miss Stewart would be with you?"

"Only till the day after Boxing Day," said Jean, with a chuckle to herself at the would-be disinterestedness of his tone. "She goes to London after that, for the Chelsea School. Then she has to visit some relatives, and will not be back till the Saturday before term begins again."

"I see," he said. "And is your small niece looking forward to Christmas?"

"I should think so!" laughed Jean. "She's wild with excitement about the tree, and Father Christmas, and all the other dear traditions we have told her of. She was most agitated yesterday about his coming down the chimney. It's only a small fireplace in her room, you know, and the fire is on night and day, of course. She kept saying, 'But he'll be burnt — I know he'll be burnt!' Mollie got out of it at last by saying he was a fairy, and fairies didn't mind flames. She was so relieved!" She burst into silvery laughter, and he joined in.

A bus laden with passengers went by them at this moment, but neither noticed it, nor saw the baleful face at the window as they stood there for a moment, laughing together in that intimate fashion. Jean was too much absorbed in Allie's Christmas to heed, and Mr Benson was deciding that, next to Mollie Stewart, Miss Jean McCleod was the nicest girl he had ever met.

When they reached Storms, Jean again invited the young man to come in for tea, but he held resolutely to his refusal. He said "Goodbye", and

tramped off cheerfully down the road, while Jean
went in.

She was thankful five minutes later that he had
not come, for she found alarums and excursions
going on in the house. From Allison's room came
wails and sobs, and she went flying upstairs at once.
In the passage, she met Morag, who was coming
away with a certain fierce resoluteness of mien that
startled her; but the next minute, she was in the
room, and found Allison crying hysterically, while
Oona and Moti strove vainly to calm her. At the
sound of Jean's footsteps, they both drew away a
little, and she had the child in her arms in a
moment.

"Allie! What is it, dawtie? Tell Auntie Jean! What
has gone wrong with my darling?"

Jean's tones were full of tenderest mother-love,
and Allison clung to her, sobbing piteously. "Auntie
Jean — oh, Auntie Jean!"

"Hush, dearie! Don't cry like that. Tell Auntie
what it is. It's all right, darling. There — there,
Auntie's little girl! Don't cry so!"

It was some time before Jean could get the child
sufficiently soothed to make any sense of what she
said. Allison had no idea of self-control, and she
sobbed until the three women were at their wits'
end to know what to do. Finally Oona came to the
rescue with a glass of water.

"Allison," she said quietly, "You are to stop crying
like this and drink some of this water. Come! Sit up
and sip it at once."

Thus adjured, Allison made a desperate effort and
sat up, but she was so shaken by her sobbing that
her teeth chattered on the rim of the glass and Oona
had to hold it for her. She was too worn out to tell
them anything at first, but presently Jean, holding
her close, caught a gasped out, "Morag! She said —

it was all — a pack — of — lies!"

"What was, darling?" asked the girl.

"Father Christmas. She said he — wasn't. It was — you — and Auntie — Oona — and — Auntie Mollie. It wasn't — true, and — you oughtened — to teach — me — such — lies."

"Did she indeed?" said Jean, a note in her voice that made Oona jump. "Never mind, Allie. Morag doesn't know everything — not by a long shot. You wait till Christmas Day, and then you can laugh at her for being so silly as to disbelieve in him."

"Really?" A gleam of hope came into Allison's eyes, but it faded almost at once. "Oh, Auntie Jean, she said there wasn't! Oh, I want there to be — I want there to be!" They assured her over and over again that it was all right. All was unavailing. The child had cried to the point of exhaustion and was in no mood to be reasonable. She refused to heed either Jean's coaxing or Oona's quiet commands, and it was long ere they could get her calmed. Then, just as they were beginning to hope that she was falling asleep, she sat up.

"If I can't believe in Father Christmas, I won't believe in God either," she said.

"Hush — hush!" said Jean softly. "You must believe in both."

Allison lay back. "Why must I?" she demanded. "I won't."

On the last word, she dropped off, and presently Oona took her gently from Jean, and laid her down on the pillows. Then she gave Moti some murmured instructions, and drew the girl from the room.

"Come and have tea, Jean. She will probably sleep for hours now; she is worn out, poor bairn."

"I am going to speak to Morag first," said Jean icily. "She knew what my wishes were on this subject, and she has chosen to ignore them. It is

quite time that she learnt that she is not the
mistress of this house. Allison's training lies in my
hands, and I will have no interference. No, Oona;
don't try to keep me! I must have this over and done
with. So far as the child is concerned, Morag has to
understand that I am sole mistress."

And, in spite of what Oona could say, Jean
marched off into the kitchen, her face white with
anger, her eyes almost black.

It was a stormy interview, and lasted long. Morag
declared that she had only done her duty by the
child — that it was downright wicked for Jean to
tell her such stories, and let her believe them to be
true.

"I'll gi'e nae countenance tae sic lees," she said,
"and so I warn ye, Miss Jean."

"Very well, then," said Jean. "If you will not do as
I say, I shall take Allison, and leave Storms for as
long as you remain in it. Have my training of her
interfered with, I will not, and that you may as well
understand first as last! As for doing your duty, all
you've done is to kill her belief in God as well as in
Father Christmas. If that's your idea of Christian
duty, I'm sorry for you!"

"Havers!" retorted Morag. "The bairn didna mean
it."

"Oh, yes, she did," replied Jean. "She's only a
baby. She sees no reason why she should believe in
one and not the other — and I don't blame her now!
However, you have heard my last word on the
matter. Either you leave Allison entirely to me, not
attempting to controvert anything I may tell her, or
to undo any training of mine, or I shall pack up
tomorrow, and leave the house with her. And, as I
said before, if I do that I'll stay away as long as you
are here. You are to tell her no rubbish about
foredoomed to eternal damnation; you are to say

nothing about hell or the devil or that everlasting worm of yours. You are not to tell her that there are no fairies or elves. In short, you are to leave her to me."

It was a bitter pill to Morag to be outfaced by a slip of a girl whom she had helped to bring up. But, with all her austerity, she worshipped Jean, and the girl's threat to leave Storms as long as she remained there unless she would give her word not to interfere with Allison's training, told.

"Ye ought to be ashamed o' yersel', Miss Jean!" she said. "To daur tae speak tae me like that! It's more than Miss Oona hersel' daur dae!"

"That has nothing to do with the matter," retorted Jean. "Allison is my niece, and I am responsible for her. Well, which is it to be? I warn you fairly, Morag. I mean what I say. You will give me your word to leave her completely to me — or we leave the house to-morrow."

Morag was beaten, and she knew it. "Keep the bairn tae yersel' then," she said fiercely. "But it's little did I ever think tae hear sic words as ye've spoken tae me this day, Miss Jean."

"Very well," said Jean. "Remember, if you ever break your word to me I will go, and you won't see me again in a hurry."

With that she left the kitchen, and marched off to the den, where Oona was sitting with a troubled face.

Morag waited till she heard the light footsteps die away in the distance. Then she sat down.

"I'm an auld wumman," she muttered to herself. "I never thocht Miss Jean wad hae daured outface me like that!"

In the den Jean had dropped on the floor at her aunt's feet in a fit of bitter crying. "It's all my fault!" she sobbed. "If I had stayed with Allie this afternoon it would never have happened."

It was bound to happen sooner or later," said Oona. "Get up off the floor, Jean, and come and have some tea. You will feel better then. At least, Morag will have learnt her lesson now."

She had! Come what might, she would never interfere with Allison again. But it came too late to save the child's belief in Father Christmas, and the Christmas Day so happily planned by Jean, Oona, and Mollie, was fated never to take place.

CHAPTER XIV

VARIOUS DISCOVERIES

Allison fretted herself into a temperature over Morag's words, and though she was wrapped up and carried down to the Den on Christmas morning, it was a very white-faced little girl who sat in the big armchair, opening her many parcels — nothing would induce her to hang up her stocking; Morag had worked too well for that! — and smiling languidly. There was a beautiful doll from Oona, and Mollie and Jean had provided fairy-books with lovely pictures. Kirsty had sent a box of coloured pencils, and there were a jigsaw puzzle from India, a ball from Bessie, and a box of beads from Moti. Allison was pleased with them all. Only over one present did she show what had happened to her. Morag had given her a Bible, and when the child knew from whom it came, she picked it up and flung it with all her weak force across the room.

"I won't have it," she said, her baby lips pressed into a hard line that was most unhappy-like.

Oona looked rather horrified, but Jean treated it as a mere matter-of-course.

"Very well," she said, as she picked it up. "You need not. But that is no reason for treating it like that." And she quietly put it away in a drawer.

Moti had agreed to stay with the small invalid while the others went to church, and they went quite happily. Morag would never dare say anything to Allison now; and Allison would not have listened to her, in any case. The short service was soon over, and they played with Allison till her bed-time came at six o'clock. Jean bore her off, and presently came down, having left her drowsy, Moti at her side.

"Come on, Moll!" she said. "Let's entertain Oona. What about some charades?" So they promptly became children, and acted charades for Oona's benefit, till she was wiping the tears from her eyes, and holding her sides, complaining that she had laughed till she ached. They had acted the Balcony scene — or as much of it as they could remember — from "Romeo and Juliet," and it had ended in the table on which Juliet was perched giving way under her, so that she fell on top of Romeo, who collapsed under her.

"Last scene, the whole word!" cried Romeo, vanishing with his lady. Presently, the door opened, and a queer creature with a muslin curtain tied round her head and face made an appearance, followed by a monk-like cavalier, who proceeded to make violent love to her.

He had just hailed her as his "Turkish Delight" when the door suddenly opened, and Morag ushered in the doctor and Mr Benson, who had been for a run in the former's car. Something had gone wrong, just outside of Storms, and, as they were there, the doctor had decided that it would be as well for him to look in on his small patient, and see how she had stood the revellings.

The lady gave a shriek of dismay, and vanished behind a settee, where she managed to discard her extraneous wrappings. The gentleman muttered a word that was certainly not a blessing on Morag, and fled from the room. As for Morag herself, those left distinctly heard a chuckle as she closed the door behind the two embarrassed men. She had been severely cold-shouldered all the week, and this was her revenge.

The doctor stammered forth his explanation, and

Oona, pitying the poor men, at once led him off to see Allison, while Mr Benson was left alone with Mollie, who had ridded herself of her disguise, and now came to entertain him with heightened colour, and very bright eyes.

"We were entertaining Miss McCleod," she explained, as she sat down. "What is the night doing?"

"Raining," said the Rev. Charles tersely. As most of his attention was taken up with Mollie herself, it was a wonder that he managed to answer her as sensibly.

"Oh, dear!" she exclaimed. "Then there's an end to the snow."

"Yes," he said. "I'm afraid it is."

A silence fell, in which the gentleman wondered what would happen if he were to tell Miss Stewart then and there how much he loved her, and how he hoped she would marry him, and the lady was racking her brains for something that would avert that very thing. The Rev. Charles' state of mind was plain to Mollie, but she was not sure of herself yet. She liked him tremendously, but it might be only liking. She wasn't sure.

Hastily, she said the first thing that came into her head. "I expect you thought we were all mad; but it was part of a charade, you see. The word was delight and we were doing the whole of it when you came. Jean had just called me her 'Turkish Delight'. I wonder if Oona noticed? It was plain enough, goodness knows!"

"Oh, no!" said the Rev. Charles.

"Don't you think so?" Mollie sounded disappointed.

"Oh, yes!" he said fervently.

How much longer this interesting conversation may have continued there is no knowing, but just then, Jean came in, very tidy, and very fresh in her favourite jade-green frock. Oona and the doctor followed a few minutes later, and the conversation became general. Miss McCleod insisted that the two men must stay to supper, and, after formal protest, they agreed. They were quietly happy, and if the young curate seemed rather distrait in manner, no one made any remark on it. At ten o'clock, the men went off, with many thanks, and Oona suggested that, as the girls had had several late nights, and Mollie would be sure of others when she was at Chelsea, it would be as well if they went to bed.

"We'll go upstairs, anyway," amended Jean.

"Then don't stay too long talking," said Oona. "Good-night, children. Sleep well."

They kissed, and then, while she went down to the kitchen to see that Morag and Bessie had gone, they went off upstairs, first to look in on Allison, who was sleeping sweetly with her new doll clasped in her arms, and a faint flush on her cheeks, and then to sit by the fire in Jean's room, where they sat talking till long after midnight.

"Better sleep here, Moll," said Jean, when the chiming of the little clock recalled them to the fact that it was one in the morning. "If Oona hears you going back to your room at this hour, she'll have fits."

"All right," said Mollie. "Can you lend me every-thing?"

Jean nodded, and supplied her needs. Then, when they were in bed with the light switched off, Mollie turned to her friend, and spoke the fear that was ever present with her.

"Jean, do you think Mrs Taylor can do anything?"

"How do you mean?" asked Jean, sitting upright at the shock of the question. "I believe that woman's becoming an obsession to you, Moll!"

"I don't know. I'm afraid of her, you know."

"But, my dear girl, what could she do to you? She won't dare to slander you after what Oona said to her; and she can't very well go hunting for you with a meat-chopper! So why are you afraid?"

"I don't know. It's just I have a funny feeling about her. I feel fey!"

"Shut up!" said Jean. "You know how I hate that expression!"

"I know. But it's the only word that will describe my feelings adequately. Do you know, I have an awful fear that she's going to try to come between us."

Jean was silent, and Mollie went on, "I don't see how she can, of course. But I know she will try."

"Let her!" was the brief response.

"Don't you really think she can?"

"Mollie, you're getting sentimental, and I won't have it. How can she come between us? Our friendship's too old and tried for that. Now it's getting fearfully late, and I'm dead-tired. Let's go to sleep. It's the time of night affecting you! You'll be all right in the morning when you wake up."

Mollie was only half-satisfied, but she turned over and presently fell asleep, to wake no more till Morag's knock on the door, and the bump as she set down the hot-water can called them both to another day. She said no more about the matter to Jean, for she was secretly rather ashamed of herself for her feeling towards Mrs Taylor; yet it haunted her throughout the day, and she was thankful that the pouring rain made it impossible for them to go out. Allie was rather tiresome, too, for she had overtired herself the previous day, and was fractious in consequence. The girls kept her amused as well as they could, but they were thankful when she fell asleep after dinner, and slept most of the afternoon. They spent the rest of the day reading and working, and Mollie declared, when Oona hunted them off to bed at ten, that it had been as good as a rest cure. The next morning she went off to Chelsea, and Jean came to see her off at the station. "I'll drop you a card," promised Mollie, when she was in the train.

"Oh, don't be rash!" laughed Jean.

"Jean! You pig! It's as much, or more, than you're likely to do!"

"Full well I know it! No one ever yet called me a good correspondent with any truth."

"There goes the whistle! Stand back, Jean, or you'll get killed. How would you like to have twelve good men and true to sit on your body?"

"Not at all!" said Jean, promptly. "Good-bye, old thing, take care of yourself!"

The train began to gather speed. Jean waved her hand, and then turned round and went through the barrier. At the station entrance she met Mr Benson, who had been on the bookstall to get magazines for his beloved boys' club.

"I've been seeing Miss Stewart off to Chelsea," she explained, as they fell into step. "I only wish I could have gone too; but I can scarcely leave Allison yet."

"Isn't she getting stronger?" he asked.

"Oh, yes. But she needs a good deal of care, and I can't expect Oona to take it on. How is the club progressing, Mr Benson?"

"Splendidly," he said, enthusiastically. "We feed them and teach them boxing and single- stick fencing and folk dancing. They come back, and then we get them. Poor chaps! Most of them have little enough to keep them straight. They seem to think the club a foretaste of Paradise, and I'm glad you mentioned it, Miss Jean, because I want to ask you if you won't come down some night and sing folksongs to them. I know you do sing, and my lads would be awfully pleased if you'd come and sing to them. Aren't there any with choruses? Then they could join in, which is just what they like."

"Of course," said Jean, turning her sweetest smile on him. "Oona and I could come any time, I should think. She always accompanies me, you know. When would you like us, Mr Benson?"

"Next week?" he said, eagerly. "Could you come next week? What about Tuesday?"

"Yes, I think that's all right," said Jean. "I'll ask Oona to make sure, and send you a card. Will that do?"

He thanked her fervently, and then, as her car had stopped, they said "Good-bye" and he went on to his rooms, thinking what a sweet girl she was, sweet and genuine.

"No wonder, though," he thought. "She has Her for a friend. Any friend of Hers would be out of the common run of girls."

Not even to himself did he specify who "Her" was; but he glowed at the thought that, by next Tuesday, Jean must have heard from Mollie, and might, perhaps, tell him her news. Of such stuff is love, that it can feed and flourish on the poorest things.

After that it seemed to Jean that she was always meeting Mr Benson when she was in Aulmbermouth. It did not take her long to realise what was at the bottom of it all, and she rejoiced, for she liked the young man, and he seemed to her nearly good enough for her friend. Mollie had managed to keep her promise to the extent of two postcards and one note, and Jean passed on their information to Mr Benson, so there was news for him, even if it was scanty.

Jean had contrived to write, telling her of the concert, and naughty Mollie had replied with the pious hope that the "poor lads won't all be forced to fly."

Jean showed this to Mr Benson when she met him in the street, and they laughed over it together. Mrs Taylor saw them out of the window, and her face grew evil. She bided her time and the next time the doctor came to see her sprained ankle she sent her first shaft.

"I hear Miss Jean McCleod is going with our Mr Benson," she said with a smirk. "I wouldn't wonder to hear that was a match."

She looked narrowly at him, but for all the effect her words seemed to have had on him she might have been commenting on the weather, which was vile.

"Ah, really?" he said, quietly. "Well, Mrs Taylor, I think the ankle is going on all right now. Don't try to do too much on it, though. That was a nasty sprain, and might have laid you up for some weeks. What dreadful weather we are having just now! I hear the Volunteer Life Brigade was up all last night and the night before. If this wind continues I suppose they will have to keep vigil again to-night."

He got up from his seat, and began to draw on his gloves. Mrs Taylor realised that he was not going to be drawn, so she said no more. But when he had gone, she limped to the window and watched him through the curtains.

"Ah, my fine Miss Jean McCleod!" she thought to herself. "You'll take my lodgers away, will you? Well, I've put a spoke into your wheel with him — and maybe a spoke or two into hers, as well! I'll teach you!"

The next time Jean met the doctor was on the doorstep of Storms, where she was standing after saying "Goodbye" to Mr Benson, who had come round about the concert. She smiled at the doctor, and waited for him to come in.

"Allie was wondering if you would come to-day," she said, with her pretty friendliness. "She is devoted to her doctor, you know! Come along to the Den! She is there to-day."

He followed her, his face set in grim lines which only relaxed when Allison, throwing down her book, ran to greet him. Then he smiled down into the little face which was beginning to show a faint tinge of colour, and sat down with her on his knee.

"And how are you to-day, lassie?" he asked, running a hand over the short, linty hair.

"Very well," said Allison. "Auntie Jean says she thinks if the wind would stop, I might go out soon."

"Yes; when the wind goes down, you may certainly go out," he said. "But now, stop wagging that tongue and let me look at it for a change."

Allison obligingly shot it out as far as it would go, and stood patiently at his side while he took her pulse, sounded her, and otherwise examined her. When he had done and Jean slipped on her little jumper again, she slipped a tiny hand into his.

"Stay to tea," she pleaded.

He shook his head. "Not to-day, Allie. I have such a lot of sick people to see, that I must go now."

Allison stared. "But you always stay much longer when Auntie Oona is here," she said. "Do stay a little, please do, Doctor dear!"

"Nonsense, Allie!" said Jean sharply. "The doctor is very busy and hasn't time to stay to- day. Perhaps he will another time, though."

Allison said no more, and he picked up his stethoscope, and put it back into his pocket.

"Shall I see you presently, Miss Jean?" he asked.

Jean nodded. "Play with dollie, Allie," she said. "I will come soon."

Allison gave the doctor an elfin smile for good-bye, and he went out after Jean with a pain gnawing at his heart.

"Yes; she is practically all right now," he said. "I hope that she will do well here. Once she is acclimatised, I think it ought to suit her. She will never be robust, of course; but she seems healthy enough, and that is the great thing. Keep her out of draughts; don't let her overtire herself; give her plenty of milk and eggs and nourishing food. She ought to be out in the open-air as much as possible; but it's unthinkable just now, of course."

"When will you come back?" asked Jean, with a curious sinking at her heart. Never had she known him so remote — so gravely professional, as he was to-day.

"Oh, I don't think there is any necessity for me to come again," he said, looking down at his hat. "She should do very well, so long as she doesn't catch any fresh cold. But send for me, of course, if you feel at all anxious about her. Prevention is better than cure, any day in the week, and Allison is a delicate child at present. Now I must not encroach on your time, as I am sure you are very busy. Also, I have a heavy round awaiting me. Good afternoon, Miss McCleod."

"Good afternoon," said Jean gravely.

She watched him going round the house, and then came in and shut the door. It seemed impossible for her to go straight to Allison. She ran upstairs to the big attic that had been converted into a nursery, and sent Moti down to the child. Then she went to her own room, and locked herself in.

"What is the matter with me?" she thought, as she sat in the window, wide gaze fixed on the tossing sea outside. "Why am I so horribly unhappy all at once?"

Enlightenment came, as she sat there, going over that chilly interview, and she suddenly cried aloud in the pain of understanding.

"Oh, no — no!" she cried.

For minutes together she sat battling with this new knowledge that threatened to overwhelm her, and turn her world upside down. She had liked him — always. She had thought he had liked her. Certainly, he had come to Storms a great deal oftener than seemed warranted by Allie's illness. A sudden thought struck her. Could it be Oona he came to see? Allison's words, and his own behaviour, bore that out.

"But Oona could never be anything to him," she half-whispered as she sat there. "She has never forgotten Ben — never will forget! Then he will be hurt! Oh, I don't want him to be hurt!"

She bowed her head on her locked hands, and fought with rising pain. She gained the victory at last, but it left a scar, and the Jean who presently went down to tea was not the Jean who had locked herself into the room when the doctor had left Storms.

CHAPTER XV

Those were sad days to the three most concerned. The doctor, noting Jean's meetings with the young curate, made up his mind that Mrs Taylor was right, and that, before very long, their engagement would be announced. He was a strong man, so he simply buried himself in his work and tried to find solace therein. To a certain extent, he was successful, but there were moments when Jean's face would rise up in his tobacco smoke or the flame of his driftwood fire, and then he was fain to get up, and put on hat and coat, and try to walk it off.

Jean, being a woman, was not nearly so successful. She led the people at Storms rather a dance with her moods. Oona wondered at first if she were missing Mollie, for that young woman, having contrived to put on a spurt with her correspondence during the first week of her absence, never sent a line for the rest of the holidays, and they had no means of knowing if she were with an aunt, or the Gorgon, her father's cousin. The one tentative remark the elder woman ventured to make was laughed at, however, so she was fain to try some other cause. She hoped that her niece was not falling in love with Mr Benson, for his state was plain to be seen — he had thoughts only for Mollie. Then, there was the puzzle of the doctor. After being almost unnecessarily attentive for several weeks, he suddenly left Storms severely alone. Oona became thoughtful on this point and began to question whether Jean had anything to do with it.

She had fancied that he had been attracted by the girl, though he was not the man to give himself away as the Reverend Charles had done. And Jean, too, had seemed to like him. Could he possibly have said anything on that afternoon when she had been out, and Jean have repulsed him decidedly? And if so, was the girl regretting it now and was that the cause of her unusual depression?

Oona's own code forbade her speaking to Jean on the subject, but she felt sorely troubled. As for herself, no such idea had ever entered her mind. Her conversations with him were mainly concerned with Allison, his work round and about Hasnett, and the weather! She liked him, and would have been well-content if Jean were to marry him; but beyond this her thoughts had never gone.

So they were all at cross purposes, and the only happy one of them all was the curate, who had eyes only for Mollie, and who liked Jean because she was able to tell him about her friend. Not that Jean gossiped; but her whole life for the last few years had been so bound up with Mollie's that it was natural for her to talk of her as she would have done of a sister.

A week before Mollie was expected back, Mrs Semple, wife of the vicar of Hasnett, called to see Oona about some parish matter, and, as Miss McCleod happened to be out, she asked for Jean. Morag ushered the lady into the drawing room where Jean and Allison were building card-houses on the floor, much to the annoyance of Jean, and the disapproval of the visitor.

Jean rose to her feet, and offered an unwilling hand. "How do you do?" she said stiffly.

"How do you do, Jean?" said Mrs Semple. "Yes, I called to see your aunt about those tiresome Stoddarts. The man is in prison again — drunk and disorderly — and his wife does nothing but cry — so bad for her when the baby is only three days old! I thought perhaps Miss McCleod would have some influence over her, and go and show her how thankful she ought to be to have George Stoddart out of the way for a while."

Jean shrugged her shoulders. Then she turned to the child.

"Run along to Moti, Allison. It is nearly teatime, and she will be waiting for you."

Allison gathered up her possessions, and went off, closing the door quietly behind her. It was never any use attempting to make her even decently civil to Mrs Semple, whom she hated. They had attempted it twice, and the result had been a scene each time. Mrs Semple hated children, though she considered that she knew all there was to know about their upbringing, and she made no attempt to win the child's friendship.

"Won't you sit down?" asked Jean, pulling a chair nearer the fire. "It is so cold to-day, isn't it?"

The Vicar's wife sat down, unfastening her coat, a procedure which Jean watched with horror, for it betokened her intention to stay to tea. However, one could not be rude, so she said, "Won't you take your coat off? and your hat?"

Mrs Semple refused. "No thank you, Jean. It will do if I loosen the coat, and I have no fancy for removing my hat continually. It disarranges my hair — I have not shorn off my glory." Her eyes went disapprovingly to Jean's short, silky crop.

"Yes; shingled hair is a great relief that way," said Jean wickedly. "It is so easy to keep in order."

"That is as may be. I can't say I approve. It seems to me to be flying in the Face of Providence," rejoined the lady. "And, speaking of order, that reminds me, I hope you are looking after the welfare

of your little niece properly? I hear she did not even
say her prayers when she first came to you. Most
reprehensible of her mother not to have taught her!"

With a smothered groan, and a wish that she
could choke Morag — who had soon learnt of
Allison's shortcomings in this line, and who had not
ceased to groan about it, and to prophesy that the
youngest Miss McCleod was, in her opinion,
foredoomed to what she called "The Pit" with
ghoulish relish — Jean answered that she did her
best

"I hope you do," said her visitor dubiously. "You
must remember, Jean, that you are responsible for
her now. You must always endeavour to set her as
blameless an example as possible. What you are,
she will be in the days to come. Train up a child in
the way he should go, and in his manhood — er —
er — he will not depart from them! That is what
Solomon tells us."

"I don't think anyone could say Solomon was
particularly successful with his own children, do
you?" said Jean demurely. "I am not awfully well up
on that part of the Bible, but I seem to remember
that his son was a bad lot."

Mrs Semple looked shocked — as well she might.
"You are very flippant," she said severely, "but I am
speaking for the child's good and yours, Jean, when
I say that I think you ought to be very careful how
you train her. Such a babyhood as she has had,
waited on hand and foot, and allowed her own way
in everything, will mean that the evil in her has had
a chance to grow strong. Ill weeds grow apace, you
know. Do you know anything about psychology and
the development of character?"

Jean did not, and said so curtly.

"I thought not," said Mrs Semple complacently. "I
was going through my book-shelves to-day to see

what I had that would be useful to you, and I found these books and pamphlets."

She felt in her capacious pockets and presently drew out a couple of books and some pamphlets with which she presented the startled Jean, who gasped out a "thank you!" "Read them, my dear," said the complacent lady. "You will find they will repay study. You will have, I fear, a hard task with Allison in any case. These will show you how to deal adequately with her."

Jean regarded the innocent books as if they were so many snakes, and wondered how she was going to get rid of her unwelcome guest. Luckily, Mrs Semple was quite happy to continue talking, and never noticed how silent her young hostess had become. She prosed on about the necessity of considering a child's individuality, and the care needed in the training of such a child as Allison, till Morag appeared with tea. After that she left her lofty perch, and descended to Guides.

"I do wish the dear Vicar had not seen fit to establish a company in connection with the church!" she sighed.

Jean sat up and demanded why in no measured accents.

"Ah! You are one yourself, and cannot, therefore, be expected to regard the matter with unprejudiced eyes," returned the lady. "Now, I consider they are bad for girls. The children learn all kinds of military ideas from the company — "

"Excuse me, Mrs Semple," interrupted Jean with some rudeness, "but what do you really know about the Movement?"

Mrs Semple looked offended. "My dear Jean! Naturally, I am interested in all parish matters."

"Do you know the first thing about Guides?" persisted Jean. "Can you, for instance, tell me what the Guide Law is?"

Mrs Semple could not. She hated to show herself ignorant of anything connected with "the parish", but Jean stuck to her point, and finally dragged out of her that beyond a vague idea of the uniform, and the fact that their own Guides met on Monday nights, she knew really nothing about them.

"But I consider that it is apt to make the girls discontented," said the lady.

"The Guide Movement is one of the finest movements ever organised," declared her hostess. "It teaches the girls loyalty, honour, oneness, and self-reliancy. As soon as Allison is old enough, she shall be enrolled as a Brownie, and I only wish every girl I know belonged to us."

The Vicar's wife rose, looking offended. "Thank you, my dear Jean. I see you are quite impracticable. I had hoped that a little chat with me would have convinced you that it would be better to give up this affair, and let us stick to the G.F.S. alone. Since you are determined to hear nothing but your own side of the matter, I must let it alone."

"I have nothing against the G.F.S.," said Jean, calmly, "but I still consider that Guiding gives the girls something no other movement has ever done. Also," she added mischievously, "Both Princess Mary and the Duchess of York are Guides, and surely, what is good enough for them is good enough for us!"

Mrs Semple sniffed, and fastened her coat. "It is growing late," she said coldly, "and Miss McCleod has not yet come. I think I must leave what I have to say to her till another day. Please don't trouble to come downstairs with me; I can find my own way out quite well."

Jean calmly followed her downstairs and sped her on her way despite this remark. When she had gone,

the girl collapsed on the old chest in the hall in fits
of laughter. They soon died away, however, when
she recalled the fact that the Vicar was wife-ridden
and that, if she chose to make it unpleasant for
them, he might quite easily refuse to let them have
the parish hall for their meetings.

"And then we shall be done!" she thought, as she
made her way back to the drawing room. "I rather
wish I hadn't said so much!"

She sat down with a worried air, but all the
thinking in the world would not help matters now.
Presently, to get away from her thoughts, she picked
up one of the books on psychology and began to read
it. Oona found her still at it when she came in at
eight o'clock, and inquired what she was reading
with such interest.

"The Growth of Character," replied Jean absently.

"What? My good child, where did you get that?
And what possessed you to read psychology of all
things?"

"Mrs Semple brought it this afternoon," said Jean,
closing the book. "She wanted to see you about
something or other. As you were non est, she
inflicted herself on me. She gave me this and some
more with the remark that they might help me with
Allie. I thought I would just see what they were
about. This doesn't seem bad, and it really gives one
some quite decent hints about looking after
children. There's one thing, Oona, it has convinced
me that I mustn't expect too much from the poor
little thing. See here!" And she held out the book,
having flipped over the pages to find what she
wanted. "See what it says about a child's moral
sense."

Oona glanced at the sentences, and then put the
book down. "My dear Jean, you knew all this
already. Of course it is impossible to expect a child

to know right from wrong without teaching. If that's all you're going to get from it, then I think it's a waste of time to read it."

"Oh, but it isn't! Look at this about punishment. You see it says it is far better to reason with a child than to punish it for naughtiness."

"You can't always reason with children — not with children of Allison's age, anyway. Your books may be all very well, Jean, but personally, I think that if you teach a child to tell the truth and be obedient, you've got enough to go on at first."

Jean sighed. "I thought you'd be interested!"

"I am. But I honestly think you'll do better by using your common sense than by worrying over this kind of rubbish."

"Well, I don't! I'm going to give it a fair trial, anyway."

Oona smiled whimsically. "Poor Allie! Well — was that all that Mrs Semple said?"

"No. Oh, Oona, I've had rather a fuss with her about the Guides, and I'm a little afraid she may try to persuade the Vicar to stop our using the Parish Hall."

"Jean! What have you been saying?"

Jean gave an account of what had passed, and Oona groaned aloud. "I wish you'd try to control your tongue sometimes! The Guides are doing the girls all the good in the world and now you may have made it very difficult for the company to carry on."

"They shall come here if she really makes a fuss!"

"You mayn't find it so easy to manage if she really makes the Vicar disapprove of them."

Jean coloured guiltily, and wished she had held her tongue. She knew just how far the Vicar was able to withstand his wife's wishes, and if Mrs Semple were really annoyed, it was quite likely that things might be made awkward for them. She turned back to "The Growth of Character", and said no more on the subject.

But oh! How the entire household grew to hate those books of Mrs Semple's during the next few days!

Jean read them all, and took notes from them. She tried faithfully to follow out their teachings, and made more blunders than she had ever done before. One of them said, "Never leave your child with servants. The best servant in the world is incapable of doing for it what you can. You must be prepared to sacrifice everything for its welfare."

Jean sacrificed two pleasant invitations and also kept Allison at her side morning, noon and night, even moving the little bed into her room, much to Moti's grief.

One of the pamphlets advocated the simplest food for children, even stating that butter was bad for them. On the fifth day, Jean instituted this new rule, and Allison, deprived of butter on her bread, raised an uproar, and refused to eat it. Jean, profiting by yet another maxim, "Never punish your child when you are angry with it. Send it from you till you have full control over your own spirit before you do anything. Then, go to it, and explaining that the punishment is given in no spirit of vindictiveness, let it understand that sin always brings its own reward," carried Allison upstairs to the bedroom, and shut her in there. Later, on going upstairs to reason with her, she found that the young lady had been improving the shining hour by cutting a pattern in the counterpane — a new one — with Jean's embroidery scissors. It is lamentable to have to state that Jean forgot the maxims and slapped the designer's fingers soundly, whereat Allison roared like a small bull of Bashan.

Luckily for them all, Mollie came on the Saturday to finish her holidays at Storms, and in the interest of hearing all about Chelsea and the Folk-Dance School, Jean forgot her books for the time being, and Allison went back to accustomed ways, greatly to the relief of everyone else.

Mollie looked white and tired, and owned that the Gorgon had been more trying than usual.

No one, however, thought about it till the Sunday afternoon, when she fell asleep on the drawing room couch, and woke up looking flushed and poorly. She ate nothing, but drank several cups of tea, and Oona, touching her hand accidentally, gave an exclamation of horror.

"Mollie! You are burning with fever! What is the matter?"

"I am rather hot," said Mollie, "and my head aches. Don't bother, Oona. It's only a headache. It will soon pass off. I think I'll go and lie down for a while."

"Better go straight to bed," said Oona sensibly. "Go and get undressed and I'll get a hot water bottle from Morag, and put a match to the fire."

Mollie went without argument, and, when Oona had left her safely tucked up, she seemed drowsy and inclined to sleep. But when the elder woman went in an hour later, she found the girl tossing about, talking rapidly in her sleep, and looking so flushed and unnatural that Miss McCleod went straight to the telephone, and rang up the doctor. He was in, and promised to come at once. Oona turned away from the telephone, and went to seek Jean.

"Mollie is ill, I'm afraid," she said. "She is certainly running a very high temperature." Allie, who was with her aunt as usual, looked up with interest. "Is Auntie Mollie very cross?" she said.

"No, dear, only not very well," said Oona. "Don't bother, Allison, but run away to Moti. You ought to be in bed, now — it is nearly seven."

"I was reading to her," said Jean apologetically. "What do you think is wrong with Mollie? Is she badly ill?"

Oona shook her head. "I don't know. She is very flushed and restless and, I think, is inclined to be light-headed. I'm rather afraid of influenza. At any rate, Allison's bed must be moved back into her own room, for I shall want you to help me with the nursing, and you must not run any risks with her. Will you see to it, Jean? Morag is lighting the fire and Bessie will help you to carry the things in. I have sent for the doctor, and he will tell us what to do about Mollie. Allison, did you not hear me tell you to go to Moti? Go at once, dear!"

Allison obeyed with some reluctance, turning at the door to ask, "Will you come and say goodnight, Auntie Jean?"

"Yes; but run along now," replied Jean with some impatience. Then, as the child went, she added to her aunt, "Do you think Allie had better be sent out of the house? I don't want to run any risks with her."

"I don't think so," said Oona. "We can keep her in the new wing, and she will be clear from infection then, if it is influenza. She would only be unhappy with strangers and is better here. However, we will ask the doctor what he thinks. Now will you see to moving the child's bed? I must go back to Mollie."

They separated, Oona going back to Mollie, who still slept restlessly, and Jean running down to the kitchen to ask Bessie to come and help her move the little bed into the rosy room again. They had just finished, and Moti was undressing Allison before the fire, when a ring at the bell heralded the doctor, and Jean ran down to admit him. It was the first time the two had met since that rainy day when he had pronounced Allison well on the highroad to good health, and the colour came into the girl's face as she opened the door. The doctor himself looked quite unperturbed and wished her "Good Evening" in his usual voice. He shed his cap and coat, and then followed Jean upstairs to Mollie's room.

She was awake now, and was sitting up in bed, her cheeks flushed, and her eyes overbright. She gave Jean a little smile, but said nothing. The doctor came quickly forward. "Good evening, Miss Stewart. I am sorry to hear you are not well. What have you been doing with yourself?"

While he talked, he quietly possessed himself of her wrist and was taking her pulse, noting, with quiet face, its rapid leaping. Her temperature proved to have risen another point or two, and he felt pretty sure that it would go up further during the night. His questions soon drew from her all he wanted to know, and then he bade her take off her dressing jacket, and lie down.

"Miss Jean will stay with you for the present," he said. "I shall see you downstairs, Miss McCleod?"

"I'm so thirsty! May I have a drink, please?" asked Mollie huskily.

He nodded, and took a little bottle from his pocket, which he handed to Jean. "Give ten drops of that in a tumblerful of water."

Then he left them, and Oona followed him downstairs to the Den.

"It's flu," he said. "It will be a sharp attack, but it is only a question of nursing. Do you want me to send a nurse in?"

"No thank you," said Oona. "Jean has all her Ambulance certificates, and Morag is equal to twenty nurses in case of need. I have my St. John certificates, too, and have done a great deal of nursing one way and another. There will be no need for a stranger, I think."

He nodded relievedly. "It's just as well. Nurses are at a premium just now! Well, there is not much to do. Keep her quiet; give her milk, lemon water or beef tea — nothing solid. I will send down a cooling medicine, but really, Nature must fight her own battles in a case of this kind. Keep the room at an even temperature. I will call in the morning; but if the temperature seems likely to go much higher, send for me. And she must not be left to-night. Someone should sit up with her."

"I will arrange all that," said Oona quietly. "Then that is all. We will see to it. And what about Allison? Should she leave the house?"

He gave the suggestion his consideration; then he negatived it. "I think not. You can keep her in that wing you don't use as a rule, and she can be with her ayah completely. This form of influenza is attacking adults more than children, and you tell me the child has not been much with Miss Stewart to-day. Keep away from her for the present, and let Moti have charge of her altogether for the present. She ought not to come into contact with anyone having anything to do with Miss Stewart."

"That can be managed," said Oona. "Bessie must be kept away, too, of course, so she can wait on Allie and Moti, and Morag will look after us. I'm afraid the ordinary work must go a little for the present. That is all then, Doctor?"

"Yes, I think so. I will send the medicine as soon as possible." He was out of the room by this time, and struggling into his coat and cap. Oona saw him leave the house, and then returned to the bedroom, where Mollie was tossing about. She looked up as the door opened.

"What is it?" she asked.

"Influenza," replied Oona. "Jean, will you send Morag to me? Tell Moti she is to take complete charge of Allison for to-night, and to-morrow, we must move them into the new wing. Now, Mollie, let me put your bed straight, dear. You will be more comfortable directly."

Jean vanished from the room, and Oona, with a deftness that told of much experience, turned the pillows, and pulled the tumbled sheets and blankets straight. Then she brought hot water, and sponged the burning face and hands. By this time, Morag had put in an appearance, and Miss McCleod gave her the orders about the new wing, and asked her to bring certain requirements to the bedroom. Bessie was not to come near them, and Allison was to be kept strictly to her new quarters. Jean was sent downstairs to have a good supper and ordered to drink some strong coffee.

"You must sit up with Mollie for the first half of the night," said Oona. "I will come and relieve you at one." She glanced at the patient who had sunk into a half-doze, and was muttering again.

Jean nodded, and went quietly out of the room. She was unaccustomed to sick nursing, but she was not a Guide for nothing. She did as she was told, and when she came back she was prepared to sit up the whole night if necessary.

Morag was busy, Sunday as it was. She had pressed Bessie into service, and, together, they were preparing the rooms for Allison and Moti. Fires had to be lighted, for the new wing was seldom used, and the rooms struck cold. Luckily, they were dry, and good fires all night would soon make them fit for the child. Her nursery was over the room occupied by Mollie, so all her toys must be brought down to one of the big bedrooms, where the bed was taken down, and a drugget was laid over the carpet.

Oona saw to it all, after she had given Jean her instructions, and left her sitting by the fire with her book and work at hand, a shaded table lamp giving her the light she needed, and leaving Mollie's bed in the shadows.

When one struck, Miss McCleod came in, clad in a cotton frock, and looking very fresh and fit, and Jean departed to bed. The patient was still in that half-doze that bordered on delirium, and still muttered, as she tossed about. Throughout the night, Oona kept watch while her temperature rose, and Mollie rambled. Sometimes she fancied that she was teaching and issued commands and criticism. Once she laughed a little, startling Oona. Then, it passed, and she was quiet for half an hour. After that, however, she rambled again, and Oona's tender heart was hurt as the girl uttered aloud the fears of her landlady that had lately obsessed her mind. Mrs Taylor had become a bogey to her, and once or twice, she cried out in terror. Luckily, she drowsed towards dawn, and when she woke up, she was conscious again. She begged for water in a thick voice, and once more dozed off. Her talk this time was of Mr Benson and Oona learned a secret that she had half-guessed. When Jean came in at eight, fresh and looking ready for anything, however, she was sunk into a state of coma.

Oona went off to bed for a couple of hours, and Jean took charge, but Mollie remained silent for some hours. The doctor arrived at half-past ten, and looked grave. The fever was running very high, and, he was afraid, would go higher. He said little, but promised to call in again later on. Then he went off, taking with him Allison and Moti. He would drive them a short way, and then drop them, and they could walk back. It was a fine day, and the child ought to be out in the open air as much as possible.

In the afternoon, while Morag took charge and Oona slept, so as to be in readiness for the night-watch, Jean went into Aulmbermouth to buy some things they needed. In the High Street, she met Mr Benson, looking very jolly. He stopped when he saw her, and asked for news of his pet, Allison.

"Allie is quite well," said Jean gravely, "but Miss Stewart came back on Saturday and brought influenza with her."

The cheeriness left his face. "I say! Is it bad?"

"A sharp attack, the doctor says. She's rather ill, I'm afraid," said Jean, with pity in her heart for the young man. "I've nearly finished my shopping now, and then I'm going home. Would you like to come back with me and see how she is? She may be better now. The worst thing is the temperature. It is so high already."

"I'll come," he said, misery in his eyes.

Jean's heart smote her. "Don't look like that," she said impulsively. "She is ill, of course, but Mollie is wiry, though she is not robust. She'll soon get over this, and then I expect, we'll have a nice time of it, when she is convalescent! People are always so miserable after flu!"

"Do you really think so?" he asked eagerly. Then as she nodded, he looked at her gravely. "I never meant to mention this to a soul till I had see her, but you must have known how it is with me, Jean. Do you think I have any chance?"

Jean raised her candid eyes to his. "I don't know," she said gently. "Even if I did, how could I possibly tell you? Mollie doesn't dislike you — but that's all I can say."

He nodded, a strangely determined look settling down on his boyish face, with its wholesome "doggy" ugliness. "I must do my best. You will stand my friend, I know."

"Of course I will," said Jean. She held out her hand to him. "I wish you — your heart's desire!"

"Thank you," he said. After which, they changed the subject, and discussed his lads and her Guides till they came to Storms.

Oona welcomed them, and raised the young man's spirits by informing him that Mollie was a shade easier just now.

"Of course, the fever must run its course," she said, "and she is very ill just now. But that's only what we may expect. Come out and see us again, Mr Benson."

He smiled, and went off a shade happier than he had been. The other two discussed Jean's purchases, and then Jean went off to prepare herself for the evening in the sickroom, while Oona sat by the fire, and mused over Mr Benson and Mollie.

For the next few days, Mollie was decidedly ill, and gave her doctor and nurses a good deal of anxiety to bear. Then the fever went down, she slept several hours, and woke up on the road to convalescence, and very mournful. This was only a phase of the illness, and it soon passed, for Mollie was a cheery person. She was still tied to her room, as the doctor refused to let her go downstairs until the weather became better. Mr Benson met Jean continually, and asked about her, and since it was for her friend's sake, Jean was pleased to let him go with her to carry her parcels, and to escort her home when he could. She meant it well and so did he, but both forgot that there are many tongues, evil and otherwise, in the world, and, in a small place like Aulmbermouth or Hasnett, gossip is almost invariably rife.

CHAPTER XVI

GOSSIP AND ITS CONSEQUENCES

A week after the end of January saw Mollie downstairs, looking rather washed out, but practically well again. She had an excellent constitution, and now made rapid progress. Allison, released from the new wing, was full of high spirits and inclined to be naughty. Luckily, Jean had forgotten all about psychology and the books, and Oona had taken the opportunity to return them when Mrs Semple had called to inquire after Miss Stewart. "Allison is going to be brought up in the good old-fashioned ways," she observed to her patient. "I've no faith in all this modern rubbish about studying the characteristics of the child! Allison is simply a naughty little girl, who has been spoilt by her life in India, and the only thing to do is to teach her to be obedient, truthful, and plucky. No books are needed for that. If she is naughty she will be punished, unless there is a very good excuse for the naughtiness. If she is good, she is not going to be praised for it. That would be the very way to turn her into a self-righteous little prig. Of the two, I would rather she were an imp."

"Don't worry! She's that all right," laughed Mollie.

However, when Jean had time to think of her small niece's training, she made no mention of the books, and they returned to the old ways with sighs of thankfulness on the part of the rest of the household. A few easy lessons in the morning were instituted by Oona, who insisted that Mollie and Jean should go out then when it was possible, and

who also had no great faith in Jean's patience when
it came to teaching a fidgety child her letters and
figures. As for Allison, as soon as she grasped the
fact that Auntie Oona could be neither coaxed nor
intimidated, she submitted with fair placidity, and
soon was able to read easy words for herself.

Six weeks after Mollie reached Storms, she
returned to her rooms in Field Terrace, where Mrs
Woodhouse welcomed her gladly, and even stayed a
few minutes to discuss the news with her — a thing
she had never done before. Mollie had come alone,
because poor Jean had been obliged to pay another
visit to her dentist in Noviam, and Oona had gone
with her to buy frocks for Allison, who had suddenly
begun to grow, and was shooting out of her things.
Mrs Woodhouse made a few comments on various
small events that had occurred since Christmas,
and then said, "So there's to be a wedding at Storms
soon!"

Mollie gasped in surprise. She had heard nothing
of it, and she was sure that it was neither Jean nor
Oona. She could only believe that Bessie must have
been "keeping company" for it was certain that it
was not Morag, who had a well-founded distrust for
the best of men.

Mrs Woodhouse, not noticing her surprise, went
on, "Yes; there's many have seen it coming for some
time now. I say he's a lucky man who gets Miss Jean
McCleod. She's a lady, and she's pretty, though I like
a little more colour myself. She's very sweet, too.
I've heard the Rector doesn't approve of the clergy
marrying, but I don't think even he could object to
Miss Jean."

Mollie sat in stupefied silence while the little
woman prosed on. She could not believe her ears.
Jean — Jean, of all people, to marry a priest! It was
unthinkable! She had often said that she pitied the

wives of the clergy, since they could never call their souls their own, but were the cynosure of all the parish. Mollie remembered how she had enlarged on the subject one day.

"It's all very well," Jean had proclaimed. "If you're a parson's wife, you're expected to be an unpaid curate. As if that wasn't bad enough, you also have to set an example to the parish. Any personal gifts you may have — music, or painting, or sewing, must be given up to the parish. Your children are the care, and form causes for interference from all the old tabbies in the place. Your private affairs are discussed, and turned inside out and upside down half a dozen times a day. Your house isn't your own — there is always something or other going on in it — Mothers' Meetings, or Bands of Hope, or things of that kind. Your very husband isn't your own, for he's expected to be at the beck and call of all the old freaks who belong to the church. You are expected to give — and largely, too — to all the subscription lists, whether you can afford it or not. And you are supposed to be on hand and able to advise whenever required. No, thank you! That sort of life may suit some people, but I bar luxuries!"

Mollie had laughed, and cried, "Hear-hear!" for this had occurred last year, before Mr. Benson came into her life. She thought of all this, and then heard Mrs Woodhouse's voice saying something that sent a dagger through her heart.

"Of course, Mr Benson will try to get a church of his own, now."

"What on earth has Mr Benson to do with it?" demanded Mollie sharply.

"Well, my dear, seeing he's the fortunate man," began Mrs Woodhouse, but Mollie interrupted her.

"Rubbish! Mr. Benson! Why — ?"

Her voice suddenly faltered, and she stopped. Mrs

Woodhouse looked at her in surprise, but fortunately laid her startled air to the shock of hearing
that her best friend was engaged — or about to be
— from an outsider. It was quite plain to the
goodhearted landlady that Mollie had no idea of it.
She stopped her friendly gossip, and said, "I'm very
sorry, Miss Stewart. Naturally, I thought you would
know all about it, you being such friends. I hope I
haven't said anything I ought not?"

Mollie waved her excuses away. "No, Mrs
Woodhouse, I'm sure you have been most kind. May
I have my tea now, please? I have to get to the class
rather early, you know." Mrs Woodhouse promptly
hurtled off to prepare a good meal, and Mollie sat
down by the fire and tried to clear her head.

Jean was practically engaged to Mr Benson! All
the place was humming with the news! Oh! it
couldn't be true! And yet she had very little really
on which to go — only Jean's own character, and the
look he had given herself the last time they had
met. What had she done? "Oh," cried Mollie to
herself, "What a little ass I have been! What an
utter fool!"

She had to go to class that night, and she must be
the same to Jean, even though she felt at the
moment as if she never wanted to see her again.
For, whatever had happened, it could not be Jean's
fault. Mollie partook of a scanty meal, and went
upstairs to change into her dancing frock. She
arrived at the High School with very few minutes to
spare, and taught the elementary class so languidly,
that they took alarm, and thought she had come
back too soon.

When the sword class began without any Jean, it
felt better; but just before it ended, Jean came in,
squired by Mr Benson, and both were laughing
heartily. How was Mollie to know that they had met

on the steps outside, and Jean had given the curate a brief but lurid account of her afternoon's visit at the dentist's?

Jean changed her shoes quickly, and went into the hall as the sword class broke up.

"I am so sorry I've missed swords," she said to Mollie. "That wretched dentist kept me ages, stopping the brute, and then we had to get Allie's frocks."

"It is a pity, of course," said Mollie. Try as she would, she could not keep a coldness out of her tones, and Jean stared at her in surprise.

"What is the matter? I'm sorry I couldn't get here in time, but I really couldn't help it."

"I know. You've said so already," replied Mollie, in the same cold tones.

She could have beaten herself for her behaviour, but she was sore and miserable still, and Jean's moonlight loveliness, thrown up by the severe lines of the gym-dress and square-necked white blouse, was hurting her as it had never done. Jean looked at her. She could not imagine what she had done, but it was obvious Mollie was upset about something. It struck her that her friend was whiter than she had looked when they had parted earlier in the day. Perhaps she was tired. She had had a nasty bout, and was not yet really strong. It must be that. And, seeing that Mollie would rather be left alone, she turned away from her and began a half-chaffing conversation with Miss Farrar.

Mollie called the class sharply to order, and bade them form sets for "Argeers", which they had not yet learned. In the stress of teaching, she forgot her unhappiness for a while, and became more like herself. But she left Jean's set severely alone, and never once came near them.

After "Argeers", she took "Parson's Farewell", and

then went through one or two other dances. Morris class came next, and they were all severely drilled in "Glorishears" and "Lumps of Plum Pudding". The class was very weary when she dismissed it, and very much puzzled as to what had happened to their jolly little teacher. Miss Stewart had never laughed once, and she had been severely business-like all night.

When it was over Jean, with a final effort, followed Mollie to the classroom where she changed and said, "Oona wants to know if you're coming to lunch tomorrow, Moll."

"I'm afraid I can't," said Mollie, who, by this time, was only holding back her tears with an effort. "I'm very busy. Don't keep me, please."

Jean gasped, as well she might, and a tart answer came to her lips. Luckily, she checked it and went away in silence.

Mr Benson, coming to ask permission to escort Miss Stewart home, fared no better, and was left wondering if he had made a mistake, and she didn't even like him. He went off feeling unhappy, and Mollie betook herself to her rooms and bed, where she cried herself to sleep. The next few days brought no alleviation, and when a whole week had passed, and the girl had not been near Storms, Oona was seriously worried about her. Jean's reports were not consoling, either. She said that Mollie had seemed upset about something, though what it was she had no idea. Anyhow she had been as icy as possible, and the whole class was concerned about her.

"Are you sure you've said nothing to tease her?" asked Oona. "You know you can be rather merciless at times, Jean."

Jean shook her head. "I haven't teased her for ages. It began last week after she left Storms. She was all right when we said farewell to each other.

When I got to class in the evening she was as chilly as an iceberg. I was late, I admit, but that wouldn't have made her like this. No; there's something behind it all. I've a good mind to go into Aulmbermouth this afternoon and ask her what it is. I hate going on like this! It almost seems as if Mollie hated me!" Her lips quivered as she ended. She was worried about her friend, and she loved Mollie very dearly. Theirs had been a perfect friendship till this happened and it made her miserable to be treated like this — especially when she had no idea what was wrong and so was unable to put things right.

Oona was careful to make no comments. "I think that a good idea," she said. "Allison and I are going to tea at the Vernons this afternoon. Why don't you catch the twenty past two tram and see Mollie. Go in your gym things and then you can have tea and go to class together."

Accordingly, a quarter to three saw Jean, case in hand — she had decided to change in the town — walking briskly down Field Terrace. Mrs Woodhouse admitted her and sent her straight into Mollie's sitting room, where that young lady was crouching unhappily over the fire, a book in her lap and tear-marks on her face.

Now, all the way to Aulmbermouth Jean had been emulating the famous Meg and John Brook in "Good Wives", and had been telling herself that she would be "cool and calm." But when she saw that wretched little figure by the hearth, all her resolutions vanished. Flinging her case down on the nearest chair, she swept across the room, dropped on her knees beside her friend, and slipping an arm round her, said coaxingly, "Mollie — Mollie Creina, what's wrong? Tell me, Honey!"

Mollie had had no time to make plans. She was

quite unstrung and had been working far harder than she ought. Influenza had taken it out of her far more than she had realised, and she was utterly miserable. So, instead of repulsing Jean, as she might have done if she had had time to think, she simply laid her head down on her friend's shoulder, and said with a sniff, "I—I think y—you might have t—told me about your engagement y—yourself!"

"My what?" Jean nearly let her fall in her astonishment. "My what, did you say? My engagement? Mollie Stewart! Are you wandering? I'm not engaged — I've no intention of being engaged! Who on earth has been telling you such rubbish?"

"Mrs Woodhouse," faltered Mollie. "She said everyone was talking about it."

"In-deed! And may I enquire who the happy man is?"

But at Mr Benson's name, she went off into a wild yell of laughter.

"Mr Benson! A parson! Mollie Stewart, how could you credit such a thing! You know my views on the subject as well as I do myself! Oh, Mollie, you ass!"

"Well, Mrs Woodhouse said you were always meeting; and you went to sing to his boys," protested Mollie, sitting up, and looking more like herself than she had done for days.

"What idiots people are!" said Jean scornfully. "Of course I was always meeting him! I don't believe I ever stirred out of the house that I didn't meet him — while you were ill! Mollie darling, don't you know how it is with him? Haven't you realised yet that he thinks my Mollie the sweetest and best girl in the whole world — as she is!"

"Well, I couldn't know," said Mollie, looking at Jean with all the old fondness in her dark eyes. "You are so lovely, Jean. I could never have blamed him if he wanted you."

Jean gave her a hug. "Oh, Mollie, how easily things can go wrong! Just that silly little fact of his meeting me to ask how you were, and we've both been desperately unhappy all this week! Oona's been awfully anxious too. She was quite worried about you."

Mollie returned the hug, and they stayed in silence for a few minutes. Then Jean, with a little laugh, withdrew her arms, and got to her feet.

"I can stay for tea, can't I? I've brought my things to change here, so I'll have to!"

"Of course you can," said Mollie. "I'll just run and tell Mrs Woodhouse, and then we'll have a good gossip. I want all the Storms news!"

Since they talked without ceasing up to the time they reached the High School it may be taken for granted that Mollie got all the Storms news, and class that night was one mad rush — so the others declared. Mollie was at her merriest, and maddest. She taught them fresh dances, laughing over their mistakes, and when they went wrong in a new figure of "Running Set", she came in to show them how to do it, and then bade them do it again — "without the variations, this time!"

Perhaps Mr Benson guessed something. At any rate, when the evening was ended, he marched her off, leaving Jean to go to her tram unescorted. She reached home, and reassured Oona as to Mollie.

"Just some silly gossip. It's all right now!"

But when she was in bed that night, she lay awake a long time. "This is the end of the old times," she thought to herself. "Mollie will never belong to me again!"

CHAPTER XVII

KIRSTY COMES TO STORMS

Mollie put in her appearance at Storms the next afternoon. She was very shy, and very sweet and looked prettier than Jean had ever seen her. On her left hand glowed a sapphire which had not been there before. She showed it half-proudly, half-bashfully when she had been kissed and welcomed back to the fold.

"Charlie went into Noviam this morning to get it," she said shyly. "Isn't it beautiful?"

"Not a bit too beautiful for my Moll," said Jean affectionately. "I hope you'll be very happy, Mollie."

"When is the wedding to be?" asked Oona.

"Quite soon," said Mollie blushing. "Charlie wants it at Easter; but I told him I must finish the year's teaching."

"I should hope you did!" cried Oona. "Easter, indeed? How did he imagine you could be ready by then? You'll have it at the end of July, Mollie, and from this house. You don't want to be married from the Gorgon's or your aunt Meg's, do you?"

Mollie shook her head. "Oh, no! This is my home. I was going to ask you if we might have it here."

"Well, it won't be from anywhere else," said Jean vigorously.

"And I want a folk-dancing wedding," added Mollie.

"How do you imagine you're going to manage that?"

"Oh, easily! We'll have a party out on the lawn after the service, and dance wedding-y things. 'Step and Fetch Her', for instance. And 'The Triumph' and 'Winifred's Knot', and 'Christchurch Bells', and — oh, heaps of others!"

"And 'Sellenger's', to finish off with," supplemented Jean.

"Of course! We couldn't end up without 'Sellenger's'!"

"Are you going to invite the classes?"

"Well, I think we might ask the Aulmbermouth ones. We don't want an awfully swagger wedding, you know. Morag shall make my cake — I'm sure she'd never let us buy one! — and you shall be my bridesmaid, and Allie shall be Page, though I've no intention of wearing a train."

"But you'll wear white, Mollie, and have a veil and orange-blossoms?" pleaded Jean. "You needn't have a gaudy rigout, but you must be in white!"

"Of course I shall. But it will be a sensible frock, that will be some use to me later. Picture frocks are charming to look at, but Charlie and I are not going to be rich, and I am going to get things that will wear! But we won't have a big show, Jean. My people are all scattered, with Dad in India, Jim in Burmah and Alec exploring somewhere up the Amazon. Charlie's folk are all in South Africa, too, so barring the Gorgon, and Aunt Meg and Uncle James, there are no relations to ask. I'm going to have a pretty wedding, and one where I'll be able to think what I'm doing — not a tamasha where I'll have to be wondering if I look gorgeous enough."

Jean nodded. "I understand."

"I don't think weddings like that are — are — well, sacramental enough," said Mollie, her face pink with blushes. "I want to feel that my wedding is a real sacrament; and so, Oona, I don't want gorgeousness."

Oona's eyes had darkened. "I agree with you,

Mollie. You shall have your happy, quiet wedding with folk-dancing and friends and home-made cakes. It is what I would have had myself." Two pairs of girlish arms were round her; two girlish voices were murmuring to her. Oona laughed a little.

"You are dear girls, both of you. Don't think I am unhappy because things haven't fallen out as I had hoped. Heartbreak doesn't often occur outside of novels. I am very happy in my life here, with you to love and to love me, and my daily work, and daily duties. Yes; you may screw up your face as you like, Jean, but when you have lived as long as I have, you will find that duty is a very real help. Now, forget the might-have-been, and let us go on with Mollie's plans. Where are you going to live, Mollie?"

"In Percy Square," said Mollie promptly. "One of those houses on the West is vacant, and Charlie has taken an option on it. We went over this morning when he came back from Noviam. He wants you to see it, Oona, in case there should be anything wrong that we've missed. If you approve, we take it."

"Jolly good," said Jean. "They are nice houses those and they have good gardens behind. They have decent windows, too, and the kitchens are on the same floor as the sitting-room, which is an advantage."

Then Morag came in with tea, and Allison made her appearance and had to be told all about it. Mr Benson rang at the bell at the same time, and had to be congratulated, and treated to a lecture by Jean, who ended by blessing them both. After that, he escorted Mollie to the station, and Jean retired to put Allison to bed. The engagement created a nine days' wonder in Aulmbermouth. Thanks to Mrs Taylor, it had got round that Mr Benson was in love with Jean, and when it was announced that the lady of his choice was Mollie, there was a great deal of talk. People were not ill-natured, but it was not human to assume there could be no feeling on Jean's part at all after all that had been gossiped. Some said she was bearing the disappointment splendidly. Others, less kind, declared that she had only been flirting with the curate and deserved what she got. The people who knew and loved the two girls were indignant at the conflicting reports that went round, and did their best to stop them. But the gossip had its way till the daughter of a leading solicitor eloped with one of her father's clerks, when it was neatly diverted.

Unfortunately, the person most concerned with Jean — to wit, the doctor — was still feeling too bitter to listen to anything that was said. With his many good qualities, he was pigheaded in the extreme, and his attitude towards the girl he had once hoped to make his wife was as icy as it had been since the end of the year. He was very busy, for an epidemic of influenza had broken out, and he was worked off his feet. He was not well, and he was unhappy. Jean, too proud to make the first advances, copied his attitude. So things were no better between the pair.

Meanwhile, Jean had something else to think about. Half-way through March, a letter came from Fareham. Usually, they heard once in every three weeks from Kirsty, who seemed to be getting on well. She was at a little day-school, but was to go to a High School in either Portsmouth or Winchester when she had been in England a little longer. She had made friends with one or two children, and was allowed to have them to tea occasionally, or to go to tea with them. On the surface, it seemed as if everything was going well with her, but Jean sometimes wondered if those laboriously-penned letters were quite genuine. Then, for five weeks they heard nothing of her, and just as Oona was beginning to hint that it was time for Jean to write and enquire about her, a letter came from Mrs Page. Kirsty had been ill — she had had chicken- pox and had been quite ill with it. Now, she was better, but the doctor thought she ought to have a change of air. Therefore, her aunt was writing to enquire if the McCleods would take her for a few weeks. If no reply came before the Monday of the following week, Kirsty would be despatched north.

"Well!" cried Jean, when she had read this. "I must say she doesn't give us much time to decide! This is Friday!"

"You don't need any time," said Oona, calmly. "Of course the child must come here. 'A few weeks?' I wonder what that means!"

"Anything from a month to the whole of the summer," returned Jean. "Well, I had better see Moti and tell her her other nursling is coming, and also break the news to Morag."

Allison took the matter coolly when she heard. "Where will she sleep?" was her one question.

"In the little blue room," Jean told her. "Would you like to come with me to meet her?"

Allison considered this, and then shook her head. "No, I'll wait here with Auntie Oona."

"You won't even do that," said Oona. "Kirsty won't be here before eight o'clock, and you will be in bed two hours before that. She will be so tired with the long journey, that I expect she will want to go to bed, too. It will be much nicer for you both if you meet in the morning."

When the child had gone to get ready for a walk with Jean, Oona turned to the girl.

"What were you thinking of, Jean, to suggest that Allison should go with you to Noviam? I daresay

Kirsty will be all right — indeed, I am sure she will. But we cannot afford to take any risks with Allison. She will not see her sister till the doctor has been and assured us that there is no danger of germs."

"Never thought of it," said Jean, airily. "Oh, all right, Oona. If you think so, we'll leave it at that. Now I must go and get ready or I shall keep Allison waiting, and she hates it."

"You must not give into her," said Oona. "You are beginning to think, Jean, that Allie's convenience is the only thing to be consulted. She has been spoilt enough, and we are having to undo it all. Don't spoil her in another way."

Jean laughed. "Oh, I'll be careful! After the way I sent her from the table at breakfast, for rudeness, you can't say I'm very likely to spoil her!"

"Oh, you are particular enough over her manners," returned Oona. "Also, you have done much towards curing her of selfishness with her belongings. But it is quite possible to indulge her too much in other ways." Jean laughed again, and left the room to get ready, and the subject of Kirsty's arrival was more or less shelved till Monday, when Allison was so excited as to be positively naughty. Oona settled her in the end by threatening her with bed an hour earlier, and Allison, who loved early bed no better than most children, calmed down after that. She was packed off at her usual time, Oona superintending the going to bed, since Jean had already set off for Noviam, as she wanted to buy one or two things there before the shops closed.

Sitting in a corner of her compartment, the girl wondered to herself how the past months had affected Kirsty. She had been a spoilt, pert child when she arrived in England; but, from her recollec- tions of Mrs Page, Jean imagined that the child must have altered in a good many ways. Allison was changed from the spoilt, rude baby who had come to Storms, and it seemed to the girl that their gentle regulations would have considerably less effect on any child than Mrs Page's undoubtedly severe ones. Kirsty, in all probability, had learnt a good many lessons by this time.

"I'm sure Allie is a great deal nicer than she was when she first came to us," thought Jean as she moved so as to keep her coat from damage from the swinging feet of a small boy who sat opposite her. "I hope to goodness Kirsty is improved, too. I can't imagine that woman indulging her in many ways. If she's been ill, she'll be rather subdued, poor kiddy!" Then she turned to glare at the small boy who was now trying to see how far he could stretch out his feet, and was wiping his boots on her in the process. His mother, a feeble ineffective creature, said "Don't be so naughty, Alfie!" but it had no effect. Jean got up with some dignity, and removed to the other corner, thinking contemptuously, "What a fool!"

However, they had just reached Noviam and she had to hurry to the London platform, as her train was late, and she had a good deal to do. She found out when Kirsty's train was due, and then raced off to do her shopping. She did it in record time, and was back at the station just as the London train swept in. She hurried up and down it, looking for the small guest, but nowhere could she see a child who in any way resembled Kirsty. She was just about to give it up under the impression that the child was not coming till the morrow, when she heard a voice say in apathetic tones, "That's Auntie Jean."

She swung round and saw a grave, elderly lady, with an anxious face, and by her side, a lanky, thin-faced child, whom she had already glanced at, and passed. It was Kirsty! The lady came hurrying to her, and accosted her eagerly. "Excuse me, but are you Miss McCleod? You are? Oh, I am so glad! I was beginning to be afraid that no one had come to meet Christina, and I did not know what to do, as I must go on to Edinburgh to-night. My son has broken his leg, and I did not want to break my journey if I could help it. This case is Christina's, and she tells me her trunk was sent in advance."

"Yes; it arrived this morning," said Jean. "Well, Kirsty, I am very glad to see you, dear."

She bent down and kissed the child, who made no response, but stood looking at her with dark eyes that seemed too big for her face. Jean slipped an arm round the thin shoulders, and drew the little girl to her, as she thanked the kind chaperon for looking after her, and hoped the lady would find her son well on the way to recovery when she reached him. Then they said "good-bye", and the girl took Kirsty off to have some hot milk and biscuits while they waited for the Aulmbermouth train.

As she sipped the coffee she had ordered for herself, Jean kept looking at the child in bewilderment. There was nothing in this scrawny, lanky creature before her of the pretty, rosy child she had met on the steamer. Kirsty was thinner and more sallow than Allison, now, and her long, brown curls had been cropped, boy's fashion, close to her head. She had obviously been very ill, but that seemed scarcely sufficient to account for her shrinking timid manner, and the startled look that came into her eyes when she was suddenly addressed.

In the train, she fell asleep, and Jean slipped an arm round her, finally lifting her to her lap that she might rest more comfortably. The light weight horrified her. Allie was almost as heavy. Kirsty slept till they reached Aulmbermouth where Mollie had come to meet them, and put them into a taxi. Kirsty

awoke then, and the way she shrank from Jean's
encircling arms hurt the girl horribly. She felt that
there must be something all wrong with a child who
was so obviously afraid of being held by anyone.

Charlie Benson was there, and he was ready to
treat the little girl with same jolly kindness that he
showed Allison, who already called him "Uncle
Charlie", and took all kinds of liberties with him
unless her aunts checked her. Kirsty shivered away
from his big hand outstretched to pat her cheek as if
she feared he would strike her, and he stared at her
in amazement.

"Kirsty is tired," said Jean swiftly. "You must
come over to-morrow and see her. Now, I think she
wants bed more than anything else."

He nodded, and put them into the taxi carefully. A
quarter of an hour later they reached Storms, where
Oona was waiting for them. Kirsty was asleep again
and scarcely woke up when they undressed her and
tucked her into bed. Jean was disgusted at the sight
and feeling of the rough and ready clothes she wore.
Allison was as plainly dressed as could be, but she
wore the best of everything. Kirsty was clad in
home-knitted knickers, vest, and stockings, and
they were of a harsh wool that must have tormented
her tender skin. She had only flannelette night-
dresses, and they were forced to put her into one till
they could get her some little sleeping suits of the
soft Indian cotton that Allison always wore. The
younger child's would never have fitted her, she was
so much grown. Finally, they lit the nightlight, and
Moti, whose mattress had been moved into the
room, prepared to go to bed, too.

Oona and Jean went off to the Den. Then, they
looked at each other in silence which Jean was the
first to break.

"Poor little kid!" she said. "Poor little kid!"

CHAPTER XVIII

Kirsty slept late the next morning. Allison was up by seven, and demanding imperiously to see her, but was told that her sister was not to be awakened, and Jean had, perforce, to take the child into her own bed and tell her stories to keep her quiet. The household was up and about its usual duties, and Miss McCleod had gone off to the village, taking Allison with her, when Kirsty opened her eyes, and looked round languidly at the unaccustomed surroundings. A dark face bent over her, and she gave a little cry.

"Moti — Moti-ayah!"

"My Kirsty-baba," said the soft, murmurous voice she had missed all these months. "Lie still, my little princess, and Moti will bring thee chota-hazri!"

The gentle hands were already brushing the untidy hair out of her eyes, and Moti was mourning the loss of the beautiful curls which she had been used to tend so lovingly.

"Aunt Gladys said she hadn't time to fuss with it, so she cut it off," explained Kirsty.

"The evil of it! My little princess had such hair!" said Moti, as she laid down the brush. "Lie still, my Missie-baba, and I will call the Mem, who will bring food. The dakitar-sahib comes later, and will say how we may make thee well and strong, so that thou mayest play even as in the old days in Hind across the Black Water."

Kirsty lay back, and presently Jean arrived, bearing her breakfast on a tray. Such a dainty meal,

fit for a princess! There was a spoonful of porridge
in an old silver bowl from which McCleods had
supped their porridge for nearly three centuries. A
tiny, pinky-brown egg was in a deep blue egg cup on
a plate wreathed with roses. Another plate to match
held bread- and-butter of wafer thinness; and there
was a cup just the same, full of rich milk. The china
was old, and so thin as to be nearly transparent.
The tray was covered with a finely- embroidered
cloth. Kirsty, with a sudden memory of a red tin
tray, thick ware mug, and food prepared with little
thought of tempting a sickly appetite, suddenly
burst into tears. Alarmed, Jean set her burden on a
nearby table, and hurried to take the child in her
arms.

"Kirsty, honey, what's the matter?"

"It's — so — p-pretty!" sobbed Kirsty.

Jean understood at once. The child's words only
emphasised the tale told by her garments, and the
girl felt a wave of hot anger at it. After all, the child
was not dependent on the Pages; she had money of
her own, and they had the handling of it. There was
no reason why she should have been clad in such a
poor way, nor treated as it was evident she had
been. She laid the little girl back, and went away, to
return with a jug of hot water, and a parcel.

"Sit up, Kirsty," she said, briskly. "I am going to
sponge your hands and face, and then we'll put this
on, and then you'll see how much better you feel! I'm
sure you'll want your breakfast then. See, we'll set
the porridge and egg in the fender to keep hot while
we are busy. Now, make haste!"

Thus adjured, Kirsty sat up, rubbing her eyes
with the back of her hand, and Jean made haste
with her toilette. When the washing was done, she
slipped off the pink flannelette nightdress, and put
her into a little sleeping suit, which Bessie had just

bought from Aulmbermouth. It was creamy-white, with blue bands, and was soft and dainty. Kirsty looked at it.

"Oh, how pretty!"

"And here's a little bed-jacket to go with it," said Jean, helping her to put it on. "Now for the bed-table, and then we'll see about breakfast."

Jean tucked the pillows in and arranged the dainty tray, and Kirsty, with the first appetite she had shown since her illness, ate every scrap of it. Jean watched the little wasted hands, the hollow face, and remembered the emaciated little body, with every rib visible and dips under the collar bones, and was furious. Even a severe attack of chicken-pox should not have made that difference in the plump little girl she remembered. Allison, who had seemed to them shockingly thin, even now, was far better covered than her step-sister. The girl said nothing, but she thought the more. On one thing she was determined, Kirsty was to go home better in every way. If Mrs Page wrote for the child to return before she was up to the standard, then the doctor must be prevailed upon to forbid it.

When the meal was ended, Kirsty lay back against her pillows, and watched Jean as she tidied up the room, and pulled the bed to order. The child was very weary, but she liked the quiet movements, so different from Mrs Page's bustle and flurry. The room was so pretty, too, with its blue walls and white draperies. There were blue rugs on the polished oak floor, and the pictures on the walls had dark oak frames. Tall slender vases, filled with daffodils, stood on the mantelpiece, and the muslin curtains let in a flood of March sunshine.

"This is such a pretty room, Auntie Jean," said Kirsty, suddenly.

"Glad you think so," laughed Jean. "There; now

are we all ready for the doctor when he comes,
Auntie Oona will be in soon with Allie, and if it's all
right, she shall come up here to play with you —
what's that?"

It proved to be the doctor, rather to Jean's dismay.
She had reckoned on his being much later than this,
and not coming till Oona had returned. As it was,
Oona was not likely to return for a good half-hour,
and she must receive him herself. With a hardening
of her face, she turned from the bed to greet him.

"Good morning, Doctor. You are very early."

"Good morning," said the doctor. "Yes; I am early,
but I had to call at the Stoddarts — Tom is ill again
— so I thought I would come here, as it is only a
little way, before my morning round. Is this the little
girl?"

"Yes, this is Kirsty. Say 'Good morning' to Dr
Errington, Kirsty."

Kirsty lifted her brown eyes to his face, and
promptly fell in love with him, as most children did.
She was very good, and let him examine her
thoroughly without making a murmur. When he
had finished, and was putting his stethoscope away,
she looked at him. "May I get up to-day, please?"

"Well, not to-day, I think," he said, smiling down
at her. "You need a good rest after that tremendous
journey yesterday. To-morrow, if you are good, and
eat up all your breakfast, you may get up for a
while. Shall I see you downstairs, Miss McCleod?"

"Certainly," said Jean. "I will come at once."

He held the door open for her, and she preceded
him to the Den, where she waved him to a seat,
herself sitting down and looking past him to the
window.

"About that child," he began. "She is tired out,
and seems very run down. Keep her quiet for a day
or two, and don't let her do too much. Nourishing

food — eggs, soup, milk — and so on. I will send her a tonic which ought to pull her up. Avoid damp, of course, and see that she is wrapped up when she goes out. I will call again in a few days' time to see how she is progressing. In the meantime, there is nothing to worry about. She will be all right in a week or two."

"Thank you," said Jean, rising with the air of a princess. "It will be quite safe for Allison to be with her sister?"

"Oh, quite. But see that they don't excite each other. Well, I think that's all. I must not be late for surgery, so I will bid you good-morning."

"Good morning," said Jean. She rang the bell for Morag, who promptly appeared. "Please show the doctor out, Morag. I will tell my aunt what you say, doctor."

He bowed, and followed Morag. Jean turned to the bookcase at once, and was very busy choosing books for Kirsty's amusement when the old woman came back.

"Yon's a fine mon," she said, apropos of nothing.

Jean took no notice.

"I said yon's a fine mon, Miss Jean."

"I heard you," said her young mistress calmly.

"Ye didna agree wi' me, though."

"Because I saw no reason to do so," replied Jean, selecting the books she wanted with great delibera-tion. "Also, I do not agree with you. He is quite ordinary in my opinion."

"Hoots! Ye wi' an opeenion!" sniffed Morag. "Whit can a bairn like ye ken aboot a fine mon or a bad yin? Answer me that, wull ye?"

"I never pretended to be a judge," retorted Jean, closing the doors of the bookcase. "It was you who asked my opinion. Now you've got it. Also, I prefer not to discuss people behind their backs. It is neither kind nor in good taste."

For a moment Morag was nearly breathless at Jean's temerity. But she speedily recovered her breath and preceded to demolish that young lady's argument to nothingness.

"'Tis a peety ye dinna think o' that when ye talk aboot yer vicar and his gude lady! I've heard ye say mony a sair thing agin the baith o' them!"

This was carrying war into the enemy's country with a vengeance, and Jean was silenced for a moment. Morag noticed it and made the most of her opportunity. "Gin ye were to luk for a gude mon, Miss Jean, ye micht gae farther, and fare worse nor the doctor. Ye shouldna delay ower lang, ye ken, and I wadna like tae see ye an auld maid."

But this was too much, and Jean signified it by her speech. "That will do, Morag! You may be my old nurse, but that gives you no right to be impertinent to me! I must go to Miss Kirsty, so if you have nothing of importance to say to me, I should be glad if you would let me pass."

Morag fell back before her dignified air and Jean swept out of the room, and left the old woman looking after her with reluctant admiration in her gaze.

"Ay! ye're a McCleod, every inch! Ye're high, lassie — terrible high, and ye winna pit oop wi' a word, but I likit fine tae see ye the noo! Ye micht ha'e bin the laird himsel' the way ye left me! I doot ye'll be a crouse handfu' for ony mon to master, but," with an uncanny chuckle, "mastered ye will be! Aye, and by yon mon ye scorn noo. For he's the mon for Miss Jean McCleod, and I ken it as weels I ken ma awn name!"

With this she turned and left the room, and went to make Bessie's life a burden to her by her stricture on careless dusting.

CHAPTER XIX

A REUNION AND TWO PUZZLES

But though Jean carried matters with a high hand where Morag was concerned, she was not able to do so with her own heart. That troublesome organ had given a sudden and most disconcerting leap at Morag's praise of the doctor, and she was beginning to learn the truth of the old saying "Speak ill o' ma love; speak well o' ma love; but aye speak o' him." She had a fine colour in her face when she reached Kirsty's room with her books, and the little girl looked at her with admiration.

"Auntie Jean, how pretty you are," she said.

"Nonsense, Kirsty!" said Jean, impatiently. "See, I have brought you some fairy-books. Allison will be in presently, and then she shall come and play with you. Moti will stay with you till she comes, for I have work I must do. Send her to me if you want anything." Kirsty nodded, and settled herself with "My Own Fairybook" quite happily, while Jean went off to attend to company accounts. Allison's arrival with Oona half an hour later solved any trouble in keeping her occupied. The two children seemed overjoyed to be together again, and spent a merry time playing with coloured chalks, jigsaw puzzles, and beads. Mollie ran in for tea, and was escorted up to the bedroom to see its occupant. Kirsty met her with a beaming smile, and chatted happily to her. When the two girls had left the children, however, Mollie proved that she was not deceived.

"I though you told me Kirsty was chubby, Jean," she said accusingly. "Why, there's nothing of her but skin and bone! Allison at her worst never looked like that!"

"She didn't, either, when I last saw her," replied Jean. "She was plump enough then. I suppose it's this illness she's had. The doctor says she'll soon pick up, though. What I'm wondering, is how long we are to keep her. We don't know anything definite yet, you know."

"I should write and ask," advised Mollie.

"I mean to. Come in here, Moll. I want to show you these things."

She exhibited a small pile of underthings, and Mollie regarded them with wondering eyes.

"What on earth do you want to show me these for? Are they for one of Oona's protégés?"

"No! These are Kirsty's things," said Jean in a choked voice.

"Kirsty's?" Mollie picked one up and felt it. Then, she suddenly flung it down. "Jean! You can't mean it! Why, it's the kind of thing the very poor put on their children. And anyway, her sleeping suit seems alright."

"She wore a flannelette nightgown of the vilest pink last night," said Jean.

"Flannelette? I thought it was more or less considered a deathtrap for children!"

"Evidently Mrs Page doesn't fret about that!" said Jean with sarcasm. "Can you imagine it, Mollie? Can you get anywhere near the thought of what clothes like that must have been to a child accustomed to the best of everything? Allie's things were almost fit for a little princess — the finest of silk and cotton — nothing coarser. Of course, Kirsty must have had the same. Then because she outgrew what she had — I should think she's about an inch and a half taller than she was when she came to England — that wretched woman puts her into rubbish like that!" She waved her hand towards the despised garments. "The kid told me quite naturally that her aunt said she couldn't have her pampered as she has been. Isn't it wicked?"

"Steady on, old girl! You're getting all worked up, and it's not necessary. The Pages may be poor, you know."

"I can't help their poverty. But I do know that Alastair left Kirsty two hundred a year — or rather, it goes to her guardians till she comes of age. They are supposed to use it for her benefit. Don't tell me that two hundred a year only runs to things like that for the child! She is going to a day-school of some kind — private, I believe. Well, the term's fees can't come to more than eight guineas at her age — not even if she took all the extras — which she doesn't. She doesn't even learn music. That's twenty-four guineas a year. Where is the rest?"

"I didn't know your brother had left the kid anything," said Mollie.

"Oh, yes. He knew there would be plenty for them all. Allison will be an heiress in a small way, you know, for Doris' share comes to her as well. Then Kirsty has a little from her own father — I believe another hundred a year. So, you see, there isn't the faintest need for the child to be dressed like that. However, I'm not going to allow it any longer. She shall be properly fitted out while she is here, and Oona is going to Alastair's solicitors who are trustees for the children, to ask them to see into matters. His money is not going to enrich the Page family if we can help it!"

"Well," said Mollie, "if you put it into the solicitor's hands I don't see that you can do any more. I should get the child what she needs, and leave it at that. She seems happy enough here, anyhow. So come down off your Rosinate, and discuss pleasant things,

Donna Quixote."

Jean gave a half laugh, and turned to the window, to look out at the sea, with its white horses which were dashing against the cliffs. "You think me quite insane, don't you, Moll?"

"No — absurd," said Mollie tranquilly. "Let's go into the garden and see if the scillas are coming up."

"Come along, then. Tea is at four to-day, as I have to change for class after. How is the house progressing?"

"Very nicely, thank you. The bedrooms are finished, and they are papering the drawing- room to-day. But I don't want to talk house with you just now. Let's talk flowers."

They had reached the garden by this time, and were pacing slowly up and down the paths. Jean forgot Kirsty's wrongs for the time being while they hunted for signs of early flowers. Oona called them in to tea presently, and they went with excellent appetites.

"By the way," she said, as she filled the cups, and handed them round, "I have some news for you both. Mrs Taylor is leaving Aulmbermouth."

"Cheers!" cried Mollie, waving her cup in the air. "Now I feel as if the last of my troubles had gone! When is she going, Oona?"

"Next month, I'm told. Mollie, if you smash my cups, I shall tell Morag to set one of the pewter tankards for you!"

Mollie hastily returned her cup to its saucer, and became normal. "Who told you?"

"Mrs Semple. I met her in the village, and she was full of it. She said that Miss Venn of the High School told her."

"The Head? Oh, then, it's sure to be true!"

"I'm jolly glad to hear it," struck in Jean. "That woman is a blight to me."

"Who? Miss Venn?" asked Oona, severely. "Really, Jean, your speeches are most confused on occasion."

"Don't preach!" retorted Jean. "I say, Mollie, where will Charles go?"

"Back to the Clergy House, I should think," replied Mollie. "It's only for a short time."

The chiming of the clock recalled them to the time, and they made haste to finish their tea. As they stood at the tram terminus, waiting for their car, the doctor flashed past in his little runabout.

"I wonder when he intends to return to classes?" said Mollie. "He hasn't been all this term."

"How should I know what he means to do?" said Jean irritably. "Do give that man a rest!" Mollie glanced at her. She knew that all was not well with her friend, but, in her own happiness, she had been rather blind lately, and it was only this moment that she had any inkling as to why Jean had changed so of late. It was a subtle change, but it was there. Mollie turned the conversation at once, but she thought the more. When the evening ended, and the doctor had never turned up, she made up her mind to find out why. She had had an idea that he and Jean might be attracted to each other, and, like Morag, though she worded her thoughts differently, she considered that it would be ideal. But this term they had been chilly to each other whenever they happened to meet. What had taken place? Funnily enough, she never connected her own trouble at the beginning of term with what seemed to have gone wrong, so she had no clue to the trouble.

"I must ask Charlie somehow," she thought. "I shall have to be very careful because Jean must be kept out of it. I shall manage somehow, I suppose. He'll help, I know." However, the help was to come from neither herself nor the Rev. Charles when come it did. It lay in far other and unwitting hands.

CHAPTER XX

KIRSTY

Kirsty had been at Storms three days when Jean
finally made up her mind about her. Life at
Fareham had not improved her. She had better
manners, and rarely if ever obtruded her opinions;
but boldness had given place to a shrinking timidity
which hurt Jean. She was sly, as well, and, living in
constant fear of punishment, had learnt to be
thoroughly deceitful. She told lies with an
absolutely straight face, and stuck to them, adding
untruth to untruth to support her statements till
Jean and Oona were at their wits' end to know how
to deal with her.

"Weep her," Morag counselled. "A lying bairn
should be wheepit."

But Jean and Oona thought otherwise. Together
with Mollie and the Reverend Charles they
discussed it over their tea the first Sunday
afternoon after the child had come. The children
had had theirs with Moti, and were supposed to be
in the nursery, reading "Sunday" books till it was
time for them to come downstairs to the drawing-
room for hymns.

"I wonder what has made her so untruthful,"
mused Oona.

"Terror," said Mollie. "If you want to know, I think
she has been frightened into it. Probably she has
been severely punished for the slightest thing, so
that now she lies involuntarily to save herself any
trouble."

"But to tell lies about an accidental smash!" cried

190

Jean. "It's such a — well — a footling thing to do! She was the only person in the room when my little blue vase was smashed. It is plain that she was the only one to do it. Why couldn't she say so, and tell me she was sorry — as she obviously was?"

"I'm afraid that the excuse of an accident has not been taken by Mrs Page," said Oona. "If the poor bairn has been slapped for every fault, I expect she got into the way of denying everything to save herself."

"Oh, she's been slapped all right," said Jean. "When I did get the truth out of her about the vase, the only thing she would say was 'Don't whip me, Auntie Jean! Please don't whip me this time!' It made me feel sick! I told her that we didn't whip people here unless they were cruel to anything weaker than themselves. I don't approve of it, anyway."

"I agree," said Oona. "I think there are far better ways of managing children. Deprive them of some pleasure, or their pocket money, or some dainty. Put a child to bed for temper — ten to one, it is tired or poorly, and is the better for an hour or two's rest — but corporal punishment should be resorted to in the final case. As for Kirsty, I don't see that we can do much beyond being patient with her."

Mr Benson nodded. "Patience is the only thing in a case of this kind. I think — "

But what he thought, they never knew, for at that moment there was a bumping sound followed by several crashes and wild yells as though someone was being murdered. The four people in the drawing room rose with one accord and dashed to the rescue. The shrieks came from a spare bedroom, into which everyone — including Morag and Moti — rushed, and there, they found a sight which caused Jean and Mollie to collapse on the nearest chairs in fits of laughter.

On the bed, tangled up in the clothes, was a weird and dishevelled object with painted face and wildly glaring eyes who, on examination, proved to be Allison. A pile of chairs surmounted by a forlorn-looking towel-rail was at the foot of the bed, and mixed up in it was Kirsty, airily attired in a couple of bath towels. A clean sheet was draped over the collection of furniture, one end of it being attached to the luckless towel-rail. Several bundles of firewood adorned the bed, and there was more on the floor. Jean's hockey-stick and tennis racquet were tied to the posts at the head of the bed, and sundry artificial flowers, reft from goodness knows where, were twined through the bed rails. Allison, when freed from her wrappings, was found to be as lightly attired as Kirsty, for she wore only her combinations and a wreath of ivy taken from an old hat of Jean's. Both children were bare of arms and legs, and both looked as if they had been mixed up in several violent earthquakes.

Oona's first care — Jean was speechless with laughter — was to snatch up something to wrap the pair in, while Morag stalked forward to the mess at the foot of the bed with a horrified exclamation of "Ma best sheets. Wull ye be lukin at that, Miss Jean! Eh, ye bad bad bairns! Ye deserve a gude skelpin' baith the pair o' ye!"

"What on earth were you doing?" asked Jean when the pair had been made decent once more.

Kirsty shrank away from her with a scared look in her eyes. Allison, who had nothing to fear and knew it, flung herself on her aunt, exclaiming soothingly, "Oh, Auntie Jean, it was such a nice Sunday game! All out of the Bible!"

"Did you ever hear the like?" gasped Morag who, of course, was present at the trial. "Ye bad lassies!

'Tis fair blasphemous ye are!"

"We aren't," cried Allison. "I don't know what it means, but we aren't, Morag! Kirsty was Solomon going to Hiram, King of Tyre for cedarwood, and I was him! Only the nasty old ship broke up," she added mournfully, "and then I got twisted in the sails, and Kirsty was in a mess."

"And who suggested this beautiful game?" demanded Jean, briskly.

There was a silence. Then Kirsty broke into a howl. "It — it wasn't m-me!" she wailed. "I didn't think of it! It was Allie!"

Allison looked at her sister in blank amazement. "Why, Kirsty — " she began.

Jean hushed her. "Be quiet, Allison. Oona, take her away, will you? Kirsty, come to me, child!"

Kirsty came, but she flinched when Jean stretched out a hand to draw her closer in a manner that showed what she expected her portion to be. Jean lifted the child to her lap, giving Mollie a look that made that young woman grab her fiancé, and hustle him off.

"Why are you so afraid?" asked Jean, when she was alone with the child.

"I thought you would slap me," sobbed Kirsty. "Aunt Gladys does, and she has such hard hands, and it hurts so!"

Jean produced a handkerchief. "Dry your eyes and stop crying. You need not be afraid of that kind of punishment here unless you hurt anything weaker than yourself on purpose. We don't punish little girls that way at Storms."

Kirsty sat up, and turned a face of blank amazement on the girl. "Not really?" she gasped.

"No," said Jean decidedly. "If you are naughty, you will be punished, of course. But not that way."

Kirsty thought this out. Jean waited; then she

added, "Try to tell the truth, Kirsty. It pays in the end."

"Are — are you sure you won't hit me?" asked Kirsty hesitatingly.

"Certain."

"Auntie Oona?"

"Nor she, either. Promise, Kirsty!"

"I will, then." Kirsty bestowed a hug on Jean.

"That's right. Now go and get your story-book, and come down to the drawing room till bedtime."

Kirsty did as she was told, and when she came down with Jean, she brought a beaming face with her. The two little girls spent a happy evening, and went off to bed at peace with everyone.

For some days after that, everything went well, and Kirsty really seemed to be trying to overcome her fault. Then there came a dreadful day when everything went wrong.

It began with Jean waking up with a nasty, grumbling toothache. Her face was a little swollen at breakfast, and Oona counselled a visit to the dentist before it got any worse. Jean refused, however. She had a healthy horror of her dentist and all his works, and, on the occasion of her last visit there — to have a wisdom tooth extracted — had suffered so much, that she had vowed not to go near him again except in the direst need.

"I haven't an appointment," she said.

Oona offered to ring him up and make one for her, but she refused.

"Your face looks so funny, Auntie Jean," said Allison at this point. "It's all on one side."

"Go on with your breakfast, and don't make personal remarks!" said Jean tartly.

Allison obeyed, but Morag, who came in with the marmalade just then, proceeded to add fuel to the flames by remarking, "Tooth-ache, Miss Jean? Ye'll be needin' to be awa' tae the dentist."

"Mind your own business!" retorted Jean, who was in a bad temper between pain and an uneasy conscience.

"Ye've got up the wrang side o' yer bed, I doot," said Morag imperturbably. She saw no reason why she should submit to Jean's rudeness.

For reply, Jean got up from the table and marched out of the room, slamming the door behind her. She did not do it so quickly, however, that she did not overhear Kirsty giggle as she went, and her temper was by no means improved by the sound. She went into the Den where a sulky fire was burning and raked at it with such vehemence that she put it out. Oona, coming in twenty minutes later, found her huddled up in an armchair, wearing a look of martyrdom that made her aunt long to smack her.

"You had better go back to the dining-room, Jean," she said quietly. "The table is cleared and Moti has the children, so you won't be disturbed, and you ought not to stay here with toothache."

"I'd rather stay here," said Jean sulkily.

Oona opened the window, and gently repeated her suggestion. Seeing no help for it, Jean marched herself to the dining-room, where a blazing fire helped to relieve her woes a little.

Miss McCleod put in an appearance a little later with a cup of hot coffee and made her drink it. Then she arranged cushions, so that Jean could rest the burning cheek against them, and left her alone to try to sleep. Jean spent a miserable morning, with her face becoming more and more puffed out, while the swelling did little to relieve the pain. She ate no luncheon, however.

"Why not go to bed?" suggested Oona.

"I'm not ill," was the brief reply.

"Indeed, Jean, I think you are. You certainly are.

You certainly aren't well. Come, dear, let me run upstairs and light your fire, and Morag shall fill the hot water bottle for you. You will be far more comfortable in bed than you are like this."

Jean's nerves and aching face yearned for the peace and comfort of bed, but she had a strain of obstinacy in her, and she refused it. Seeing she was determined, Oona gave it up, and after luncheon, dismissed the children to get their toys, since they must play in the Den as the nursery was being turned out. Jean sat down in her armchair, and tried to amuse herself with a book. Oona sat down with some sewing, and there was peace for a while. Then some imp inspired Kirsty to suggest that they should build a Tower of Babel with their bricks, and, just as it was finished, an incautious movement of Allison's brought it down with a crash that made Jean and Oona jump, and set the tooth aching worse than ever.

Allison burst into a roar. Some of the bricks in falling had struck her. Kirsty, who was annoyed at the destruction of their beautiful tower, slapped her, and Allison yelled the harder. Oona settled things by putting Kirsty outside the door, and bidding Allison remember that she was too big to cry like that. Allie relapsed into injured silence, and Jean hunched herself over the fire with a resigned manner that made her aunt yearn to box her ears.

The silence lasted for ten minutes, and was broken by another crash, this time of breaking china. Jean sprang to her feet, stalked to the door and flung it open. There stood Kirsty, a scared look on her face, and, on the floor, in several pieces, was one of Jean's much- prized rosebowls, swimming in a puddle of water, while jonquils lay round among the debris.

"Kirsty, what were you doing with that bowl?"

demanded Jean in no measured accents.

Alas for Kirsty! She had never seen her aunt like this, and the unwonted spectacle frightened her.

"I never touched it — it fell itself!" she said nervously.

"Christina, how dare you tell me such a lie? Answer me at once! What were you doing? Haven't I told you and Allison that you are not to touch the vases and bowls? What do you mean by disobeying me in this fashion?"

Thoroughly demoralised, Kirsty burst into tears, and stuck to it that she hadn't laid a finger on the bowl — it had fallen itself. A fresh twinge of toothache helped to blind Jean to the fact that the child's lack of truth was largely her own fault on this occasion and she shook her.

"You wicked child! I wonder you aren't ashamed of yourself! I won't allow you to associate with Allison as long as you tell such awful untruths! Go to bed, and stay there until you are prepared to tell me the truth!"

Kirsty fled, crying bitterly, and Jean returned to the room, looking like a thunder-cloud personified. Morag brought in the tea ten minutes later, and laid the table with indescribable sniffs all the time. Jean, whose head was aching in sympathy with her tooth by this time, ate nothing, but when Oona again suggested retreat to bed with a hot water bottle she received such a snub, that she left the girl alone for the rest of the meal, and Jean found herself in Coventry. After tea, Miss McCleod took Allison off to the nursery and went to see Kirsty. She found that young lady in her right mind, but very subdued, and soon coaxed the truth out of her, and got her promise that Jean should be told the next morning. Then she returned to the Den, to find that Jean had gone off to her room after all.

Morag had to be soothed next, and a nice piece of work Oona had of it! The old woman was decidedly on her dignity, and vowed she wasn't going to have doors slammed at her, nor a bairn like Miss Jean talking at her that way, either! After talking herself nearly hoarse, Oona got Morag to admit that if Jean had not been in pain she would not have behaved so badly.

"Though, mind ye, Miss Oona," said Morag. "I'm no sayin' I wis wrong. Gin Miss Jean had been a sensible lassie she wad ha'e gone to the dentist and had yon tooth pu'ed oot!"

Oona agreed with this in her secret heart, though she was not going to say so to Morag, so she left the kitchen and went up to Jean's room where the patient, easier now that she was safely in bed, listened to what her aunt had to say half-sheepishly.

"I didn't mean to scare the kid into lies," she admitted. "It was the noise upset me. It went through my tooth like a red-hot knitting needle."

"I have made an appointment for you with Mr Tomlinson for to-morrow afternoon," said Oona calmly, "and Jean! In the morning just accept Kirsty's apology and say no more about it. She is very sorry for everything, and remember, if you had not lost your temper with her, she would probably have told you the truth at once."

Jean's temper was over. "Poor lassie!" she said. "It was more my fault than hers this time. I've given you all the benefit to-day, I'm afraid. I'm awfully sorry, Oona."

Oona bent to give her the kiss of peace before she said, "Never mind now. Go to sleep, and you will probably feel all right in the morning."

CHAPTER XXI

AN UNFORTUNATE ENCOUNTER

The next morning, peace was made, and Kirsty owned to having taken the bowl in her hands to admire it. Jean apologised for losing her temper — much to Kirsty's amazement, and all was well between them. After breakfast, Jean went off upstairs to get through her duties for the day, and twelve o'clock found her in the train for Noviam. Her appointment was for three, but there was shopping to be done for the children and Oona, so Jean had lunch in a pretty café, and then went to buy stockings and frocks for the two little girls, and handkerchiefs for her aunt. Half-past-three found her outside Mr Tomlinson's door, the troublesome tooth well and truly filled, and prevented from giving any further trouble. She still had one or two commissions to execute for Oona, so she finished them in leisurely fashion, and then had tea before she strolled down to the station, pausing en route to buy a copy of a new novel she saw in a shop window. It was that pause that brought about all that happened next, for it made her just too late to catch the train she had intended, and she had to wait for the next. When it came, she settled herself in the corner of a first-class carriage, and opened her book.

Just as the train began to move, she heard the sound of flying feet, the door of her compartment was jerked open, and a gentleman dived in, assisted by a porter, who slammed the door. Jean looked up, and was nearly petrified to behold Dr Errington putting his bag on the rack. Just as she raised her eyes, he turned and saw her, and his face changed.

"Good afternoon, Miss McCleod," he said, coldly.

"Good afternoon," she replied, in even colder accents.

There was an awkward pause while he sat down, then Jean returned to her book, reflecting ruefully that this was an express train, and that neither would be able to change carriages as the first stop was Aulmbermouth.

"Oh, hang!" she thought viciously. "What a horrid situation! I suppose we shall sit here like a pair of icebergs all the time. Why on earth did I bother about buying the book? If I hadn't, I should have caught the last train and all this would have been avoided."

The doctor's thoughts were running on much the same lines. "What ghastly luck!" he thought.

Jean tried to read her book, but it was no use. She went over and over the first paragraph, and was no wiser when she had read it for the third time than when she had begun it. She shut the book, and took to gazing out of the window. The doctor was doing the same thing on his side of the compartment, for he had been so late for the train that he had had no time to buy an evening paper as he had intended. They sat like this in blank silence for ten minutes; then Jean's sense of humour came to her undoing.

"How priceless we must look!" she thought, her lips twitching. "Anyone could see that we know each other, and here we are, sitting like two stuffed fishes!"

She glanced across at her fellow-passenger to find that he was looking at her. Both looked away at once, but the girl's self-control was rapidly deserting her. Presently, she stole another peep at him. He was sitting staring straight ahead, his lips compressed, his brow drawn together in a scowl.

As a small child, Jean had had a bad habit of copying the expression of anyone to whom she sat opposite. At this moment, the old habit reasserted itself, and the doctor, glancing her way, was stunned to see her face twist itself into a frown which he easily recognised as an imitation of his own. The disgusted look that crossed his face as he grasped this was too much for Jean, and she burst into shrieks of semi-hysterical laughter which only redoubled themselves as his disgust grew.

"You are amused!" he said at length, in tones calculated to subdue the most daring.

Jean made a valiant effort to pull herself together, and after nearly biting her tongue off, she succeeded in controlling herself.

"I—I beg your pardon," she faltered. "It—it—is—so—funny!"

"May I inquire what it is that strikes you as 'funny' about the situation?" he demanded bitingly.

"You—me—us!" stammered Jean, losing her head completely.

"Indeed? Permit me to congratulate you on your sense of humour!" he retorted. "I can see nothing 'funny' as you call it about it!"

"N—no?" gasped Jean.

"No! And that you should do so, does not commend you to me!"

Jean began to be angry. She sat up, and tucked some loose hair under her hat. "I regret that I cannot return the compliment on my sense of humour," she said. "I can only commiserate with you on your obvious lack of it."

Now the doctor prided himself on his ability to see a joke, so Jean's remark was the one best calculated to rouse him. Never an easy tempered man, he was tired and over-worked, and not fit to meet the girl at the moment. Accordingly, he, too, lost his head, and answered as he was later ashamed to remember.

"Doubtless Miss McCleod has a poor opinion of my sense of anything!"

"May I ask what you mean by that?"

"Surely you must remember that there was a time — not so long ago — when I exhibited my folly to you pretty freely. May I ask if that memory has occasioned you as much amusement as, apparently, my personal appearance does?"

Jean was puzzled, for she had no idea what he meant. She was furious also. How dare he speak to her in that tone? She raised her eyebrows, and drawled in her most insolent voice, "I'm afraid I've no special memories of you. You flatter yourself too highly."

Her tones flicked the doctor on the raw. "So much the better for me," he said, his almost ungovernable passion mounting in his voice as he spoke. "I am glad to hear it!"

Jean bowed. There was a painful silence: then he spoke again.

"After this, I am thankful to know that I saw you in your true colours before making an abject fool of myself to you."

"Then what do you call your present exhibition?" queried Jean, who was certainly possessed of a devil just then.

He nearly choked, and he sent an agonised glance at the station through which they were whirling.

"I regret," he stammered at last, "that I ever met you!"

"Oh, don't say that!" said Jean in gently ironic tones. "Think how much you would have missed this afternoon! It must be a great relief to you to cast off the outward seeming of a gentleman occasionally! — To have such a good excuse as this — "

"Better be a brute than a heartless flirt — as you

are!" he interrupted her, madly.

Jean sprang to her feet. He rose to his. Man and woman, they stood there, rage gleaming in their faces. She was nearly as tall as he, and her eyes were almost on a level with his. He almost shrank, appalled at the fury of their green depths. And he was as much startled by the devil she had aroused in him.

"You cad!" she said at length, in low tones of concentrated anger. "I didn't think even you could sink to such depths! Thank heaven, I have learnt what you are!"

He was about to utter the final words that would have ended everything for them. Then something restrained him. With a short laugh he sat down.

"This conversation had better cease," he said gratingly.

Jean sank back into her seat. She was still trembling with passion, and she dared not trust her voice. Picking up her book, she read it industriously for the rest of the way — upside down! The doctor sat buried in his thoughts. At Aulmbermouth, he opened the door for her, and waited till she had passed the barrier before he followed her. Then he strode off home at such a rate that he nearly knocked down Mrs Taylor, whom he chanced to encounter on the way. He had no idea that he had done so. He strode on, and Mrs Taylor, recovering her equilibrium, stared curiously after him. Then she went home to spread a new scandal — a last one — about the new doctor whom she had met, and he had been so drunk that he had nearly knocked her over!

As for Jean, she took a taxi to Storms, for she felt quite unable to walk even the short distance to the trams. The children had gone to bed, so there was only Oona to exclaim at her white face, for Morag was out at the prayer-meeting at her particular tabernacle. Oona was startled, and full of commiseration for what she must have undergone at the dentist's. "I wish I had come with you," she lamented, as she took the girl upstairs to bed. "Come along, and get to bed. I'll bring you some hot milk, and then I hope you will soon feel all right! My poor Jean!"

Jean let her have her way. At least this was better than Oona knowing what was the real cause of the trouble. She submitted meekly to being put to bed, and given hot milk which she loathed. When Oona had made up the fire, and seen that she had everything she was likely to need that night, Jean turned over and pretended to fall asleep. Oona was deceived and stole out as noiselessly as possible.

But when the last sounds of the household had died away, Jean turned her face to the pillow, and wept bitterly. Everything was at an end now. Nothing could wipe out what had been said to-day, and she had killed her own happiness. Long after Oona had fallen asleep, Jean sobbed against her pillow. Finally, when the grey dawn was stealing in at the windows, she made an effort, and pulled herself together, and got up to deposit her soaked handkerchief in the linen basket, to sponge her face, for she was determined that her aunt should never know of this, and to cool her hot head against the glass of the window. Then, once again her unconquerable gift of laughter came to her aid.

"What a pair of idiots we must have looked!" she thought. "It's as well no one saw us!"

It was well Jean could manage a laugh; there were days of heart-sickness before her.

The next morning, when Jean awoke after a short uneasy slumber, the sun was shining and the sea was sparkling and dancing gaily. She felt as if it ought to have been a grey day to match the greyness of her outlook on life. She had yet to learn that old Dame Nature pays no heed to our troubles. From the next room came the sound of Allison's laughter as Moti dressed her, and on the windowsill a saucy robin perched and whistled merrily. She got out of bed, and went over to the dressing-table. From the mirror, a pale face with heavily-shadowed eyes looked back at her mournfully. She studied it with interest for a moment. Then she flung back the silky, untidy hair from her eyes.

"It's no use, Jean," she said. "You've made a fool of yourself, and lost the best chance of happiness through your own fault. It's up to you to keep your troubles to yourself. Don't whine, my girl!"

With this bit of bracing advice, she turned away and made for the bathroom. Half an hour later she was downstairs, racing the little girls through the garden as if she hadn't a care in the world. The children thought her extra jolly that morning, and told her so. Jean did not worry, so long as no one knew what she was feeling.

"I'm like a sick animal," she thought with dreary humour. "I want to creep away into the darkness and lick my wounds."

She took the children back to the house and was the merriest of the merry during breakfast. No one noticed that, in spite of all her nonsense, she was eating next to nothing.

Allison was seized with a sudden dislike of her porridge, and the subsequent battle between her and Oona took Miss McCleod's attention off her niece. After breakfast, the usual duties had to be gone through, and, since Oona was called away to a newly-made widow, whose man had gone down in the grim North Sea overnight, there were the children's lessons to superintend. Choking back her

longing to get away somewhere and break her heart
in peace, Jean sat and heard them read, and helped
them with sums and writing.

When the afternoon came, she felt she could stand
it no more. Calling to Oona that she was going for a
walk, she hastily effected her escape, and was soon
flying over the sands. The sun had vanished at
noon, and there was a grey sky overhead. A low
moaning of the wind told her that a storm was
coming up, and the sea was uneasy. Of all these
signs, however, she took little notice, as she sped
over the firm sand, obsessed by the feeling that only
in rapid movement could she get any relief.

Luckily, the beach was deserted, or people might
have taken her for an escaped lunatic. As it was, the
only living thing in sight was a mongrel dog, who
romped clumsily alongside of her, and yelped with
joy. She paid no heed to him at first, but his frantic
pleasure roused her, and she paused in her breathless flight to gentle him. As soon as she stopped he
slunk aside with a movement that told what he
expected, and Jean, tender-hearted where all
animals were concerned, stood, self-forgetful, for the
first time that day. "Poor old man," she said. "Come
along, good dog!"

He eyed her distrustfully from a distance. He was
a young dog, but his short life had taught him to be
suspicious of all human things that stood still to
take any notice of him. The girl dropped to her
knees, and held out her hands. "Come, then, old
man."

He sidled a little nearer. The sweet voice seemed
friendly enough, and, at least, she could not kick
him in her present attitude. When he was just out of
her reach, he stopped looking at her timidly, and
wagging a tentative tail. She made no effort to grab
at him, well aware that this would frighten him

sooner than anything else. Still in her kneeling position, she spoke to him soothingly, noting the while how thin he was, and the marks of sores on him.

"Poor old man! What have they been doing to you? Are you afraid of me, old fellow? Come and make friends with me, doggy!"

She crept within touch, and she laid a gentle hand upon his yellow head. The next moment he was fawning on her, licking at her with his long, red tongue, and assuring her as best he could, that he was her friend for life. A sudden splash of rain on her face awoke Jean to the fact that the storm was near at hand, and she was a good two miles from home, with little shelter anywhere, for at this point of the coastline the cliffs rise almost precipitously from the shore. She rose to her feet and looked round. The sky was black with clouds, and the waves were lashing themselves to fury. She could not stay where she was, so she decided to race home along the beach. Unfortunately, she had tired herself by her former flight, and she soon found that her knees were beginning to give from sheer weariness, and she could scarcely keep her feet. Her run became a stumble in the sand, and then a walk; and all the time the rain was driving in from the sea. She would have to climb the cliff, for the east wind was driving the sea as well as the rain, and she knew that she could not get round the point that jutted out to form the small bay where she was.

She must climb the cliff path, and it was more than a hundred yards back. She turned and trudged back to the place where it began, fighting against the wind, which came swooping down on her like a living thing. From the way things were working up, she judged that at high tide the beach would be covered. She reached the bottom of the path and began the climb upwards. It was not an easy one at any time, for it was little more than a goat track, but to-day, with the wind and the rain, and her own weariness, she was ready to sit down and cry from sheer fatigue more than once. Luckily, she kept her head, and did nothing of the kind. She struggled on till she was at the top, the dog following her with a meekness that told her he adopted her for a mistress, whatever she might think on the subject. Having ended the climb, she felt that she could not go a step further, and sank down on the soaking grass, her heart pounding in her ears as she lay. The sound of an approaching car forced her to her feet, and she stumbled across the road, with some idea of begging a lift to Hasnett. Then, as she saw and recognised the doctor's little Morris-Cowley, she drew back, flushing. He saw her, of course, and even in the present state of their relations with each other, he could not ignore her. He pulled up a few yards ahead of her, and called to her as she drew level, "Miss McCleod, what are you doing out in all this rain? May I give you a lift to Storms?"

There was no defence for Jean in what followed. As she owned later, she behaved like a spoilt child of six. Instead of thanking him, she merely said, "No".

The corners of his mouth went up in an unpleasant smile. "In fact you prefer to court certain pneumonia to being indebted to me for anything?" he drawled. "I regret I cannot see it in that light. Will you please get in at once!"

"I am going to walk," said Jean stubbornly; and began to do so.

Like a flash, he was out of the car, and at her side.

"Pardon me, Miss McCleod, but you are going to do nothing of the sort. You are going to get in beside me, and let me drive you home as quickly as possible. You will be ill if you stay in those wet things much longer!"

"That is my concern," said Jean icily.

"Oh, pardon me, it is surely your aunt's as well," he said suavely. "Perhaps it may make it easier for you if I tell you that I should do the same for an old fishwife whom I had met under like circumstances."

For reply Jean hastened her steps. It had no effect. He was with her in a moment, and it was obvious from his face that he was very angry.

"Will you come?" he said in repressed tones. "Or must I carry you?"

That turned the scale as he had known it would. Without a word, she swung round and retraced her steps to his car. She got in, disdaining any assistance from him, and the long-legged cur followed her. She lifted him into her lap, and the doctor, without a word, got into the driver's seat. The run lasted about fifteen minutes and none spoke. The dog was the only contented member of the party. He felt himself in Paradise already, and was inclined to doubt his luck.

At the door in the Storms' wall, the doctor drew up, and Jean got out. She was boiling by this time, and her rage gave an added poison to the verbal shafts she flung at him. "I hope you feel like an Ethel Dell 'strong, silent' hero! You have certainly acted like one — even to the point of forgetting the courtesy every lady expects to receive from a man who has any pretensions to being a gentleman."

With this, she stalked off, her dignity somewhat marred by the excited leapings of the dog. As for the doctor, that final taunt of hers sent the angry blood leaping to his face and he drove to Aulmbermouth at a speed that narrowly escaped bringing him before the magistrates. Once Jean was in the house, she raced up to her room, and locked the doors. She was in no mind to be interrupted by anyone. She had sufficient sense to get out of her wet things, and go and have a hot bath. An illness would not help matters in the least. When she was warm and dry once more, she turned her attention to the dog who had watched her proceedings from beneath the dressing-table.

"I don't know whose dog you were," she said, "but you are mine now. Come along downstairs, and let's break the news to the family."

She marched down to the Den, the yellow animal following her closely. Oona was there with the children, and they all gasped when they saw her escort.

"Oona," she said, "I've adopted this dog."

"Good heavens!" gasped Oona.

"What's his name, Auntie?" demanded Kirsty, who, with Allison, was hugging him.

"Waif," said Jean. "Oona, he's not a beauty, I know, but he seems faithful, and we do need a dog."

"You must settle it with Morag," said Oona. "So far as I am concerned you may keep him."

For reply Jean marched off to the kitchen, Waif beside her, and informed a startled and indignant Morag that he was to make his home at Storms.

Morag had plenty to say. The unfortunate part — for her — was that she was not allowed to say it. She had barely got out her first indignant sentence, before Jean's voice, cool and cutting, checked her.

"That will do, Morag. Waif stays at Storms, and I will have no further trouble about it. Is that clearly understood?"

Morag muttered something to the effect that it was. She could not make out Miss Jean these days, but it is certain that she had never so admired the girl before. Oona, for all her quiet dignity, would never have spoken like this. Morag would not have allowed it. But Miss Jean was a stronger character, and the old woman was forced to recognise it. Not that she was reconciled to the new member of the family for long enough. She spoke of him bitterly as "yon tyke", and swept him out of her kitchen with the nearest broom whenever he was misguided enough to poke his nose round the door. But she made no attempt to turn him adrift.

Having settled the question of Waif's right to a home at Storms, Jean went back to the others, and passed a peaceful evening. She caught no cold, as she richly deserved for her adventure — indeed she seemed better than she had been before. Mollie vowed she had never known her friend to be so brilliant, so gay as during the succeeding weeks. Then April brought a change to Storms. Mrs Page wrote to say that Kirsty had been away long enough, and must return at the end of the week. Looking at the child's blooming cheeks, and her healthy plumpness, Jean was fain to admit that she was right. So Kirsty, amid many tears, went south again, having been promised that, by hook or crook, she should be at Storms for "Auntie Mollie's" wedding. She also went with a new trunk filled with pretty clothes, and the assurance that hereafter, she should be clothed as became her position. Oona had written to Alastair's solicitors, and one of the firm had travelled to Fareham to interview Mr and Mrs Page, and warn them that the money left Kirsty by her step-father must be used as he had directed. Kirsty was to be properly dressed, and she was to be taken away from the private school where she was learning nothing, and sent to a good boarding-school next term.

Allie missed her horribly, and was so dull, she was driven to the companionship of "the lass". This was not without results which were to have far-reaching consequence in her aunt's life. Bessie was well-primed with stories of the coast, for her father and two brothers were all fishermen, and she had lived all her life in the district. Among other things, she told the small girl of the smuggler's cave that existed somewhere between Hasnett and Blyton Sands. Allison was delighted with her stories, and finally extracted from the little maid a promise that they should go to see the smuggler's cave as soon as possible. It was only possible to see it at low tide, so they had to wait a week. Then, one fine day at the end of April, Bessie fulfilled her promise, and the little girl came home with bubbling tales of "a big hole in the cliff" and "seaweed all round, ever so high up". Jean paid little heed to it. She was working hard, trying to work off her misery. She kept her secret carefully, but Mollie and Oona both realised that something had happened between her and the doctor, though none knew what it was.

As for the doctor, he never came near any of them at Storms. There was no need, for one thing. Allison was much stronger, and was beginning to lose the fragile look that had worried those in charge of her all the winter. She was going to school in September, and Moti was going back to her own country before then. Besides this, none had ever seen him at classes since Christmas. Mollie, busy with her own affairs, had little time to think of it, though she felt vaguely worried. As for Oona, she had long ago learned the art of leaving other people to mind their own business, and if she was anxious at Jean's unusual loss of flesh, she said nothing.

So matters went from day to day, and when the summer term was drawing to a close, and Mollie was looking forward to her wedding day, it seemed as if they would continue this way for ever. They did not; but much was to come before that time.

CHAPTER XXII

A FOLK DANCE WEDDING

"Now for the veil, and then the bride is ready."
Jean McCleod, in soft white georgette, with
touches of green bringing out the delicate colour in
her face, lifted the lacy mass of the veil and
proceeded to arrange it on Mollie's head.

"Hold up your head, Moll; I can't see how this
goes. Through here? Good! Wait a minute and let me
drape the folds. There; now look at yourself!"

Mollie Stewart turned to the long mirror on the
wall, and looked at the reflection of herself in soft
ivory satin, with long lace veil frosting her dark
hair, and the warm flush that happiness, excitement, and shyness combined had brought to her
face. It was a lovely little bride that stood there,
while Jean put the finishing touches to the dainty
dress.

"There's Oona calling," said the bride suddenly.

Jean nodded, caught up her gloves, and set her
hat straight. Then she took the bride in her arms.
"Kiss me, Moll. Mollie Stewart will never do so
again!"

"Mollie Benson will, though!"

Their lips met, and then Jean drew back. "Well,
after that piece of sentimentality, I think I'd better
go," she said. "Bless you, Moll!"

She ran hastily out of the room, and Mollie was
left alone. There was the sound of the children's
voices; then the shutting of the door, and the sound
of taxi-wheels on the drive. Mollie put on her gloves,
and took up her bouquet of old-fashioned lilies and

roses. She slowly left the room, and went down to the drawing room, where her Aunt Meg's husband awaited her. He was a pompous little man, whom Mollie disliked, but he was the only male relative she had in England, so it had been decided that he must give her away. Oona had invited the pair of them for three days, and he had spent all the previous day fulminating against "the absurd arrangements you have been making for your wedding!"

He looked appraisingly at her as she entered, and as his eyes fell on her unconventional cluster of flowers, his brows met in a decided frown.

"My dear Mary. Surely you might have had a proper bouquet!"

"I might," said Mollie tranquilly, "but I prefer these dear things, which I gathered myself this morning, with the dew on them."

"But it looks so — er — well — poverty-stricken," he complained.

"Rats!" said Mollie briefly. "Come along; it's time we were going. I don't want to be late."

She turned out of the room, and Uncle James followed her, grunting in a dissatisfied way, and sat down beside her in the car.

It was a glorious day — real bride's weather, as Jean had proclaimed at six that morning when she had stuck a ruffled black head out of her window to sniff the early morning incense of summer flowers. The sun shone brightly, and the sea lay blue and sparkling below; at their doors, the fisher-folk gathered to watch the car as it flashed past with the white-robed bride in it. Mollie looked at them, smiling as she passed. She knew from Oona how hard their lives were, and she knew how they would have liked to see her in her bridal finery. She decided that when she and Charlie came back from church, the car should be stopped, and she would get out and let them examine her daintiness.

Ten minutes later they were at St Simon's, and Uncle James handed her out with great empressement. She took his arm, and they were in the church porch, where Jean and the children were awaiting them: Jean, lovely with the loveliness of a flower; the little girls wild with excitement and clutching their nosegays of roses feverishly.

The organ pealed forth, and, to the strains of "Haste to the Wedding," Mollie passed up the aisle on the arms of an Uncle James, who was nearly stiff with horror at the idea of a dance being played in church.

They reached the chancel steps, and Mollie was aware of her tall bridegroom standing beside her. On his right hand stood the doctor, who had been forced into acting best man. The service was a very happy one. They sang two hymns — the old "Hierusalem" of Elizabethan times, and Herrick's lovely words,

"I sing of Brooks, of Blossomes, Birds and Flowers." The organist had set it to an old canon, and it went well.

The vows were exchanged; the ring was slipped on to Mollie's finger; the final blessing was uttered, and they were going into the vestry to sign the register. Then the bride and bridegroom passed down the aisle, and out into a blaze of glorious sunshine, where small children were gathering to make the usual Northumbrian demand, "Hoy oot!" in the hopes that the happy man might have some spare halfpence to cast forth as largesse. Finally, they drove away, and through Hasnett, where Mollie got out of the car for long enough to let the women see her.

It is to be feared that the chauffeur exceeded the

speed limit in order to get them back to Storms before the rest of the party arrived there; but they did it, and when the bridesmaids, with the best man and the groomsman, arrived, they found the leading lady and gentleman already established beside the centre bed in the garden.

Gradually, the taxis and cars unloaded their burdens of well-dressed people at the Storms entrance, gradually, the garden filled up, and the buzz of gay chatter mingled with the murmur of the sea. Then the bride suddenly clapped her hands, cried, "Take your partner for 'Haste to the Wedding'!" and swept into line with her husband, while two violins and a 'cello, situated beside some laurel bushes, struck up the tune. They all danced after that. Those who did not know the dances relied on those who did, and a very merry time they had of it, till Mollie and Charlie led the way to the house, and tea. It was a hurried meal for the bride, for they had danced later than had been intended. At last Jean hurried her off, and the white-clad lady was exchanged for one in soft pinks. Jean took the slim hand in hers and looked at the lovely face under the rosy hat.

"May all your days be as gay as this," she said tenderly. "Even if your feet are not dancing, then may your heart!"

Mollie lifted to hers dark eyes full of happy tears. "Oh, Jean! And I hope and pray the day may come soon when I shall dance at your wedding! There's none will do it with a gladder heart than I!" They kissed, and then the bride ordered her friend off, to call the other unwed people into the hall, for she was going to fling her bouquet down in accordance with the old custom, to see who would be next to follow her into matrimony.

She came to the top of the stairs — a human rose

rather than a girl, her big cluster of garden flowers loosely held in her hand. For one moment, she looked down at the merry crowd gathered there, then she called, "Catch, someone!" and flung the flowers down.

As they fell, they parted, for Mollie had previously untied the bouquet. Pretty Miss Radley got the giant's share, at which everyone laughed appreciatively, for she had become engaged recently. Jean caught the red roses in the held-up skirt of her frock; and one sprig of white heather alighted on the doctor's shoulder.

Mollie sailed down the stairs smiling. "Two weddings," she remarked, as she joined her husband, "will arise out of this one."

"Auntie Mollie can't count," said Kirsty audibly at this point. "Three people caught the flowers!"

Oona suppressed her, but the three most concerned had heard, and one went white, while the other two coloured furiously.

There was no time, however, to think of it, for the car had come to the door, and the newly-wed pair were running the gauntlet of confetti, rose-petals, rice and — old shoes! Morag flung one of the latter with such accuracy, that it caught Mr Benson squarely in the stomach, and caused him to collapse on the step of the car with a startled grunt. However, no damage was done, and he was up again the next moment. A cheer arose, and, while several people suddenly struck up, "For they are jolly good fellows!" the chauffeur started her up, and they rolled away.

Mollie's wedding was over.

CHAPTER XXIII

It was arranged that Kirsty was to spend all her summer holidays at Storms. The Pages were going to the Channel Isles for their holidays, and had no desire to have a restless fidgety child with them. The McCleods were not going away till September, when Oona was going to old friends in Edinburgh, and Jean was to pay a series of visits to school friends. While they were absent Morag was going to have her idea of a perfect holiday, and clean the house from top to bottom. She would meet them on their return with a complacent smirk, and a house so appallingly neat that they would be almost scared to sit down in it at first. Not that that would last long. Jean was not born tidy, and Oona was not far behind her in that respect. Still, just at first it would be a trial. Then gradually they would slip back into the old ways, and Storms would become itself once more.

This was the arrangement to which they had come. Allison was to go with Oona, and see "Auld Reekie", and its many interesting spots. She was wildly excited about it all, and chattered away to Kirsty till that young woman was nearly green with envy.

"You do have nice times, Allie! I wish I was you!" she said wistfully.

Allison looked at her doubtfully. "Shall I ask Auntie Oona if you can come too?"

Kirsty shook her head. "It wouldn't be any use. Aunt Gladys would never hear of it. Why, King

Arthur used to live at Winchester, and she won't take me there, though you can see his castle, and the Table Round, and lots of things."

"She must be horrid," said Allison, with more candour than manners.

Kirsty sighed. "Well, I'm with you now, anyway, and she did let me come for Auntie Mollie's wedding."

"There's posty!" said Allison, forgetting the subject, and scrambling down from her perch on the low front wall, to race to meet him. Kirsty followed her, and the good-natured postman gave them the letters between them, asked them if they had seen a mermaid lately and then bade them "good-morning", and left them to carry the mail in to Oona. "I'll take the big fat one, and you can have the others," suggested Kirsty. Allison gave in willingly, and they ran to present the letters.

"Letters, Auntie," said Allie, dropping her handful on Jean's lap.

"And another big one," added Kirsty, offering it.

Jean took it, and looked at it thoughtfully. "From Jersey," she said. "Something from your aunt, Kirsty."

"From her? Oh, Auntie Jean!" Kirsty's voice rose in a wail of distress. "Oh, do you think she wants me to leave here?"

"Silly Kirsty! I don't expect it's anything of the kind," laughed Jean. "She's asked us to keep you all the holidays, you know, as they didn't want you in the Islands. I expect it's just to ask how the wedding went off, and if you are being a good girl." She sorted out the letters on her lap, and gave Allison two or three. "Take those to Auntie Oona, Allie, and then sit down, both of you."

They did as they were bidden, and breakfast went on quietly, till Jean announced that they were going to take lunch down to the sands at the foot of the cliffs, and stay there till tea time. Then the children were so excited that they could scarcely sit still to finish their meal, and they were sent off in order, as Jean said laughingly, to let their elders eat in peace and quiet.

Jean skimmed through most of her correspondence before she went to find the tent they were taking down. Mrs Page's letter she slipped into her pocket, being sure that it would be uninteresting. Then, led by the excited children, they left Storms, and descended by the narrow path to the shore, whence the receding tide was drifting out. The sand was already hot with the August sun, and by the time the tent was up, Jean declared that it was warm enough to bathe. They all went in, Jean climbing over the rocks, far out, to dive off them, and come up again with laughing face; Oona keeping closer in, with one eye on the two little girls, who scrambled about, and splashed each other, and had a splendid time of it. When they came out, Oona and Jean dried the two children, and dressed them, and then attended to their own toilets. After this, they had luncheon, brought down by Bessie, and when it was eaten, and the little girls were cuddling down for an hour's rest on which Oona insisted every afternoon, Kirsty remembered the letter, and asked about it.

"Did Aunt Gladys only say what you thought she would, Auntie Jean?"

"Mercy me!" exclaimed Jean. "I forgot all about it till you spoke."

"Have you had a letter from Mrs Page?" asked Oona.

"Yes, but I forgot all about it. I'll skim through it, and then you can see it."

Jean produced it from her pocket, tore it open,

and proceeded to "skim" it. When she had finished, she glanced at the two children, who were both drowsing comfortably.

"Oona, come with me and get some rosy seaweed, will you," she asked quietly. Knowing it to be an excuse, Oona rose at once.

"What is it, Jean?" she asked when they were out of earshot of the children.

"Sit down," said Jean. "I want to read you this."

They sat down, where they could still watch the two little girls if it were necessary, and Jean read aloud the letter.

" 'Dear Miss McCleod, — It is some time since I last wrote to you, but I have been so busy, lately, and there has been so much to see to, especially since our lawyer made such a fuss about Chrissie's school.' — That's one to us, Oona! — 'Letter-writing seems to get crowded out, and I have been able to attend to only the important' — nasty for us — 'correspondence. But I am sure you will understand. We are having a very pleasant time here. Jersey suits both of us, and though we are naturally disappointed that the additional expenses we have had lately with Chrissie had put our idea of going to Madeira for a holiday out of the question, still we are not doing so badly.

'While we have been here, we have met with some very nice colonial people from South Africa — perfect ladies and gentlemen, you understand. I am not one to mix myself up with everybody, and Mr Page is the same. We like these people very much, and what they have told us of their district interests us. In fact, we have been more than interested. Mr Page has become so keen on the idea that he has written to London for all details, and I think after reading this, you will not be surprised that we are going there ourselves as soon as possible. There

seems to be very little doing in England, and as we
have all the extra expense of the child, things have
been worse for us' — I like that! What about her
father's hundred a year, to say nothing of poor Lal's
two hundred! — 'and it seems better to leave the
country.

'Under the circumstances, you will realise that
Chrissie will be a greater burden than ever. She is
growing fast, and is not so very strong. I am not
sure that Africa will suit her. Also, it seems a pity
that she should be so completely parted from her
sister. Finally, as you have shown so much interest
in the financial side of her affairs, it struck me that
you would probably prefer to keep her in your own
hands altogether. That being the case, my husband
and I have made up our minds to renounce any
claims we may have on her, and make her over to
your guardianship. I feel sure you must have
expected this after your behaviour in the matter of
her schooling, and the small legacy left her by your
brother. I am not one to say much, but I feel it only
right to let you know that your treatment has hurt
me very much, and Mr Page, too. It looked as if you
thought we were trying to pocket the money.

'So it is all arranged. We shall sell everything, and
leave for Cape Town in early September. Under the
circumstances we think it would be as well for
Chrissie to stay where she is. I will send all her
things to you, as we shall have nowhere to put
them. Mr Page and I are leaving Jersey to-morrow,
and hope to get rid of the remainder of the lease of
our house almost at once.

'So, from now on, Chrissie will have to look to you
for all she requires. She has a little money from her
father, as I daresay you know. With what your
brother has left her she ought not to be a great
expense to you unless you bring her up to be extrav-

agant, and put silly notions into her head. But that will be your own affair.

'I hope you will punish her well if she tells you lies. I may say I have found her disgracefully deceitful and untruthful. She is also cowardly and sly. Where she gets it from, I cannot imagine. I am afraid her poor mother was a weak woman.' — Oona! I'm not going to read all this rot about poor Doris! The woman has no sense of decency! Of all the abominably insulting letters! And to drop the kid on us as though she were a bundle of old clothes! What a beast of a woman she must be!"

"Give it to me," said Oona, holding out her hand for the letter.

Jean passed it over, and Oona read the remainder in silence. Then she folded it up, and gave it back to its owner.

"Well?" demanded Jean.

"I have nothing to say. I am very glad Kirsty is not going back to the writer of that letter. She would have no chance of growing up a decent woman. It will be as well for Allison to have a sister, for then they will have to give and take at home. Kirsty will be no expense to us but for what we choose to give ourselves. Thanks in the main to Alastair, she has three hundred a year of her own, safely invested, so she will never come to want."

"Just as well the babes know nothing of this," said Jean, casting a glance to where they lay sound asleep. "I'm glad we are to have Kirsty. I've always felt we shouldn't have separated them."

Oona nodded. "And now what about rousing those children and moving our possessions? The tide is coming in, and we don't want to be overtaken."

Jean agreed, and they woke the two children, and then set to work to get the tent down.

"What about holidays?" asked Oona.

Jean glanced round to see where Kirsty and Allison were and finding they were climbing the path to Storms, carrying the luncheon basket between them, replied, "They can go to Mollie while we are away. You can't drop two children on the Frasers — it wouldn't be fair, and they can't come with me. I'll promise them both a trip to Edinburgh next Easter and they shall both go to the High this term. Mollie won't be bothered with them much in the daytime, for they will be there all the morning and afternoon."

They left it at that and later on in the day, Jean told Kirsty that she was to live at Storms for the future as the Pages were going to Africa and couldn't take her with them. Kirsty was overjoyed. "Oh, Auntie Jean — Auntie Jean! It doesn't seem possible it can be true!"

"It is true," said Jean, taking her on her knee. "We are very glad about it, all of us. Auntie Oona and I have always felt you belong to us and wanted you."

So Kirsty's cup of joy was full.

CHAPTER XXIV

THE ARRIVAL OF ANGELA

When life goes on quietly from day to day, there is not much to chronicle. Jean found that during the months that followed their undertaking the guardianship of Kirsty. The children went to school in the September, and, for the whole of the winter, their lives were made up of little happenings. There were no bad illnesses to worry over, for even Allison indulged in very few colds, and Kirsty bloomed in the bracing air of the North Sea coasts. Away from the fear of her aunt, she was turning into a nice child, and took care of Allison in the most motherly way. So the months passed, and spring came to give place to summer, and summer came with unusual heat and sunshine for this part of the world. The children spent all their time on the shore, and both were brown and rosy. Oona went off for a long visit to some of her mother's people, who lived in Shetland, and Jean decided that when the children's holiday came, they should go to the lakes for a holiday.

"I don't want to be away longer," she said to Mollie one June afternoon, when they sat discussing it in the garden of the old house in Percy Square. "For one thing, I don't like leaving Morag alone any longer. She's getting an old woman now, and if she isn't watched, she will insist on working herself to death. For another, I like to be near you as much as I can. Also, the children have done a good deal of travelling already for such youthful people, and I do want them to love their home."

"They do that all right," said Mollie, putting down her sewing, and getting to her feet.

"Where are you going?" demanded Jean. "Sit down again, Moll, and tell me what you want. You do far too much running about!"

"I was only going to tell Annie to get tea ready," said Mollie, meekly obeying her. "The children will be here presently — it's nearly four. You know, you and Charlie are simply absurd about me! I wonder you don't bottle me in spirits of wine, and put me under a glass shade!"

"You ought to be grateful to us!" retorted Jean, as she went towards the house. "You are nearly as much trouble to look after as Allie or Kirsty!"

When she came back, she found the Rev. Charles Benson, sitting on the arm of his wife's chair, whistling gaily.

"Hullo, Jean," he said. "Has Mollie told you the news?"

"No," said Jean.

"I thought you'd rather tell her yourself," explained Mollie.

"What is it?" demanded Jean. "You look very thrilled, both of you!"

"Oh, we are!" cried Mollie. "Guess what it is — Don't tell her yet, Charlie."

Jean leaned back in her chair, and crossed her ankles. "You might as well tell me, for I've not the slightest intention of trying to guess."

"Aggravating imp!" declared Mollie. "Tell her, then, old man!"

The Rev. Charles extracted a letter from his pocket, and tossed it over to Jean. "There you are! Read it, and tell us what you think of it."

Jean grabbed it, and eagerly devoured the contents. The next moment, she was careering over the lawn in a wild travesty of a morris jig.

"Cheers — cheers! I knew the Semples were going, but I never thought of anything so delightful as you and Mollie coming to Hasnett! The Bishop is a dear to think of you, and his character must be as nice as his face — and I've always said that, outside a stained glass window saint, I never saw anyone with such a beautiful face."

"Woa there, you crazy thing!" cried Charlie. "Sit down, Jean. Here's Annie coming with the tea-tray, and she'll think it's permanent insanity this time."

Jean sat down and fanned herself with her handkerchief.

"Ouf! I'm hot! It's topping news! Fancy having Mollie close at hand all the time!"

"It is nice, isn't it?" said Mollie eagerly. "And then the house is so old, and so pretty, and the garden is lovely."

"It's nice all round," declared Jean. "When will you move? You'll have to leave all the work to us, Mollie. We'll have to send you to Storms while Charlie and Oona and I do the moving. You mustn't try to do too much, you know!"

Mollie laughed, and the arrival of the children put an end to the conversation.

The year had made a big difference in both. Kirsty was once more rosy and plump. Her brown hair floated in curls over her shoulders, though in school it was tied back. She was slowly overcoming her dread of consequences, and learning to speak the truth on all occasions. Allie had lost her look of terrible fragility, and had lately begun to grow. She was not pretty, but she had a quaint elfin air about her that made people look at her a second time. This pair tore across the lawn, and flung themselves on Jean, screaming, "Auntie Jean — oh, Auntie Jean!"

"Well, what is it?" asked Jean, catching them in her arms. "Who's been killed?"

"Kirsty is in the third eleven at school!" shrieked Allison.

"Third Eleven?" asked Jean, puzzled.

"Well, Third Form Eleven," amended Kirsty. "Isn't it splendid, though? 'Cos I never thought I would be."

"Jolly good," said Mr. Benson. "How many are there in your form, Kirsty?"

"Thirty-one," said Kirsty, solemnly.

"Then it is very good. But I thought your bowling and fielding practice might just turn the scale. Well done, little girl!"

Tea, which Annie brought out at this point, was a very jolly meal, though Mollie refused to let them sit over it.

"No, it isn't fair to Annie. This is her night out, and she has developed a young man, lately, and I expect he'll be waiting for her. Take the cake back to the house, Kirsty, and put it away. You can carry the biscuits, Allie."

The children trotted off with their burdens, and Jean was about to follow them with some fruit dishes, when the gate opened, and Bessie came rushing in, waving an orange-coloured envelope at Jean.

Jean snatched it from her, and ripped it open, while the "lass", scarlet-faced and breathless, waited.

"What is it, Jean?" cried Mollie, as her friend's face suddenly grew white, "Oh, what is it, my dear?"

"Oona," said Jean, in a stunned voice. "She has had a bad accident — fallen on the rocks. I am to go at once!"

Mollie rose from her chair and pushed her friend forcibly into it. "Charlie, go and get the sal volatile. Then you had better get out the time-tables and look out the trains and boats. Bessie, go back to

Storms, and tell Morag that Miss Oona has had an accident, and Miss Jean has to go at once. Ask her to begin to pack for Miss Jean. Jean, don't look like that, dear. It will be all right, I know. Charlie will take you to Noviam, and see you into the Aberdeen train. The children will stay here, of course. Morag is too old to be bothered with them, and it will really be better while this hot weather continues, for getting into school."

Too stunned by the shock to think for herself, Jean fell in with these arrangements, and that night saw her leave Hasnett for many a long week. Oona was badly hurt. The spine had been damaged in the fall, and for some weeks it was feared that she would never walk again. When, at length, that dread was overcome, they moved her by easy stages to Storms, where they found Allison and Kirsty awaiting them with news that brought pink to Jean's white face and a light to her heavy eyes that had been missing for many a long day. Early that morning, Mollie's little daughter had arrived, greatly to the joy of all concerned.

"Uncle Charlie said that I was to tell you that he would come up this evening, Auntie Jean," said Kirsty. "He will tell you and Auntie Oona all about Angela."

"Angela — is that to be her name?" asked Oona with a smile from her couch.

"Yes — 'cos it's St Michael's and All Angels," said Allison.

True to his promise, Charlie Benson turned up after Evensong that evening, and after he had exchanged greetings and enquired about Oona, and learnt that the doctor hoped that in a year she would be all right again, he told them about the baby.

"And she is to be called Angela?" said Oona.

"Angela Jean," he replied with a smile. "Of course she must have her godmother's name."

"Oh!" Jean went pink. "How nice of you and Mollie!"

The next day she went into Aulmbermouth, and was allowed a tiny peep at Angela Jean, but it was another three days before they let her see Mollie.

"Only a short visit," said Nurse, as she admitted the girl. "And don't let her talk too much."

Jean promised, and then she was bending over the bed where Mollie, with the old stars in her dark eyes, lay smiling at her.

"Mollie Creina!" said Jean, bending to kiss her.

"Hullo, Jean! Oh, it is so nice to see you again. I wanted you ages ago, but they are so fussy! What do you think of baby?"

"She is a darling," said her godmother. "Thank you for the name, Moll."

"What else could she be called?" laughed Mollie.

Jean sat down, and took the baby. "Now you must lie still and let me tell you about Oona. You haven't heard yet, you know. No; you're not to say a word."

And for the rest of the visit she talked about Oona, and Mollie had, perforce, to listen in silence.

When nurse came to intimate that it was time Mrs Benson rested, Jean got up, laying the baby in her mother's arms. "Mollie, I'm awfully glad! You know that?"

Mollie smiled. "Of course! I've only one dream left unfulfilled now, Jean."

"Oh? What's that?" But Mollie would not tell her.

Jean went away, with a last kiss, and Nurse darkened the room, and laid Baby in her cot.

But when she was alone Mollie smiled to herself.

"When you and Kenneth Errington come to your senses, and I dance at your wedding, I shall be the happiest woman on earth, Jean, my dear!"

CHAPTER XXV

TROUBLE AND A RECONCILIATION

"**A**-ah! Ya-ah!" "O-o-o-h! Kirsty, you pig!" "Children! What is the matter with you now?" Jean flung down her pen and went into the hall where the two small girls were scowling at each other. A silence followed her question. Tale-telling was forbidden at Storms. Also, neither was very clear as to what really was the matter. Jean waited two minutes, then she said firmly, "I mean to know. Why are you crying, Kirsty?"

Kirsty stood on one leg like a contemplative young stork and then said, "It's so dull in the house and I want to go out!"

"Well, you can't! The rain is pouring down, and it's blowing a gale of wind into the bargain, so I'm afraid you must content yourselves indoors — at any rate for the present."

"Well, I want to go out," drawled Allison.

"I've already said you can't. Run away to the nursery and play there. If it clears up in time, I'll take you for a run before dinner. Now then — run off!"

They went with an ill-grace and Jean returned to the Den and Company Accounts, with which, since she was no mathematician, she was making heavy way.

She groaned as she sat down. "Why, oh why, did I never learn book-keeping at school! Oona, what happens when you are in debt to the extent of seven and fivepence and yet seem to have one and a halfpenny in hand?"

Oona smiled. "You begin again."

"I thought so! Well, here goes!"

She began again, and had just finished, when Morag came in to say that Miss Farrar was enquiring for her, and that she had put her in the drawing room.

"Farrar! Oh, what fun! She must have called to tell us about Radley's wedding!" cried Jean. "I'll bring her here, Oona, shall I?"

Oona nodded, and Jean went off, to bring Miss Farrar down to the Den to tell them about pretty Miss Radley's wedding, which had taken place the previous Saturday.

"You'll stay to lunch," said Jean hospitably. "Oh, yes, you must!"

Miss Farrar agreed, and they sat talking things over, and never noticing that the rain was gradually ceasing, though the wind still continued to blow great guns. During the course of the morning, the door opened and a little face peeped in, but the three were deep in conversation, and never noticed it. When the gong sounded for luncheon Jean arose, laying aside her sewing.

"Come along, Farrar, I expect we shall find the babies waiting for us ravenously. Why, it has stopped raining. We must get them out this afternoon. They are such open air little people, that the confinement to the house of this past two days has upset their tempers, I'm afraid."

She led the way into the diningroom, and then stopped short in blank dismay. Instead of the two neat little maidens she had expected, there was only Waif, who seemed unhappy about something, for he was sitting on the windowseat, whining.

"Why, where are the children?" cried Jean.

She rang the bell, and Bessie appeared. "Bessie, run up to the nursery, and tell the little girls to be quick. Come over here, Farrar," she went on, as the maid left the room. "It's very tiresome of the pair to be late. And it's not like them, either!"

She served the soup, but she and her guest had barely tasted it before Bessie appeared. "Please, Miss Jean, I can't find Miss Kirsty or Miss Allie. Will they be with Miss Oona?"

"Nonsense, Bessie! Miss Farrar and I have just left Miss Oona. They must be somewhere in the house. Go all over and seek for them."

But twenty minutes later, Bessie came back to say that the children were nowhere.

"Their hats and coats is gone, Miss," went on Bessie. "I looked special into the cloakroom to see, and Miss Kirsty's red tam and Miss Allie's blue one, and their blue coats is missin'."

Jean turned rather white. Then she pulled herself together. "That means we must seek them outside," she said. "Farrar, would you mind coming? Or, rather, would you go one way while I go another? Goodness knows where they've got to — tiresome little monkeys!"

Miss Farrar nodded. "They might have gone into Aulmbermouth," she suggested. "I'll walk in and make enquiries, and you go the other way to Blyton Sands. I don't suppose they can have gone far. After all, they are only little girls."

"I'll go down to the Vicarage first," said Jean. "There's just a chance they may have gone there. They adore Baby Angela, and spend half their time playing with her."

She ran down to the kitchen to tell Morag to keep Oona quiet, and not to let her know about this latest freak of the children's if it were possible. Then she hurried upstairs and put on her outdoor things.

She and Miss Farrar went on in silence till they came to the Vicarage, where they turned in. Mollie came to the door herself, exclaiming with pleasure at seeing them, but her face fell when she heard what they wanted.

"No; I haven't seen anything of them since the day before yesterday. They certainly haven't been here to-day. But I'll ask Charlie if he knows anything about them."

She left them in her pretty drawing-room, and went away, to come back with her husband.

·"They won't have gone along the cliffs, will they?" he asked when he had greeted the two.

"I hope not," said Jean in dismay. "Why, they couldn't keep their feet; there's a heavy gale blowing."

"No; of course not," he said. "Well, look here. You, Jean, go along the road to Blyton Sands, and enquire of all the bus conductors if they have seen them. Miss Farrar can go into Aulmbermouth and do the same. I'll come round to Storms, and go along the cliff-path."

It was the best they could do. Jean set off for Blyton Sands, while Mr Benson got into his cap and coat, and made for the cliffs, and Miss Farrar started on her long walk to Aulmbermouth. Half-way there, she met the doctor, to whom she told her story, and he promptly joined in the hunt, after racing his car home at full speed.

Meanwhile, Jean had gone along the Blyton Sands road with a sick feeling at her heart. It turned down to the sea about a mile and a half from Hasnett, and if the children had followed it, they might easily have been hurt in the gale which made it hard enough for her to fight her way along. Waif, who was with her, whined occasionally as he went, but he made no trouble till they had turned down the road to the sea, and reached the coast. There, at the top of the cliffs, he set his feet, and refused to go on, barking and whining furiously.

"Oh, come along!" said Jean, going to drag him away. She laid hands on his collar. Then she suddenly stopped. Caught in the bushes at the top of the narrow track that led down to the shore was a tiny scarlet wool glove that she recognised as Allison's. Could the children have gone down? But why? And where? Suddenly, she remembered that the Smugglers' Cave was a bare half-mile away from the foot of this path. Snatching up the glove, she held it out to the dog.

"Here, Waif! Good dog! Seek, boy — seek!"

Waif sniffed at the little glove. The next moment, with a short bark, he was bounding down the path. Jean followed him as quickly as she could, and though the wind fought with her, and she felt beaten and bruised all over before she reached the bottom, she accomplished it in safety. How the children had managed it was something she could not understand, but that they had done so was evident, for she found Kirsty's handkerchief, half-buried in sand, not far away.

Jean turned, and looked at the foaming masses of angry water that were leaping nearer every moment. With this east wind, she realised that floodtide would find the whole stretch of sand where she stood covered with a raging sea. If the children were here, she must hurry and get to them, for they would have to get back to this path. Further along, the cliffs were inaccessible to small children, and no woman or child could stand up to the force of those waves. Also, if they were in the Smugglers' Cave, they stood in the gravest peril. Seaweed grew up the walls as high as she herself could reach, and she knew that with a tide like to-day's nothing could live in it through the churning of the waves in that narrow space.

She tore over the loose, heavy sand at full speed, and reached the narrow slit that led into the cave proper with leaden limbs, and pounding heart. By this time, the waters were much nearer, and she knew that it would take them all their time to get back to the path. She pressed into the cave whither Waif had preceded her, and heard his bark, and the joyous cry of two little voices.

"Here's Waif! Darling Waif! Now we'll send a message, and they'll come and get us!"

"I'm here, darlings," she called.

A scream greeted her, and she saw in the dim light, Kirsty sitting on the ground, with Allison lying on her knee. Even in that dim light, Jean realised that something was wrong.

She hurried forward.

"Darlings, what is it?"

"Allie has hurt her foot, and can't stand," said Kirsty. "Oh, Auntie Jean, what is that awful noise?"

Jean got to her feet. She could never hope to get to the path in time if she had to carry Allison. They could barely have done it if the child had been all right. She gently lifted the little girl from her sister's knee to lay her down. Allie gave a short scream, and fainted.

"Get up, Kirsty," whispered Jean. "Waif, on guard!"

Waif knew what that meant. He dropped down beside Allison, and Jean, with Kirsty's hand in hers, made for the wall.

"We can't get out, Kirsty. We must see if we can find anywhere above the water level where we can sit till the tide goes down. I'm going to set you on my shoulders and I want you to feel along while I go sideways along the wall."

Kirsty nodded. She was crying very quietly but something in Jean's tones told her that it was a very serious matter, and she must be as brave as she could. Stooping, Jean swung the little girl up, and got her on her shoulders. Normally, she could not have done it, for Kirsty was a sturdy, well-grown girl, and Jean, for all her height, was slenderly built. But all her reserve force came to aid her in those horrible moments. The long years of folk-dancing had given her poise and balance, and, as she moved slowly along, her hand against the wall for support, she kept steady. Suddenly, a little cry from Kirsty ran through the gloom.

"Auntie Jean! There's a ledge here that's quite dry, and no seaweed on it, either. It's pretty big, too. I believe we can all get on easily."

Jean stood still, and lowered the child to the ground. "Wait here, Kirsty, while I go and bring Allison and Waif. Don't move, for if you do, we shall have to do it all over again. Stand still, Kirsty, and pray — pray to God that we may be saved!"

Kirsty did as she was told, and Jean went back through the rapidly fading light to where Allison still lay in a death-like swoon with Waif beside her. She picked up the child, and went back to Kirsty, who was sobbing softly, while she framed the words of the Lord's Prayer with her lips.

Jean laid Allison down on the ground, and held out her arms to the elder child. "No, Kirsty. This is the last. Up you get, and on to that ledge."

Kirsty struggled up, and stretched up her hands. There was a wriggle and a kick, and she was up. Jean had intended handing up Allie next, but she changed her mind, and picked up Waif. He struggled, but a superhuman strength seemed to have come to the girl in that moment, and she got safely within Kirsty's reach, and the next minute, he, too, was on the ledge.

"I am going to pass Allie up, now," said Jean. "You

must lean out as far as you can with safety, and catch her. Waif will help somehow. After that, I will try to get up myself. But, whatever happens, Kirsty, you are to stay there till the tide goes down, or someone comes. Promise me!"

"I promise," said Kirsty, without a full understanding of what her promise meant, which was, perhaps, just as well.

Jean bent down, and picked up Allison, who roused to consciousness as her injured foot hung down, and began to cry. Jean hushed her.

"There is no time for that, Allie. Stretch up, and try to catch Kirsty's hands."

Allison stretched up, and Kirsty, leaning over at a most dangerous angle, managed to grab her frock. Both would almost certainly have fallen over, had not Waif fixed his jaws in Kirsty's skirt, and tugged valiantly till finally Allison was landed safely on the ledge.

Then Jean looked round for a means of getting up herself. The walls were almost smooth and there was no foothold here. The dim light had practically faded, and they were in darkness. The foam from the waves was dashing in, and her feet were wet. Jean knew that matters were desperate. She didn't want to die; every fibre of her healthy young body rebelled at the thought of death. She felt a yard or two further along, and so came to a little cleft in the rock. She scrambled up somehow, and then found that Kirsty had followed her, and was leaning over.

"Can you catch my hand, Auntie Jean?" said the little girl. "Waif has got hold of me, and I think we could help you."

Jean shook her head. "No, Kirsty; you might fall over." Then, with a sudden inspiration she added, "Unloose your gym girdle, and give me an end."

Kirsty did as she was told, and Jean contrived to

twist the end round one hand. "Give the other end to Waif," she called.

Kirsty did as she was told, and then, with an inward prayer, Jean let go her hold on the rock and swung up by the girdle. It was strongly woven, and it held. Waif, feeling the girl's weight dragging him over the edge, fought furiously with all the strength of his strong young muscles. Kirsty, grasping what was happening, caught at the girdle and added her strength. There was a second's hesitation. Then Jean felt herself within hand's grasp of the edge. She gripped, put all her force into her wrist muscles, and heaved herself up.

Then, she must have fainted, for the next thing she knew, a warm wet tongue was licking her face, and Kirsty was sobbing beside her. She struggled into a sitting position, and pushed the hair out of her eyes.

"All right, Kirsty. Don't cry, dawtie. Where is Allison?"

"Here," sobbed Allison. "Oh, Auntie Jean, I don't like this place! And my foot does ache so, and I want to go home!"

Jean got to her, though she felt one huge ache. She kissed her, and ran slender fingers down the hurt ankle. Judging from the swelling, it was sprained. She did not think any bones were broken. She tied it firmly with their three handkerchiefs, and then settled herself to stay where she was till the tide went down. The waves were forcing their way past the narrow entry into the cave, which was filled with the booming of their thunder. The spray, flung high into the air, wetted them at times, but they were safe enough. All round, and as far as she could feel, the place was dry and there was no seaweed at all. Having bandaged Allison's ankle, she laid her down, and told Kirsty and Waif to sit beside her.

"I want to feel along to see if we can get further from the edge," she explained. "Then the spray won't wet us."

They were very good, poor children. Allison whimpered a little with the pain in her foot, but Kirsty sat like a little Trojan, her arms around her little sister, till Jean, crawling on all fours, came back to them.

They had fallen asleep, wearied out by what they had gone through. She wondered if it would be wiser to wait till the tide fell, and go along the sands, or if she should rouse them and take them by the way she had discovered. For she had found a flight of steps, roughly hewn out of the living rock, and when she had climbed up them she had found herself in a tangle of gorse bushes which she had succeeded in pushing aside, to find that she was looking out on the wasteland between Blyton Sands and Hasnett.

The remembrance of Oona and what she must be suffering on their account decided her and she woke the poor little girls. They listened to what she had to tell them and then said they would do as she wished.

Picking up Allie and carefully edging along the narrow ledge as close to the rock as she could, Jean walked steadily to the steps. Kirsty, on all fours, and Waif followed her, and when they had reached the foot, and the noise of the waves in the cave was dying in the distance, she stopped.

"Wait here, Kirsty darling. I will carry Allie up, and then I will come back for you," she said. "You won't mind being alone for a few minutes, will you?"

"No, Auntie," said Kirsty.

Jean mounted the steps, stumbling for very weariness, and forced the bushes to one side. She laid Allison down on the short, bents grass, and turned to go back for Kirsty. A little voice checked her. "It's all right, Auntie. Waif and I are both here." The good child had struggled up to save her aunt another trip. Jean helped her out, and then followed herself. It was night, and a solemn moon was shining through the rifts in the clouds. Beneath the cliffs, they could hear the wild fury of the sea; closer at hand was the homely sound of a motor. Jean got to her feet, and lifted Allie into her arms. She must get to the road, and ask that motorist to give them all a lift home. He could not refuse when he heard their story.

How she did it, Jean never knew. Somehow, the bedraggled four reached the road, just as the motor drew level, and its occupant, turning to look at them, put on his brakes with such vim, that the car nearly skidded. He was out of it in a second, and across the road and Jean was caught in a pair of strong arms, while a voice that had last said anything of importance to her had done so in tones of concentrated fury, was calling her pet names, and a pair of lips were pressed to hers again and again.

"Oh, Kenneth, is it you?" she said faintly.

He grabbed the pair of them just in time, then Jean's head dropped on the last word, and if it had not been for the doctor, Allison would have dropped. As it was, he lifted them together, and carried them to the car. Kirsty followed, and Waif leaped in as one sure of his welcome.

It was as well that it was a clear road, and that there were no police traps that night.

CHAPTER XXVI

ALL'S WELL THAT ENDS WELL

Of what occurred at Storms that dreadful afternoon and evening, Jean never got the full story. When they arrived home to be greeted by a distracted Oona, who had rebelled fiercely at her own helplessness, and a grim Morag, who said not a word, good, bad, or indifferent, the doctor sent the children off with Bessie, and ordered Morag to see that Jean had a bath, and went to bed. Mollie had come up in answer to a telephone call from Bessie, and she took charge of Allison, who was wailing with the pain in her foot. Allie had gone back to her babyhood, and sobbed for Moti, who was far away in India. The doctor came in after they had got the child to bed, and bound up the sprained ankle properly, and then administered a sedative, which, fortunately, took effect almost at once. He had already done the same for Kirsty, for he was worried over her. She was older than Allison, and grasped the danger as the younger child had not done. He had not liked her wide eyes, and the rapid beat of her pulse. He hoped, however, that the night's sleep would calm the over-excited brain. If not, he feared an illness.

As for Jean, despite bruises and wrenched muscles, she was so worn-out, that she nearly fell asleep in her bath, and when he came to see her, she was far away.

"So much the better," he said. "She will probably sleep herself well. Of course, she will be terribly stiff and sore for the next few days, but she is level-headed, and will not fret herself into an illness. I am most anxious about that elder child. Keep her very quiet for the next few days. But I will come in to-morrow."

All through the night the trio slept, and most of the next morning. The children wakened then, but Jean slept on till early afternoon. When she woke up, it was to find Oona sitting watching her.

"Oona," she said drowsily.

Oona bent forward from her couch. "Jean, my darling!"

Jean yawned, and began to stretch. She stopped with a little scream. "Ow! my shoulders! Oh, Oona! I am stiff!"

She moved cautiously, and managed to sit up. "That's better. How are the children?"

"Getting on very nicely," said Oona. "Allie's foot is bothering her, but a sprain is always a painful thing. Kirsty is worn out. The doctor says she has to stay in bed for a few days till she gets over it."

"Poor little maid!" said Jean. She thought invol-untarily of what they had gone through the day before, and shuddered. "I am going to get on my dressing-gown and bedroom slippers and go to see them," she declared.

She got up, moving with the utmost caution, and managed to get into them, and then she limped along the passage to the two rooms. Allison greeted her with a sob, and held out her arms for a cuddle. Jean sat down on the bed, and held her close.

"You will never run away again, will you, Allie?" she murmured.

"No," sobbed Allison.

"Now you must lie down, dawtie, and go to sleep. Let Auntie Jean cover you up."

She tucked the clothes round the little girl, and had the satisfaction of seeing the long black lashes resting on the white cheeks before she left the room.

Kirsty was a different matter. In her case, it was nervous fear more than anything else. She was suffering from the awful strain, and it was a relief to lie in Jean's arms, and sob out her story. How she and Allie had been so angry because Miss Farrar had come, and Auntie Jean had not taken them for the walk she had promised, so they had gone by themselves. They had only meant to go along the road a little way, and then come back, but she had thought of the Smugglers' Cave, and had suggested it to Allie, who had agreed. They had got down to the shore by means of crawling on all fours, and then had struggled along to the cleft. Once in the cave, they had enjoyed themselves until Allison's unlucky slip had spoilt the fun. Kirsty had tried to carry her little sister, but Allie's weight was beyond her, and she had given it up, and sat down to wait till help should come.

Mercifully, until Jean arrived, the child had had no conception of the danger, or she would have suffered more than she did. It was weeks before her nerves were in order again — weeks before she could sleep without dreaming of it at least once in the night. They were very careful and judicious with her. Jean wrote to India, and summoned Moti back to England, and she came at once. Until she landed, Jean herself slept with the child, and Kirsty woke out of hideous dreams always to find herself cuddled close in tender arms. Then New Year's Day brought Jean's wedding, for the doctor declined to wait any longer, and the excitement of it all, and of going away with Oona, who was much better, and Allie, who was now quite all right, and rather inclined to regard the whole matter as a bad dream, helped her.

But this was all in the future. On that afternoon, the Kirsty who sobbed out her confession was a very

little girl, who shuddered and started at every
sound. One thing that resulted from it was that she
never could endure going to the cave till long years
had passed. Then one afternoon, Jean's children,
who had heard the story from old Morag, now
almost bed-ridden, begged Kirsty, a pretty girl of
twenty-two, to take them to see it. Accompanied by
her future husband, Kirsty agreed, and so the old
ghost was laid at last.

But on that afternoon, Kirsty knew nothing of
this, and when she said that she would never enter
the cave again, she meant it.

Jean held her close and kissed and petted her till
she was calmer. Then she said she must go and
dress but Bessie should come to sit with Kirsty till
someone else could. Then, she retired to her own
room, and, by dint of setting her teeth, she contrived
to get into her clothes. Bessie had to brush her hair,
and wash her, for the pain involved in raising her
arms was almost unbearable. But she finished at
length, and when Mollie ran in at four o'clock, she
and Oona were in the Den.

"Jean, someone in the drawing room wants to see
you," said Mollie.

Jean heaved a sigh and got to her feet. "Some
wretched reporter, I suppose. You might have
protected me, Moll!"

"Trot along and get it over," said Mollie, who was
busy removing baby Angela's shawl.

Jean went and opened the door, intending to be
very icy. But it was no reporter she saw there. The
tall figure of the doctor confronted her, and when he
came forward and took her into his arms, she gave a
little sigh of relief, and nestled to him like a child.

"Jeanie, my little Jeanie," he said tenderly.

Jean raised her green eyes to his face with a look
in them that made him catch his breath.

"Yes, I am yours," she said, and gave him her lips.

A little later, when they had more or less recovered their senses, he looked at her with a laugh in his eyes.

"You didn't look any too pleased to see me at first," he said. "Why was that?"

"That little wretch Mollie told me — or let me think — that it was a reporter," said Jean. "I was going to squelch him thoroughly."

"And you found that instead of a newspaper man it was — "

"My Kenneth!" she said, proudly.

* * *   * * * *   * * *

"I aye said sae!" remarked Morag later on. "I aye kenned that he was the mon for Miss Jean, though she wadna ha'e it! When wull she be mairrit? New Year? Aye? Well, they are no juist weddin' in haste, for he's been courtin' her this mony's a day. I wish them weel and the bonniest bairns in the warld for aul Morag to nurse. Wull ye be havin' fish-cakes or bacon for breakfast, Miss Oona?"

AFTERWORD

POLLY GOERRES

Jean of Storms is a world away from Elinor M. Brent-Dyer's school stories, being her only known pure sortie into the world of adult romance. Of course, she wrote about love in many of her other books, and the relationship between Allegra Atherton and Hugh Redmond in *Janie of La Rochelle* (1932), and the courtship of Juliet Carrick and Donal O'Hara in *The Chalet School and Jo* (1931), both illustrate that true love's course is not always a smooth one. But while the later La Rochelle titles could well have been written with the older teenager in mind, *Jean of Storms* was a newspaper serialisation to be read chiefly by adults.

Within the story, Brent-Dyer draws on many of her own life-forming experiences. For example, we know from Helen McClelland's biography (*Behind the Chalet School*, Bettany Press, 1996) that Brent-Dyer had despised a landlady she lodged with while teaching in the south. Could this have been the prototype for Mollie's nasty, gossiping landlady, Mrs Taylor, in *Jean of Storms*? The name of Elinor's landlady was Mrs Page, the self-same name used for Kirsty's fierce and immovable guardian. Mrs Page is a Hampshire lady, and the way that Elinor describes the Hampshire accent might well be indicative of her own dislike for it — in *A Problem for the Chalet School* (1956), when Rosamund begins to lose her Hampshire accent, Joan Baker sneers that she is starting to talk 'lah-di-dah'.

While Elinor was growing up, the north-east of

England was an area seething with industry and shipbuilding. It was also a seafaring community; one where Elinor's naval father had plied his trade. The local paper of the day, the very one in which *Jean of Storms* was published, was titled in full the *Shields Daily Gazette and Shipping Gazette*, and as a shipping gazette carried timetables not only of ships visiting nearby coastal ports, but also of ports around the country. We can see that this was a part of life at Storms, for when Oona, Jean and Mollie need to find out when the ship bearing Kirsty and Allison, Mollie asks: "Isn't there a shipping gazette downstairs? It will give you the Indian boats, won't it?"

By 1930, the north-east had become a troubled and hungry place. Just six years later — Brent-Dyer and her mother had by then left for Hereford — the famous marchers set off from Jarrow, a town only a few miles south of South Shields. In this area, also made popular in Catherine Cookson's books about 'The Fifteen Streets' and the television adaptation thereof, life for the working people was very hard. There was a high suicide rate among young men and a high infant mortality rate, and deaths at sea, such as that of Oona's fiancé, Ben, were common-place. Young lads were given robust exploits to keep them away from crime, such as the folk-dancing and sports which the Reverend Charles Benson tried to encourage.

Folk-dancing is a central thread throughout *Jean of Storms*, acting as the focal point for the social life of the community. We know from McClelland that Brent-Dyer was keenly involved in the folk-dancing movement of the inter-war years, teaching classes to her pupils at the Misses Stewart's school and attending events organised by the English Folk Dance and Song Society. In the book, folk-dancing classes serve as a meeting-place for women and men of the middle class and a catalyst to the love lives of four of the book's main characters.

The year in which *Jean of Storms* was published, 1930, was a momentous one for Brent-Dyer in her personal life: it was the year that this hitherto practising member of the Church of England was received into the Roman Catholic faith at the Church of St Bede's in Westoe Road. The attitude towards religion in *Jean of Storms* in view of Elinor's conversion is thus worthy of comment. One of the strongest and best drawn characters in the book is the kitchen tyrant Morag, whose staunch Presbyterian views are shown in a very poor light. She is held responsible for Allison's loss of faith in God because she tells her that Father Christmas does not exist: "If I can't believe in Father Christmas, I won't believe in God either!"

Racism is also touched on in Morag's attitude towards Moti-ayah, the gentle and loving nanny (this is of course a racial stereotype) who accompanies Allison and Kirsty back to England from her native India. Brent-Dyer seldom showed Asian characters in her work; the only notable exception is Lilamani, the Kashmiri child helped by Lavender Leigh in *Lavender Laughs in the Chalet School* (1943). So Moti, as an Indian woman, is unique.

South Shields being a seafaring community, in reality the townspeople would occasionally have met other races. There is documentary evidence, for example, that there was a strong Arab Muslim community in 1920s Tyneside. But Morag would have been unlikely to have seen an Indian face close-up, and in an episode reminiscent of Frances Hodgson Burnett's *The Secret Garden*, where the Yorkshire maid confesses to having wondered if Mary Lennox was a brown-skinned native, Morag meets Moti and rails at "yon black heathen".

Poor Moti's "heathen" influence on little Allison is scorned throughout the rest of the book by Morag, only serving to illustrate further the intolerance and unpleasantness with which Brent-Dyer treated Morag's Presbyterianism. Even the title of the chapter when Moti first appears at Storms, "Jean gives Storms a Shock", gives an indication of how the Indian servant might be received by the British servant class:

> With a face full of horror, she [Morag] turned to her mistress. "Maircy me! Miss Jean's brocht yin o' they blackies!" she ejaculated, aghast.

Eventually, because of Morag's diatribes about Moti's heathen religion, the two servants have to be kept apart.

By contrast, the attitude of the upper middle classes — Jean, Oona and Mollie — is one of cheerful acceptance. Moti's race is scarcely mentioned, save for Jean's comment on their journey from Southampton: "Moti . . . attracted more attention than I quite liked." In recognition of Moti's status as nanny, Jean, Oona and Mollie show more gratitude and politeness towards her than they would to other servants (certainly more than Jean does to Morag), ensuring, for example, that her room is well-prepared. Mollie is especially chatty to Moti on Moti's unfamiliar first night at Storms, recalling how glad she had been of her old ayah when she first came to England as a child. It is worth bearing in mind, on the other hand, that however well Jean, Oona and Mollie treat Moti-ayah, they still tacitly accept that the young woman will leave her family and home and travel half way round the world to a strange place at the whim of her employers.

Despite its background, there is much of the vintage Brent-Dyer in *Jean of Storms*. For example, in Jean McCleod and Mollie Stewart Brent-Dyer has created characters who are every bit as resistant to change and growing up as the teenage Joey Bettany in the Chalet School series; the only difference is that Jean and Mollie are twenty-three and twenty-four respectively. Mollie's utterance, when Jean first tells her that young Allison is coming to Storms under Jean's guardianship, is pure Joey Bettany: "It's going to mean changes, and I hate changes!"

The almost secondary role of Oona McCleod is also interesting for the Brent-Dyer reader. Oona has lost her fiancé at sea, and still feels the loss keenly when this story opens twelve years after the event, a fact which the far-from-mature Jean fails to grasp:

"It's some time ago," said the girl [Jean], answering that unspoken thought of her aunt's.

"What difference would it make if it were a hundred years?" demanded Miss McCleod. "You are very young, Jean, or you would not talk like that."

The implication that Oona McCleod's enforced spinsterhood is to be a life sentence is clear throughout the book; while Mollie and Jean make matches, Oona, at thirty-five, is deemed too old to do so. Hers is to be a life of committee work, helping the poor of the parish and undertaking good works for the church.

At the time of writing, Brent-Dyer was thirty-six and had taught throughout her adult life. Was Oona's status indicative of the view Brent-Dyer took of her own spinsterhood, that her chance of marriage had passed her by? There are similarities with Aunt Peggy in *Monica Turns Up Trumps* (1936), who has sacrificed her young womanhood to the upbringing of her dead sibling's children. By the time they are of an age to do without her, she is settled into the role of housekeeper and plainly considered too old for marriage. But the very young aunt- or sister-guardians, like 21-year-old Nancy Drew in *Carnation of the Upper Fourth* (1934), and Madge Bettany, who is aged twenty-four at the start of *The School at the Chalet* (1925), manage to escape their womanly responsibilities to become wives, mothers and homemakers themselves.

Another recurring theme from the Chalet School books is Brent-Dyer's unaccountable interest in India. Neither McClelland nor Fen Crosbie, who has done extensive research on the dedicatees of Elinor's works for the *New Chalet Club Journal* (December 1996), can shed any light on this. (The dedicatee of *Jo Returns to the Chalet School* — 1936 — is Lucy Violet Moore of India. Who was she?) Yet in *Jean of Storms* the sub-plot centres around relatives from India coming home to England. Jean's brother and sister-in-law have been out there with their children, Kirsty and Allison. Jean's best friend Mollie also started her life in the sub-continent.

Similarly, the central characters in the first Chalet books, the Bettany siblings Madge, Dick and Joey, are the orphan children of parents who had been out in India when they were born. Dick has returned to India with the Forestry Commission. Also in the first Chalet book comes Juliet Carrick whose parents, we are told, are "Anglo-Indians". Dick later marries Mollie Avery in India; she is his boss's daughter, and all but one of their long family are born there. In a tradition continued with Allison and Kirsty, the children are sent back to the home country for their education.

On the surface, then, a lot of *Jean of Storms* is predictable Brent-Dyer. There is a largely matriarchal family unit, a strong Indian connection, the usual 'big sister' relationship à la Joey and Madge, Janie and Elizabeth/Anne, Joey and Robin (and, in real life, Elinor and Hazel Bainbridge) which we find in Oona and Jean, and in Jean and the two half-sisters, Kirsty and Allison — and of course, the doctor as the Dashed Good Catch.

But unusually for Brent-Dyer, there is also the very dominant servant figure in Morag. One can hardly imagine the exemplary Anna, for example, challenging Joey in the way that Morag challenges Jean. When ticked off for disobeying orders, Morag retorts: "Ye ought to be ashamed o' yersel', Miss Jean! To daur tae speak tae me like that! It's more than Miss Oona herself daur dae!"

Also unusual is the relationship of Jean McCleod and Mollie Stewart. The two are the best of friends; witness Jean's comment when Mollie is reconciled to Rev. Charles Benson (which recalls Winifred Holtby's reaction to Vera Brittain's engagement), that she has lost "her" Mollie. This traditional school best-friendship is seldom seen in a Brent-Dyer book — even the twosome that is Jacynth Hardy and Gay Lambert is diluted by the presence of a third, Gillian Culver; and Jo Bettany, of course, was one of a quartet. Elinor tended to prefer triumvirates and gangs to exclusive bosom friendships. However, an exception in the Chalet series is the partnership forged between the older Nancy Wilmot and Kathie Ferrars, both mistresses at the school; perhaps Elinor was happier with adult twosomes.

The last few chapters of the story seem very hurried, with Mollie's marriage and motherhood,

Kirsty and Allison's progress at school, Oona's dispatch to Scotland, her bad accident and recovery, Morag's extremely rapid ageing process and the acquiescence of Jean to Kenneth all being crammed into the end of the tale. It is an odd end for Oona; it was not really necessary to move her away from centre stage, yet Elinor does so, almost as if to say that the spinster guardian was obstructing Jean's passage to marriage. Did she lose interest in *Jean of Storms* when she got towards the end of it? Or did she write it as it was serialised and was then unable to sustain the impetus in order to meet daily cliffhanger deadlines? Or did the paper simply give her notice that they wished to start another serial?

In conclusion, *Jean of Storms* is more than just a love story. It deals with several secondary themes including race, child-rearing and the relationship of employer to servant. It has moments of humour, too: the vicar's wife Mrs Semple is a stock character right out of Elinor's children's writing, first cousin to Rebecca Learoyd, Miss La Touche, or "that sodger".

Most of all, however, *Jean of Storms* is a novel of the north-east. The area around South Shields is known today as 'Catherine Cookson' country in honour of its other literary daughter, whose gritty tales of north-eastern realism provide perfect escapist reading. Mrs Cookson's popularity is enormous and she has also proved a great benefactress to the region. Yet *Jean of Storms* is as much a product of Catherine Cookson country as any of the Mallens or Tilly Trotter tales, and Elinor M. Brent-Dyer, till now associated chiefly with Hereford and the Austrian Tyrol, deserves to be much better known in the area of her birth. This novel can only help to enhance her reputation.